T0265578

ON THE HORNS OF DEATH

Also by Eleanor Kuhns

The Ancient Crete mysteries

IN THE SHADOW OF THE BULL *

The Will Rees series

A SIMPLE MURDER
DEATH OF A DYER
CRADLE TO GRAVE
DEATH IN SALEM
THE DEVIL'S COLD DISH
THE SHAKER MURDERS *
SIMPLY DEAD *
A CIRCLE OF DEAD GIRLS *
DEATH IN THE GREAT DISMAL *
MURDER ON PRINCIPLE *
MURDER, SWEET MURDER *

* *available from Severn House*

ON THE HORNS OF DEATH

Eleanor Kuhns

**SEVERN
HOUSE**

First world edition published in Great Britain and the USA in 2024
by Severn House, an imprint of Canongate Books Ltd,
14 High Street, Edinburgh EH1 1TE.

severnhouse.com

British Library Cataloguing-in-Publication Data
A CIP catalogue record for this title is available from the British Library.

ISBN-13: 978-1-4483-1088-3 (cased)
ISBN-13: 978-1-4483-10890-6 (e-book)

All Severn House titles are printed on acid-free paper.

Typeset by Palimpsest Book Production Ltd.,
Falkirk, Stirlingshire, Scotland.
Printed and bound in Great Britain by
TJ Books, Padstow, Cornwall.

Praise for Eleanor Kuhns

"This complex, character-driven mystery is loaded with fascinating historical details"
Kirkus Reviews on *In the Shadow of the Bull*

"Crisply drawn characters, combined with the immersive Boston setting, which beautifully delineates the life and times of the era, from the rich to the very poor, add up to a satisfying historical mystery"
Booklist on *Murder, Sweet Murder*

"The ambience of early 1800s Boston makes for an interesting read"
Kirkus Reviews on *Murder, Sweet Murder*

"This sobering look at the cultural divide over slavery in the early days of the Republic deserves a wide audience"
Publishers Weekly on *Murder on Principle*

"A complex mystery that focuses on the institutional racism still sadly ingrained in the nation's psyche"
Kirkus Reviews on *Murder on Principle*

"The story shines for its historical backbone and atmospheric details . . . Perfect for readers of Margaret Lawrence's Hannah Trevor novels and Eliot Pattison's Bone Rattler series"
Booklist on *Death in the Great Dismal*

About the author

Eleanor Kuhns is the 2011 winner of the Minotaur Books/ Mystery Writers of America First Crime Novel competition for *A Simple Murder*. The author of eleven Will Rees mysteries, she is now a full-time writer after a successful career as the Assistant Director at the Goshen Public Library in Orange County, New York.

www.eleanor-kuhns.com

ONE

L ate again, I hurried down the stony slope into the caves under Knossos. Even from the top of the twisty path, I could hear the grunting and the nervous kicking of cage walls by agitated bulls. I increased my pace despite the slippery footing. I could smell the thick coppery scent of blood, far more intense than the usual odor of damp rock. Why was there blood? Something terrible was happening.

The oil lamps in the center of the cave cast a dim smoky light, but there were several, enough to see by. Although all the bulls were restless, most of the bull leapers were crowded around the foremost pen. 'What's going on?' I asked Arphaia and Obelix as I reached the stone floor. Arphaia and Obelix had helped fill the hole left by the loss of my sisters.

Arphaia rolled her eyes at me and shrugged. 'Don't know.' A short, sturdy girl, her skin was the color of ripe figs. Obelix was taller and paler and so slim she looked like a boy from the back. Like me, they'd tied their hair back into braids. 'I'm busy here,' Arphaia continued. She was helping Obelix pull her skirt over her loincloth, and I guessed the older girl had unexpectedly gotten her monthly. It was always an inconvenience for us women on the team.

'Can I help?'

Arphaia shook her head. Glad to be excused – I was burning with curiosity – I hurried across the stone floor toward the cluster of older bull dancers by the cage. Ready for the upcoming ceremony, they wore only loincloths and boots.

'Something upset the bulls,' Geos said with a frown, running a hand over his bald head. He had trained all of us.

'Especially the bull chosen for sacrifice . . .' Elemon glanced anxiously at the pen. He was the most experienced of us but a recent injury had left him skittish.

I dropped my metal belt on the floor with a clatter and went to join the team. The bull in the pen was white – a pure white like the foam that came ashore from the sea. The largest and strongest of them all, he'd been chosen for our performance at the Harvest Festival today. After the six days of the celebration, he would be sacrificed to the Goddess. Other sacrifices would be made throughout to the Dying God to thank him for the grape harvest, and the wine he'd taught us how to make. But this bull, the greatest of all, would be sacrificed last.

I approached the pen. The strikes against the wooden planks had loosened several. I tried to squeeze into the throng at the front, but no one would move away to let me through. I went around to the side and peered through a crack.

The white bull was trotting around the pen, lashing his tail, kicking up his front feet and grunting angrily. But he did not come near this side. Hmm. Why not? I crouched down to peer through a larger gap at the bottom.

And there, right in front of me, was the body of a man. I gasped and fell back. 'Geos,' I said in a trembling voice. When he did not hear me, I raised my voice. 'Geos.'

'What, Martis?' He sounded harried.

'Come here. There is a body inside the pen.'

'What? Who is it?'

'I don't know.' I shook my head. I hadn't wanted to look. The body appeared to have been both gored and trampled by the bull. 'I think this is why the bull is so nervous . . .'

Geos came around the corner. Although, at sixteen, I stood taller than him by several inches, now he stared down at me sitting on the rock floor.

'Are you sure?' He sounded disbelieving. 'Why would anyone join a bull in the pen? These are not tame animals.'

'I don't know.' I scooted backwards so he could crouch down beside me. Groaning, he lowered himself first to one knee and then to the other. Cautiously, using both hands, he collapsed to a sitting position. From there, he looked through the breach between the weathered wooden boards.

'By the Goddess,' he muttered, 'you're right. How could this happen!' He struggled to rise. 'We've got to get that body out of there. None of the bulls will settle . . .'

Turning, Geos shouted at the other bull dancers. 'One of you, go find Tinos.'

As the High Priestess's consort and the wanax who served as the chief administrator of Knossos and its environs, Tinos would be responsible for investigating this tragedy.

I rose shakily to my feet and peered into the pen next to the one occupied by the white auroch. This one was empty. Glad to have a problem to focus on, I said, 'Maybe we can put the bull in here. And this wall' – I gestured to the partition we'd been looking through – 'is already damaged.'

Geos glanced into the empty pen and then turned his gaze on the battered fence. 'Perhaps. But first we need to pull the body out. Once that is gone, maybe the bull will settle down.'

By now, the other bull dancers had joined us. Elemon shouldered me out of the way. 'The boards are already damaged,' he said. 'Maybe we can pull them away and slide the body through.'

Geos nodded and his eyes shifted to the pen behind me. 'We can take some of those pieces and use them to barricade the hole afterwards.' As Elemon wrenched the boards away from the cage bottom, Tryphone grabbed the victim's arm to pull him through. After a few seconds of futile struggle, Thaos, one of the other men, knelt down to help him. The body awkwardly inched forward.

I could barely watch. I could see that several bones were shattered and his arms flopped limply behind him.

Once he was free, we bustled around gathering wooden planks to place over the gap. I didn't believe the bull could escape through the narrow opening at the bottom, but we covered it, nonetheless. No one wanted an angry animal charging around the caves, and he was still not settling down. Of course, the smell of blood hung heavily in the air.

'What happened?' Arphaia asked as she and Obelix approached us.

Before Geos could reply, excited chatter from the youngest of our team – all still congregated at the entrance to the arena – distracted us. Geos hurried around the pen, the rest of us following. Tinos had arrived. He was clad in a long robe banded with diagonal stripes of red and blue and wore his ceremonial knife on the belt around his waist. Apparently, he'd been pulled away from an important ritual. 'What happened?' he asked. 'He' – gesturing to Curgis – 'told me you discovered a body in the bull's pen?'

'That's right,' Geos said. 'I sent him to you.'

In his formal clothing, Tinos seemed older and much more serious than the man I knew and liked. 'Show me,' he said.

Geos glared at the kids. 'Stay here,' he said firmly. 'This is not something any of you should see.'

Thirteen-year-old Costi curled his lip mutinously but didn't argue.

'I'll watch them,' Obelix offered. She was quite pale.

Arphaia glanced at her. 'We both will,' she said.

I did not offer. Although I did not want to look at the body, I did want to be near Tinos. I quickly joined the line of bull dancers following him and Geos to the side of the bull pen.

Tinos stared at the battered and bloodied remains on the floor for several seconds and heaved a sigh. 'Who discovered the body?' he asked.

'Martis,' Geos said.

Tinos shot me a look from under his thick black eyebrows. This was not the first time I had witnessed a violent death. 'Of course, it would be,' he said.

'I could smell the blood when I got here,' I said, rushing into speech. 'And the bull was angry and upset. They' – and I gestured to Elemon and Tryphone – 'were here by the pen.'

Tinos glanced at the bull dancers, and then his gaze flicked to the pen where the white bull could be heard snorting and shuffling. 'I see.' He turned to Geos. 'That white bull can't be used in the ceremonies now.'

'I know,' Geos agreed. 'He's been tainted. But we have a few others.' He pointed to the pens at the back of the cave. 'Backups. The second choice is black, though. Not white.'

Tinos nodded. 'He will have to be the one. A bull that murdered a man is no fit sacrifice to the Goddess.'

I thought of all the bull leapers who'd been gored or trampled by a bull during the ceremony and wondered why a wounding or a death in the course of a performance was acceptable to the Goddess. Because this had not happened during the Goddess-sanctioned ritual?

'What possessed him to enter the cage?' Tinos wondered aloud, pushing his hair to the back. When no one replied to what was clearly a question without an answer, he asked, 'Does anyone recognize him?'

'I don't think any of us really examined him,' Geos admitted apologetically.

Tinos raised his brows and looked around at us. Thaos and Curgis, the newer bull dancers, shook their heads and backed away. I refused to show such weakness in front of Tinos – I did not want him to think less of me – so I steeled myself and stared down at the body. Elemon cut through the crowd and joined me.

It was difficult to recognize the victim through the blood and the bruising. I thought his skin was naturally darker than the fair Elemon, but I couldn't be sure. Finally, Elemon shook his head and stepped away to join the others. I continued staring at the body a few seconds longer – not at the face, but at the kilt around his hips. We all wore loincloths during the bull dancing. It was necessary to move freely, and we did not wear clothing like a long skirt that would catch on the horns. The victim's garment was subtly different, longer and decorated with blue stripes.

'I know who that is,' I said, my voice breaking. 'It's Duzi.'

TWO

'Duzi?' Geos said, staring at me in shock. 'Are you sure?' He too spoke softly so the others could not hear.

I nodded, too shaken to speak. I'd first seen Duzi a few weeks ago. Although my mother did not want me visiting the docks, insisting it was too dangerous, I still occasionally went. I counted Tetis, an Egyptian prostitute who worked there, as my friend. That time, as we were talking, Tetis stopped mid-word and stared over my shoulder. I turned to look.

Several Cretan sailors manhandled a prisoner off one of the slim naval ships. His heavy black beard, stretching all the way down his chest, and the battered bronze helmet with a spike in the center marked him as a foreigner. 'A pirate,' Tetis said with dislike. 'More and more of them harass Egypt.'

By the time Duzi joined the bull leapers a week later, the helmet was gone and the beard shaved away. But the kilt girding his hips was the same one he wore now.

'Who's Duzi?' Tinos asked, keeping his voice low so he could not be overheard.

'A volunteer for the bull leapers—' Geos began.

'The navy brought him here,' I said at the same time. 'I saw them take him off a ship.' My voice trembled, and Tinos raised his eyebrows at my emotion.

'Ah. The pirate,' he said. He knew my mother did not want me visiting the docks. But he didn't scold me. Not this time anyway. 'Did you know him well?' I shook my head.

'A pirate?' Geos repeated incredulously, staring at Tinos. Crete had probably the best navy in the world; our cities and towns suffered little from the depredations of pirates.

'Egypt asked for our help,' Tinos explained. 'The seafarers from the east – they target those rich cities of the Black Lands, and the cargo ships that trade with us.'

'But they don't dare attack us,' Geos said in satisfaction.

'Only once in a while,' Tinos agreed with a smile. He turned and looked at the tunnel that led to the arena. Although he couldn't see anything in the gloom, he said, 'It must be time for the bull dancing and time for me to meet the High Priestess. On the way, I'll tell the bull handlers that we won't be using the white bull and they should take out the black one instead.' He glanced first at Geos and then at the rest of us. 'Please, don't gossip about this tragedy. We don't know what happened . . .'

I sneaked a look at Elemon and the others. They didn't seem to realize the victim was Duzi – one of us.

Geos nodded. 'I don't want the kids to know either,' he agreed. 'Not until after the performance, at least. It's dangerous enough as it is, without distraction. What possessed the young fool to go into the pen?'

'And please, can we cover him up?' Tinos added as he turned away.

'Cover him with what?' Geos muttered as Tinos disappeared into the tunnel. I looked around. All the bull leapers except for Obelix and me were clad in loincloths, and I was the only one wearing a jacket and a linen blouse as well as a skirt. At sixteen, I felt awkward running through the town half-naked so I covered my loincloth with street clothes. I slipped off the skirt and held it out to Geos. Although the skirt was an old one, and both faded and shabby, I wore it often. I would not be happy if Duzi's blood stained it and made it unwearable. But right now, I didn't see what else I could do.

Geos nodded his thanks and draped the garment over Duzi's face. 'And what am I supposed to do about bull leapers,' the old man grumbled. 'Half the team is too young and untried – still basically children.'

I knew Geos did not like sending me in. Geos and my grand-father had been close friends and although we honored the Goddess with the dance, it was dangerous. Injuries and, yes, deaths were common. Geos didn't want to see me hurt. That was why he had been so ready to accept Duzi into our ranks. The barbarian was untried but also strong and lithe. He learned the acrobatics quickly. Geos had had high hopes for him.

I guessed today I would leap over the bull's back more than a few times. Although we numbered thirteen without Duzi, we were only nine once the youngest – Costi, Nub and the twins – were taken out.

I dropped my linen blouse and jacket on the belt, stripped the bangles from my arms and ran my fingers through my hair to remove the hair clips and ropes of beads. Automatically, I dropped them on my clothing. But I did not join the line of bull dancers waiting to parade into the arena. Instead, I returned to the body. Poor Duzi. At least the protection of my skirt offered him some dignity. I shifted it to cover his face more thoroughly and saw to my dismay that the cloth was already stained. I doubted the marks would ever wash out. But with the blood wiped away, the wounds on Duzi's face and chest were now more easily seen. There was something odd . . . As I bent over the body to get a closer look, Geos shouted at me.

'Martis! What are you doing? Come on. We have to go. We're late already.'

I jumped. 'Coming.' I quickly squeezed in between Arphaia and Thaos. After a growth spurt this past summer, I no longer stood at the front but in the middle.

Although it was not yet raining, the sky was overcast and the air was cool. The hot dry summer had ended, and we were moving into the cooler, wetter autumn. In another week or so, the farmers would begin sowing the wheat and barley in the fields.

But today, and for the next few days, we celebrated the grape harvest.

We were a somber group that paraded around the arena, entertaining the crowd with handstands and somersaults. As we queued up at one end of the space, and I looked at my teammates forcing smiles as they waved at the audience, I wondered how they would behave if they knew who lay dead in the bull's pen.

With a self-conscious grimace, Obelix removed her skirt.

Flowers rained down upon us – but not the brightly colored blooms of spring. Mostly narcissi and crocus bloomed now, so we were showered in yellow and purple.

A few moments later, the bull handlers released the animal into the arena. The black auroch, although not a small animal, appeared smaller to me than the white bull. But this one also seemed more energetic. He snorted and pawed the ground in the middle of the arena, watching us with his shiny black eyes.

Elemon nervously touched the thick ropy scar that twined around his torso. He'd finally recovered from the wound sustained in a ceremony seven or so months ago, but it had been a difficult convalescence.

Tinos, still in his long robe, leaned forward, his face twisted with sympathy. He was a former bull leaper himself and wore a scar almost identical to Elemon's around his waist.

Tryphone took up his position. He was two or three years older than I was and almost as dark as Duzi. Tryphone had come to Knossos from a town on the eastern side of Crete. I don't think any of us knew why he'd left Gortnya and traveled east. But Geos had been overjoyed to discover Tryphone was already an experienced bull leaper.

At Geos's nod, Arphaia moved around to the rear of the bull where she would catch us as we dismounted. Geos usually chose her as the catcher; a farmer's girl, she was cautious but not afraid of the beast. But she was graceless as an acrobat. Short and stiff, her flips over the bull's horns usually dropped her right behind the beast's head in a clumsy sitting position.

Geos looked up at the High Priestess. As usual, she did not smile, and her expression was as rigid as a statue's. Her obsidian-dark eyes flicked over us, and then she nodded. Geos gestured at Tryphone. He moved forward.

His bronzed arms reached out to grasp the bull's horns, and his legs lifted up until I could see the soles of his boots. He used the momentum from the bull's head toss to flip over, landing easily on the bull's black back. With a salute and a bow to the High Priestess, Tryphone jumped down, barely touching Arphaia's hand for balance.

Since Obelix and Thaos would jump after Elemon, who had just stepped forward for his performance, I allowed my mind to wander. Wondering what exactly Duzi had been doing in the bull's pen was so much easier than imagining his fear as the bull charged. I recalled the drying streaks of blood; he had not died much before the arrival of us bull dancers. Of course, that did not tell me when he might have gone into the bull's pen. Or how long he had been inside suffering the bull's attacks.

My mind went reluctantly to my last sight of the body. Something bothered me about the wounds. I knew what the injuries caused by a bull's horns and hooves looked like; during the last year, I'd seen more than I cared to. The blunted horns left craters and long gashes in human flesh. And the battering left by the monstrous hooves was especially memorable; the power and the weight of the bull resulted in large bruises and broken bones. But there was something—

'Martis!' Geos's voice suddenly interrupted my thoughts. 'What is the matter with you?' Coming out of my deep thought, I blinked at him. He gestured at the bull standing in the middle of the arena. I gulped. I usually spent a few minutes mentally preparing myself for the run across the sand, the careful stretch out to grasp the bull's horns and finally the leap up and over. 'Go,' Geos said impatiently.

THREE

Taking a deep breath, I rubbed my sweaty hands on my loincloth. 'Go, go, go,' chanted the crowd. I could smell the bull's pungent musk and somebody's heavy Egyptian perfume. The bull pawed the ground and grunted twice before breaking into a run. I had no time to think. He was right in front of me. I sprinted forward, automatically reaching out for those ivory spikes, my body instinctively moving into the proper position. The bull tossed his head, and I went flying, landing perfectly on his broad back. Arphaia reached out for me. I took her hand and jumped down, my legs suddenly trembling as my body realized how careless I'd been. As I reeled to the side of the ring, I scolded myself for allowing Duzi's death to distract me. I would have plenty of time to think about it after the end of the ceremony. If I survived.

'What happened to you?' Elemon asked, his hazel eyes focused on me. 'You looked Goddess-touched.'

'I was thinking,' I replied stiffly.

'Well, don't think anymore. You'll get yourself killed.'

I turned away and watched Tryphone run toward the bull's horns. He executed a perfect flip over the back.

'I want to try,' said Costi. I eyed him disdainfully. He was only thirteen, a mere child. An orphan, Costi had arrived unexpectedly during the summer and volunteered.

'All right,' Geos said now. 'But later. After the bull tires.'

Elemon and I exchanged a glance, both of us wondering if this was a wise decision by Geos. Costi could do the jump – but he was so fearless he could get hurt.

'Why don't you spell Arphaia and catch?' Geos added. 'For a little while. I need her here, leaping.' *Without Duzi.* The unsaid words hovered in the air.

Ah, I thought. That made more sense. Tryphone and Elemon performed second and third jumps, their last performances sloppy. They were already tiring, and after another few jumps they would be exhausted. Arphaia would make a good substitute, gawky though she might be.

The bull looked as though he would never tire. Younger than the white bull, and not as seasoned, he ran at us with aggressive energy. I shivered a little but told myself I was merely chilly because the breeze was drying the perspiration on my body.

Grumbling, Costi trotted into the ring. Arphaia, her face split with a wide smile, joined us in the line.

'Martis. Go.'

I moved into position for my second jump and stared at the bull. One would think that after bull leaping so many times I wouldn't be afraid. But I was. The massive beast tossed his head, and I began my sprint. He ran for me, those fearsome horns pointed right at me. A few seconds mistimed, a few steps too far to the right or left, and a bull dancer could be speared by those horns. Although cropped and blunted, they could still cause a lot of damage. I focused, reaching out until I grasped the horns, and the bull threw me high into the air. Although I feared the bull and his horns, I loved this part and always wished my flight through the air would last longer.

It seemed to me that I did not soar as high this time. Maybe the beast was finally tiring.

Geos must have seen that as well. He moved Arphaia to the front of the line.

She was the last to jump. Instead of soaring like an eagle, she lumbered through the air as ungainly as a pelican. Laughter rippled through the audience.

Arphaia landed badly as well, sliding off the bull's back. Despite Costi's best efforts to hold her, she crashed to the ground. As the handlers rushed into the ring and she limped to her feet, I saw she was weeping with frustration.

Tinos leaned over and spoke to the High Priestess. She did not look at him, nodding slightly in response. As the bull was drawn from the arena, the Lady and her consort stood up, signaling the end of the performance. I distinctly heard some of the audience grumbling that the performance was too short. Usually, we danced with the bull until we were stumbling with fatigue, a situation destined for injury. Today, the only one hurt was Arphaia, and she'd only bruised her ankle. Some flowers were thrown into the ring, and Elemon and Tryphone were called to the stands for tokens – mostly jewelry of varying value. I'd won a copper ring once from a generous fan. I doubted Arphaia would ever win much more than that.

We queued up and walked quickly out of the ring and across the ground to the tunnel. It felt even colder inside the caves, especially since we were all sweaty and panting, and I began to shiver. I hurried across the floor to my tiny bundle of belongings and quickly pulled on my old jacket.

Then I joined Geos and Tinos by the body.

'What are we going to do?' Geos asked Tinos. 'We can't leave it here. And since he's a foreigner, he has no family or family tomb.'

'He'll go to the healer first—' Tinos began.

'He was one of us,' I broke in. Now that the excitement of the bull dancing was fading, and I realized Duzi was really and truly gone, my voice broke. Tears filled my eyes. I tried to blink them away. 'We, the bull dancers, should care for him.'

Tinos looked at me. 'Was he a special friend of yours?' he asked.

'We were friends, of course . . .' As I realized what Tinos was really asking, I flushed and shook my head. 'We were not "special" friends, not romantic at all.' I did not want to marry, ever. 'I think he and Arphaia were close . . .' My words trailed away; Arphaia did not yet know the victim was Duzi.

'We'll have to tell her,' Geos said. We exchanged a glance. 'We'll have to tell them all.'

'I know.' Although I would not have to be the one who shared this terrible news – that would be Geos's responsibility – I dreaded seeing the shock and grief on my friends' faces. 'Isn't there a tomb for bull dancers?'

'Yes, for those of us who, for one reason or another, cannot or do not wish to be buried with family,' Geos said.

'But they were all stars,' Tinos objected. 'The best of the sport. None were pirates given a choice of bull dancing or execution.'

'He was one of us,' I persisted stubbornly.

Geos and Tinos exchanged a glance. 'It is an option,' Tinos admitted.

'Why did this young fool enter the bullpen?' Geos muttered. 'I thought he knew better.'

'He didn't,' I said.

'What do you mean?' Geos looked at me, his heavy gray brows rising. 'He didn't know better?'

'He wouldn't enter the cage. Or approach a bull. He was terrified of them,' I said. I'd recognized the signs. The first time Duzi saw the bull approaching, he broke out in a sweat, his eyes widening. Face ashen, he ran from the ring. I'd found him nearby a little while later, throwing up. Since that initial terror was common, Geos had not marked it as important. But Duzi's fear had not eased, and although he'd managed a few awkward jumps, I doubted he would ever become the bull leaper Geos wanted.

Tinos eyed me for several seconds. 'What else, Martis?' he asked. 'I've known you since you were Telemon's age. What are you not telling me?'

Tinos had become the High Priestess's consort just over nine years ago, when I was seven.

'I think Duzi was murdered.' My voice caught. Tinos and Geos waited while I composed myself. 'There's something wrong. Look at his chest.' I bent and removed my stained skirt. 'See the wounds. They don't look right to me.'

Tinos examined the marks I'd noticed before. 'Hmm. Those do appear to be stab wounds.'

'It's hard to see anything with the blood and the bruising,' Geos said doubtfully.

'The bull is powerful . . .' Tinos's fingers involuntarily touched the scar circling his waist. 'I'll have Potnia's healer examine the body before we send Duzi on to the afterlife. If your suspicions are correct and there's something wrong, she'll find it.'

'What will we tell the others?' Geos asked.

'That this is Duzi.' Tinos blew out his breath. 'Let them think the bull caused his death. For now, we'll let everyone think this is just a terrible accident.'

'Which it might be,' Geos said hopefully. Doubtful, I shook my head.

'We should do it now,' Tinos said. He threw a sympathetic glance at Geos. 'We'll both do it.'

'Thank you,' Geos said gratefully.

I took one final look at Duzi before Geos threw my skirt over the face once again. Then we both followed Tinos to the front of the cave.

FOUR

'No, no,' cried Arphaia. I moved forward and took her hand, my own eyes moistening.

'I did not realize you and Duzi were so close,' Elemon said disapprovingly.

Arphaia shook her head. 'We were when he first arrived. Not anymore. But we remained friends.' Obelix, now fully dressed, put an arm around Arphaia's shoulders. My nose wrinkled at the odor of fish emanating from Obelix's clothing but Arphaia didn't seem to notice.

'Do you know where he lived?' Tinos asked. Arphaia shook her head. 'Or whether he had family?' She shook her head again.

'Did he have any friends?' I interjected my own question. 'That you know of?' Both Tinos and Geos frowned at me. 'Besides us, I mean.'

'I don't think so,' Arphaia sniffed. '*We* were his only friends.'

'Ahh.' Now I understood why Duzi stayed with us, despite his terror of the bulls.

'He had to know someone,' Tinos said. He did not add that if someone had stabbed Duzi, he hoped it was not one of us. I looked around me, at the other bull dancers. Everyone looked shocked by Duzi's death, and Costi was crying. No one looked guilty. I bit my lip; surely Duzi's murderer could not be one of us. But what did I really know about any of the others? I knew Arphaia and Obelix the best. My gaze moved to Elemon. He was still the most famous of us and had been a dancer when I'd begun training and performing with them, but he'd been badly gored by a bull, and I hadn't seen him for several months while he healed. Most of the others were new. Some were even younger than Costi. Any one of them could have a secret life.

There were few of us, to begin with, fewer volunteers every year, and the rate of attrition was high. Many bull dancers died or were so severely wounded they had to retire. Others married out or, like Tinos, moved on to other pursuits. I would have to decide whether I wanted to continue next year, when I embarked on my agoge, my initiation into adulthood. Most women married afterward, and although I didn't want to wed, I would be almost eighteen then and under pressure to do just that.

There were few old survivors. Geos, the man who trained us, was one. He'd made a life teaching the next generations of bull dancers.

I stared at each of my teammates, wondering if one of them had stabbed Duzi over some as-yet-unknown conflict. The murderer had to be someone unafraid of the bulls, unafraid enough to push Duzi's body into the pen. Not the youngest. Costi was thirteen, and I thought the girl – Nub, they called her – was maybe a year younger. The twins were only eleven. None of them were strong enough to overcome a man.

Perhaps one of the men? I stared at Tryphone and then my gaze moved to Thaos and Curgis. They were all strong enough to manhandle Duzi into a bull's pen. But why? Arphaia? Could it have been jealousy? I examined her thoughtfully. Without the heavy line of kohl emphasizing her eyes, they were small and unremarkable. Her round cheeks were blotchy with weeping. I did not believe she was attractive enough to cause that kind of murderous emotion. But what did I know about the mysteries of the human heart? After all, Duzi had been interested in her.

'I don't know. I don't know,' Arphaia wept in answer to Tinos's questions. Scowling with frustration, Tinos stepped back and rubbed his face. I smiled at him sympathetically. The Harvest Festival was a busy time for the High Priestess's consort. Tinos's eyes were already heavy with fatigue. And now there was a murder.

Before he could continue his questioning, a woman accompanied by four men with a litter emerged from the tunnel. Despite the dim light, I recognized her as the High Priestess's healer.

'Where's the body?' she asked Tinos.

'I'll show her,' Geos said with a gesture.

Everyone watched the healer and her slaves follow Geos to the back of the cave.

'I'll speak with you again later,' Tinos said to Arphaia. 'Where do you live?'

She did not reply, her gaze fixed on the litter as the men lowered it carefully to the cave floor.

'Arphaia!' Tinos sounded annoyed.

'What?'

'Where do you live?'

'To the northeast,' she said, still distracted by the activity at the bull pen. 'I'm staying with my aunt and uncle.' She sobbed and continued, 'It is one of the biggest farms with a large vineyard by the road. Stone pillars by the gate.'

'I'll see you there,' Tinos said. 'Everyone, go home.'

'But I—' I began.

'Especially you, Martis,' Tinos said firmly. 'I'll speak with you later.'

I bit my lip, suppressing the argument I wanted to make. I could help Tinos solve the murder; I knew I could.

'You heard the wanax,' Geos added. 'Go home. Remember, no training tomorrow.'

Tomorrow was the second day of our harvest festivities, this time honoring Dionysus, the Dying God.

I patted Arphaia on the shoulder. 'I'll see you soon,' I whispered and stepped away.

By the time I gathered up my linen blouse and all my jewelry, only Tinos, the healer and the slaves remained. Duzi's body had been moved to the litter; the healer lowered the curtains around it, and they set off. Tinos fell into step behind them. I looked at his forbidding back, but I just couldn't obey him. I followed them through the tunnel and past the arena toward the large edifice on the other side of the square.

I could travel much faster than they could, so I raced ahead, hurrying home.

'What in the name of the Goddess happened at the ceremony?' my mother asked as soon as I stepped through the door.

'I can't talk now,' I said as I hurried into my bedchamber. 'I'll tell you later.' I grabbed the first skirt I could find although it did not match my jacket and pulled it over my hips. Still fastening the belt as I ran, I left the house once again.

When I descended the steps, I saw the palanquin moving along the southern side of the building and I quickly hurried to catch up. I followed them all the way to the western side and around to a ramp that led to the lowest level. Tinos never looked behind him as I trailed them into the basement.

This was the healer's domain. The air was aromatic from the bunches of drying herbs hanging from the ceiling. Two of the four walls were lined with shelves, and those were crowded with jars of varying sizes. Knives and other tools were hung on the third partition. A long wooden table ran down the center of the room. Mortars and pestles of different sizes were arranged on one side of the shelves underneath, while the other side held rolls of linens, rags and other supplies.

The healer gestured to the back room and another long wooden table, this one darkly stained. A window high up in the wall poured light upon the wooden surface. The slaves deposited Duzi on it, and Tinos followed the healer inside.

I took up a position near the door where I could see but was not visible to Tinos.

The healer removed my skirt from Duzi's face and chest and dropped it to one side. 'Hmm,' she said. She called for a basin of water. Taking a rag from her supply on the shelf below the table, she dipped the rag in the water and gently sponged away the blood.

'One of the bull dancers said she thought there was something wrong with the wounds . . .' Tinos said. I wanted to point out that I was that bull dancer, but I did not want to be ejected from the room, so I bit my tongue.

'She is right,' the healer said. 'Look here and here.'

Now I had to move closer to the table so I could see what she pointed to.

'What am I looking at?' Tinos asked.

'The bull's horns tore through the flesh here and left a large wound. Do you see?' the healer asked Tinos.

I nodded involuntarily. Although the hole was only a few inches wide, the damage around it was extensive.

'You can also see the injuries left by the bull's hooves,' the healer continued. I nodded again since I'd already spotted them.

'But here and here' – as she gestured to Duzi's chest, I pushed forward to see to what she pointed – 'these are stab wounds made by a knife.'

I nodded again. I could see the difference. The wounds made by a knife were narrow, deep punctures. More like slits.

Tinos took his knife from the sheath and held it up to compare it to the wounds on Duzi's chest. Tinos's knife was wider and thicker, and it did not look as sharp.

'The bull gored this poor boy,' the healer said. 'But those wounds are more a tearing. The knife pierced the chest, and that, I would guess, is what killed him. He was stabbed and pushed into the bull pen with the bull and left to bleed to death. This was murder.'

FIVE

After a few seconds, Tinos sighed. 'I feared that was so.'

'But where is the knife?' I asked, forgetting I was not supposed to be there.

'I thought I told you to go home,' Tinos said in annoyance.

The healer turned and eyed me thoughtfully. 'I guess you're the one who noticed the difference in the wounds?' she asked. I nodded.

'I found the body . . .'

'This is Martis, whose curiosity frequently gets her into trouble,' Tinos said, frowning in my direction.

'Maybe so. But she asks the correct questions.' The healer glanced back at Duzi's body. 'I am not familiar with a knife that can make those narrow wounds. It must be something long and sharp and very thin.'

'I didn't see anyone wearing a knife,' Tinos muttered.

'We were all wearing loincloths for the dance,' I said. 'There's no place to hide a knife.' Tinos and the healer nodded.

'I'll return to the caves and search,' Tinos said. 'In the white bull's pen – after he has been removed, of course.'

'What will happen to him?' I asked.

'I don't know,' Tinos said. 'Maybe he'll be purified . . .' He shrugged. 'The High Priestess will consult with the other women and decide.' He looked at the healer. 'If you find anything else, let me know.' As she nodded, he turned and left, his booted feet thudding on the stairs.

'Wait,' she called after him. But Tinos did not turn around and, within moments, the healer's chamber had emptied. 'Do you know this poor fellow's family?' she asked me. I shook my head and then reconsidered.

'Geos,' I said. 'Talk to Geos. We bull dancers were his family.'

She nodded her thanks, eying me so intently that I felt uncomfortable and stepped backward. She caught my arm as I prepared to follow the others out. 'Are you apprenticed to anyone?'

'My mother is Nephele, the weaver,' I said cautiously. 'I help her.'

'I see.' She paused and then added, 'Do you want to be a weaver?'

'No,' I replied honestly. 'Why?'

'You are sharp-eyed and not at all squeamish. You didn't flinch, not even a little, when you looked at the body. I could use an apprentice. After all, you can't leap the bulls forever.'

I stared at her. Although I'd been worrying about my future, I'd never thought of apprenticing to a healer. Did I even want to? Finally, I said, 'I'll think about it.'

My thoughts in a whirl, I walked the length of the complex back to the apartment. The intersecting halls were thronged with people, but I barely noticed them. Could I become a healer? Healers had a lot more freedom of movement than weavers.

My head was too full of competing thoughts. As I deliberated about Duzi's death, the knife and the bull, my attention kept veering to the possibility of becoming a healer. It was all very confusing.

It was a relief to reach home and try to answer my mother's questions. 'What happened? The bull dancing was so short.' She'd been pacing back and forth through the main room. 'Everyone's been talking . . .' Then her gaze took in my mismatched skirt and jacket and the grimy linen over my dirty bare shoulders. 'Martis! Where is the skirt you wore this morning?'

I opened my mouth to reply and, without warning, burst into tears. My mother rushed over and put her arms around me. She led me to the cushions and drew me down beside her.

For a few moments, she rubbed my back without saying anything. When the storm eased, she said, 'I knew something happened. The ceremony was abbreviated. Are you going to tell me?'

I nodded, trying to pull myself together. 'Nobody's supposed to know. Duzi was killed.'

'Duzi? Duzi who?'

'He's one of the bull dancers. Was.' I inhaled a shaky breath. I couldn't tell her – at least, not yet – that Duzi had been murdered.

'I see.' She still looked bewildered. 'You've never spoken of him. Were you close to him?'

I shook my head. 'No. But I knew him, of course.'

My mother remained silent for a few seconds. 'But he wasn't gored by the bull. I would have seen that.'

'No. We found him in one of the pens.' I hesitated, choosing my words carefully. 'He wasn't gored in the ring.'

'He went into the pen?'

'It looks as though he did,' I said. 'Several of his bones were broken . . .' I shuddered at the memory. 'We found him just after we arrived to line up for the performance. The bull – the white bull originally chosen for the ceremony – was agitated. Running around and grunting and banging into the fence.'

'I wondered why the bull in the ring was black,' Nephele said, her forehead puckered. 'I remember when we tested the bulls. The one we chose was white.'

'Geos sent Curgis to fetch Tinos and they said that bull couldn't be used—'

'Because he was defiled,' my mother said with a nod. 'What does this have to do with your skirt?'

'Geos took it to cover Duzi's face, and I don't want it back now. It's all stained.' I swallowed. 'With blood. It was terrible.'

My mother pushed the hair from my face. 'Don't think about it anymore. Go bathe and dress. Then we'll eat and you'll feel better.'

I wept again in the tub, but the warm water did soothe me. I redressed in a new skirt and jacket, red with blue designs, and a fresh linen bodice. I was combing my hair when my mother appeared at my bedroom door.

'Tinos is here,' she said in a low voice. 'He says he wants to talk to you. Shall I send him away? Tell him you'll talk to him later?'

I shook my head. 'I think he's planning to talk to all of the bull dancers,' I said. 'I'll talk to him now.' I quickly plaited my damp hair and followed my mother into the main room.

Because my mother hovered at the edge of the room, Tinos and I stepped outside to the courtyard to talk. Besides not telling her Duzi had been murdered, I hadn't confessed to finding the body.

Tinos still wore his long robe, but it was crumpled and smudged with dirt. A band of grime across his knees suggested he'd been kneeling on the cave floor. The three locks of hair he usually wore curled over his shoulders had been pushed back, and his mouth drooped with fatigue. I wished I could take him in my arms and comfort him, but I knew better. The High Priestess was a jealous woman. And my attraction to Tinos was something I barely dared admit even to myself.

'Did you find the knife?' I asked.

'No. We searched the cave and swept out the pen, and there is no knife.'

'The killer took it away with him,' I breathed. I raised my eyes to Tinos. 'The murder was planned.'

He nodded. 'That's my guess.'

'Who hated him that much?' I wondered aloud. I couldn't imagine. 'Duzi was a poor man, recently arrived,' I said. 'He hardly knew anyone. Who would want to kill him?' Tinos shook his head, as puzzled as I was.

SIX

Tinos and I stared at one another in silence for several seconds.

'That is what I need to figure out,' Tinos said at last. 'Let's start at the beginning. Who was there in the cave when you arrived?'

'Everyone. I was late.'

'Tell me everything you remember.'

I took a few moments to order my thoughts. 'I didn't go into the cave by way of the arena tunnel,' I began. 'Instead, I went along the path by the sea.' I paused, remembering my walk along the ridge. The gulls flying, screaming, above me. When I looked through the trees, I could see the striped sails of the fishing boats in the glittering water. Everything had seemed so peaceful then. 'When I went into the cave, I think all the bull dancers and Geos were there. He was by the pen, the pen for the white bull, with Elemon, Tryphone, Curgis and Thaos.' I closed my eyes and tried to remember. 'All the bulls were agitated, but the white one was

the most upset. I could hear him bellowing and kicking the sides
of his cage.'

'Tell me exactly where the other dancers were.'

'Um. Arphaia and Obelix were together. In front of the pen
where my sister Nuia was held. Do you remember?' I looked up
and met his gaze.

'Yes. At the bottom of the path.'

'Yes. Costi, the twins and Nub were by the arena tunnel. Pretty
far away.'

'I doubt the children had anything to do with Duzi's death,'
Tinos said in a dry tone. 'For one thing, none of them are strong
enough to drag Duzi into the pen.'

'I doubt Arphaia or Obelix could either,' I said, loyal to my
friends.

'Perhaps not.' He rolled his lower lip between his teeth.
'Neither are weak, though. After all, they too leap the bull.' He
lapsed into silence for a moment. 'All the others were with Geos,
by the gate?'

'I think so. Elemon and Tryphone were there with Geos. Thaos
and Curgis were a few steps behind them.'

'Then what happened?'

'I joined Geos but I couldn't see anything.' I stopped, remembering the thunderous pounding of the bulls' hooves. 'It was so
noisy. All the bulls were stamping and running and bellowing.'

'Go on.'

'When no one would let me through, I went to the side and
pushed a loose board away. That's when I . . .' I couldn't continue.

'When you saw the body?' Tinos looked at me sympathetically.
I nodded. 'Do you know of anyone who had issues with Duzi?'

'Not that I saw. But I didn't spend time with him or with the
other men. I really only socialized with Arphaia and Obelix. We
used to go to the market.' I smiled, remembering.

'What else, Martis?'

'I think Tryphone and Duzi went places together but I don't
know where. I never saw Elemon with anyone.'

'Tell me about your friendship with Duzi,' Tinos said.

'We talked sometimes,' I said cautiously.

'No more than that?' Tinos sounded sharp, and I hoped he
was jealous.

'No,' I assured him.

'Do you know where Duzi lived?'

'I think by the docks?' I wasn't sure and planned to ask my friend Tetis. She worked the docks and knew most of the people around there. I didn't intend to confide that to either Tinos or my mother, though.

'Did he have family here?'

'He mentioned a brother. But I am not sure the brother lived here, on Crete.'

Tinos sighed in frustration.

'Was he truly a pirate?' I asked. Tinos nodded.

'He was. They don't often attack Knossos – we have too many ships and sailors – but they go on to Egypt. Pharoah asked the High Priestess to stop them when we could. As I understand it, some of our navy saw the ships and challenged them. After the battle, Duzi was pulled from the water, along with a few others.'

'Could his murderer be one of the other sailors?' I asked.

'Doubtful. Most of them were executed.'

'I'm sorry I don't know more,' I said now. 'I would tell you if I did.'

'It's more than I heard from Arphaia.' He grimaced.

'I don't think Arphaia and Duzi did much talking,' I said acidly. Tinos laughed. Although it was nice to see his frown disappear, I immediately felt guilty for my catty remark. I doubted Arphaia and Duzi had done more than talk, and maybe kiss. A female bull dancer couldn't jump if she were pregnant; it threw her balance off. We were all very careful.

'She's from a farm on the outskirts of Knossos,' I continued more seriously. 'I believe she has several brothers and at least one sister.' I paused, wishing I'd paid more attention to her chatter. 'I remember she had some conflict with her uncle, so her mother sent her to an aunt near Knossos. That's what she said, anyway.' I paused again. The uncle was her mother's brother and, as was customary, bore some responsibility for his sister's children. 'Arphaia described him as bossy and controlling.'

'Hmm.'

'I also suspect she hated living on the farm,' I added. 'Hated the work. She became a bull dancer for the fame and the riches.'

Tinos nodded. A popular bull dancer like Elemon, or Tinos

himself when he'd performed, could find himself showered with valuable jewelry. Retirement at the top of his celebrity could mean other honors. Tinos had become consort to the High Priestess. 'I don't think either fame or riches are in Arphaia's future,' he remarked now. 'She jumps like a sick cow.'

I smiled. 'Unkind but accurate,' I agreed. 'But at least she isn't afraid of the bull.'

'I suppose you are planning to talk to her?' Tinos said.

'Of course,' I said, purposely misunderstanding him. 'I see her almost every day.'

Tinos shot me an annoyed look. 'I meant about Duzi's murder.'

Of course I was planning to question her, but I didn't want to tell him that. 'I will follow the conversation wherever it leads,' I said evasively. 'Anyway, Arphaia is likely to speak more freely to me than to you.'

Since that was true, Tinos couldn't argue. 'Be careful,' he said instead. 'She may be the murderer.'

Laughing derisively, I shook my head. Although I supposed it was possible Arphaia was involved, I couldn't see it. 'She's a young girl,' I said. 'Younger than I am. And a stabbing? Where would she hide a knife? She was wearing a loincloth.'

'I don't know,' Tinos said. 'Maybe she threw it away . . .'

'Weak, very weak. You looked for it, remember? Besides, stabbing seems more like a man's crime to me. And if Arphaia could have discarded the knife, so could any of the male bull dancers.'

'That is true.' Tinos rubbed his hand across his face. 'I won't have time to question her tomorrow. Or the next day, either.' I nodded; tomorrow was the second day of the Harvest Festival, and the day after was the third. Tinos, as consort to the Lady, had many ritual responsibilities. I glanced over my shoulder at the red sky.

'At least it looks like it will be nice tomorrow.'

He looked over my head and nodded. With the arrival of autumn and the coming of winter, Crete was moving into its rainy season. We both could remember previous years when Dionysus's ceremonies took place in the rain.

'There is that,' Tinos agreed. 'You can't think of anything else?' I shook my head. 'If you do, make sure you tell me.' He eyed me sternly before turning and striding across the courtyard, his long robe flapping.

I stared after him. Although I hadn't told him, I hoped to speak to Arphaia tomorrow and Geos and the bull leapers after that. Somebody must have seen something that would help me.

No doubt, Duzi would be laid to rest within a day or two.

I thought of him for a few seconds, my eyes burning. Poor Duzi, to lose his life so young.

As I reflected upon him, and how quickly the Goddess could snatch away one's life, I was reminded that I would have to find his lodgings and search them, hopefully before Tinos did.

I anticipated a busy few days.

SEVEN

As the smell of roasting meat wafted across the space, my stomach grumbled. I'd eaten very little at the noon meal – I never ate much before a performance – and I was ravenous now. I hurried across the courtyard to the cook. She was bending over the hot brazier, turning the strips of meat. I reached out to take a piece of bread.

'Stop,' she said, slapping at my hand. 'You can wait a few minutes.'

'No, I can't,' I said.

'You sound no older than Telemon,' the cook said repressively. Telemon was only six, almost seven. 'You're too old to whine and carry on. Anyway, you have a visitor now.'

'He left,' I said.

'Not the wanax. Your uncle Pylas.'

'Oh, of course.'

Farmers came to Knossos from miles around to participate in the festival. Offering the first fruits to the Dying God ensured a good harvest the following year. Pylas had brought figs and grapes from the villa. Also, as the remaining male member of the family, he would shepherd Telemon through the steps necessary for entry into the dorms. Boys began their agoge as seven-year-olds.

Pylas, my mother's first husband's brother, had wed my eldest sister Opis. The villa, all the fields and olive groves and vineyards around it, had belonged to her. He'd continued as manager after her death. I supposed, as I was the remaining granddaughter, the villa now belonged to me. But I had even less interest in living there than I did in taking on my mother's weaving business while I married and raised a family. Involuntarily, my thoughts flew to the healer's offer, before skittering away. I did not want to think about that now.

Uncle Pylas was seated in the main room with a beaker of wine in his hand and a plate of honey pastries on his lap. He smiled at me as I came inside. My brother sat next to him, a carved wooden bull in one hand and a carved goat in the other.

'Look at what Uncle Pylas gave me,' Telemon said, holding up his new toys.

'By the Goddess,' Pylas said, staring at me in amazement, 'you look quite grown up.' I smiled uncomfortably, unsure what to say.

'She will be entering her agoge in a few months, when she turns seventeen,' my mother said.

'I start my agoge in a few days,' Telemon announced proudly.

I saw tears fill my mother's eyes. 'He's growing up,' she said. 'My baby is growing up.'

'You still have Ria to care for,' I said. Ria was Opis's daughter, born before my sister's death, and still only seven months old.

A spasm of regret flashed across Pylas's face. As far as everyone knew, Ria was his daughter. I knew that wasn't true, but the truth was something no one discussed.

'It won't be the same here,' my mother said. I nodded. I would miss Telemon, too. And even though he would come home periodically for visits, it truly wouldn't be the same. He would grow into a different person, a young man, with a whole life we didn't know about and couldn't share. My own eyes filled but I quickly dashed them away. Telemon was so proud of himself.

'The food is ready,' the cook said from the door.

I rose early the next morning, just as the sun was beginning to rise above the horizon. I knew Tinos would have been up even before this, long before daybreak. In his role as the Dying God, he would be traveling around accepting the first fruits and blessing the harvests. I hoped to have visited Arphaia and returned home by then.

When I stepped outside, I saw a few enterprising shopkeepers opening their shops by lamplight, but the streets were mostly empty. I cut through several alleys until I reached the main road. Then I started walking, traveling east, toward the farms on the outskirts of the city.

The dirt surface was not as dusty as it would have been during the dry summer, nor as muddy as it would be later this month as the rains occurred more often. In the cool morning air, the walk was refreshing, but I was glad I wore my jacket.

I passed the cemetery and realized I hadn't visited the family, especially my sister Arge, for some time. I would have to do so soon. Arge would be interested in Duzi's murder.

I quickly left the cemetery behind. A thick band of forest separated the cemetery and the vineyards and farms beyond. These woods stretched from this northern strip to the mountains at the south. I couldn't see the snow-capped peaks over the trees, but I knew they were there. Timber came out of these forests for export, mainly to Egypt but to other nearby nations as well.

It was mid-morning by the time I left the forest behind me. Vineyards rolled over the hills to my left. I saw the gray-green leaves of growing olive trees behind the fields. Was this the farm Arphaia mentioned?

Laborers toiled in the vineyards, picking the ripe grapes. A row of people stood along the road with baskets of grapes and figs resting at their feet. These would be offered to Dionysus.

'Martis,' someone shouted.

I turned toward the sound. A young woman waved at me. Was that Arphaia? I would never have recognized her. Instead of the boy's kilt in which I'd always seen her, she wore a fine woolen skirt of a soft blue with a matching jacket. Several gold necklaces glittered over her linen shirt, and her dark hair was dressed in the latest style and decorated with clips. She looked quite pretty.

'Arphaia,' I said in amazement as I approached her.

'What are you doing here?' she asked.

'I came to see how you are,' I said. She nodded, tears flooding her eyes. With a quick glance over her shoulder at an older woman behind her, Arphaia moved toward me.

'I'm sad about Duzi.' Her tears smudged the kohl around her eyes.

'Of course,' I said. 'You probably knew him best.'

Arphaia shrugged. 'Maybe. We saw each other for such a short time. It wasn't serious.' She smiled, a small private smile that piqued my curiosity.

'Did you want it to be?' I asked. She vehemently shook her head. 'Did he?' She hesitated, her gaze rising so that she stared over my head.

'I think so,' she said at last. 'He talked about settling down and raising a family. I'm not sure I'm ready for that yet.'

I nodded. Arphaia was younger than I was, and I certainly did not want to marry and settle down.

'Not with him, anyway.' She smiled again, and I became even surer than before that she'd met someone else. 'It was you he was really interested in.'

'Me?' I shook my head. 'I don't want to marry, either,' I said.

'Is that the only reason you weren't interested in Duzi?' she asked, her smile broadening. 'I've seen the way you look at Tinos.'

Heat surged into my cheeks. Since I most definitely did not want to discuss my feelings for Tinos, I changed the subject. 'Is there anywhere we can talk?' I asked. 'I know you told the wanax a little about Duzi, but I think there's more.'

She hesitated. 'Are you hungry?' she asked at last.

'Starving,' I said. I'd left the apartments without eating breakfast.

'The Dying God will not be here for a little while yet. Let's go back to the villa and eat something,' she suggested. 'We can talk there.' She brought me to an older woman, as tanned as Arphaia and with the same pronounced cheekbones. 'My aunt.' To her, Arphaia said, 'This is my friend, Martis.'

The aunt inspected me with curious eyes. Her hair was tied back and she wore a scarlet cloth over it. 'She's spoken of you,' she said.

'We're going inside for breakfast,' Arphaia continued, gesturing to me. 'Come on.'

EIGHT

As we walked up the slope to the house, Arphaia said over her shoulder, 'We should talk in private. I don't want my aunt to send me back to my uncle.'

'I know you don't want to live there.'

'No. My uncle wants me to marry a man on the next farm over. His friend.' She rolled her eyes at me and added, 'An old man. That way, both farms will be together and much larger.'

'I suppose you will inherit when your mother dies?' I asked.

Arphaia nodded her head. 'I'm the oldest girl. Already my younger sister is married and living far away.'

I blinked at that. Arphaia was only fifteen. How old was her sister? 'What does your mother say?'

'She allows her brother to decide everything.'

I glanced at her, surprised by the anger and bitterness in her voice. 'I can't imagine my mother allowing that to happen,' I murmured.

I followed Arphaia into a large room with a stone floor. A wide table covered with dishes sat on one side. It looked as though several people had made something to eat and then left the remains on the table. I saw some kind of barley mush, flat-bread, several baskets of fruit and a dry, crumbly goat cheese. Several flagons of beer and wine and a pot of spiced meat completed the offerings. Arphaia went to a large basket of figs and scooped up a handful. I helped myself to the bread and the figs and began to eat.

'So . . . Duzi,' I said, my mouth full.

'I enjoyed spending time with him,' Arphaia said with a smile. 'But you know he was not a Cretan. He hated bull dancing.' I nodded; that I knew. 'He was looking for a wife with a farm or a fishing boat or a business. That's what he wanted.' She grimaced. 'I didn't want to marry someone who wanted my farm.' Her eyes suddenly filled with tears and she wiped them away with the back of her hand. 'I might as well have stayed home if I did that.'

'He owned nothing?' I asked as soon as I could trust my voice.

'Not a thing. Even Tryphone arrived in Knossos with some jewelry.' She shook her head.

'Do you know where he lived?' I asked. I knew Tinos would ask her this.

'Somewhere near the docks. Near a tavern.'

Since that was not uncommon, I simply nodded.

'He was too poor to buy food and was always hungry. I think Geos fed him sometimes. Like he does Costi,' she added. 'But most of all, what I liked least is that Duzi was not interested in any girl without property.'

'How did he know about your farm?' I asked.

'I told him,' she admitted, blushing. 'It was in the beginning. I said all kinds of things, hoping he'd be interested in me. It wasn't until I talked about the farm that he paid attention. And then, whenever we talked, he always brought up the farm.'

I hesitated a moment. 'I thought he was a sailor,' I said at last. 'A pirate.'

'All of his people are sailors and pirates. But they own homes and farms in their lands, too. That's what he wants.' She sighed. I nodded. What Arphaia said made sense. But I had a nagging feeling she still hadn't told me everything.

'Does Tinos know this?' I asked. Duzi had been given a lot of freedom for someone pulled out of the water after a battle.

Arphaia shrugged. 'I didn't tell him. Why would he be interested in that?'

'He'd be interested in everything,' I said tartly. Arphaia shrugged again, her gaze sliding away from mine. She was definitely keeping something to herself. 'Did Duzi talk to any of the other bull dancers?' I asked.

'Well, he—'

'Here you are.' A young man with thick curly hair and bright eyes entered the room. Ignoring me, he approached Arphaia and put a hand on her shoulder. She smiled up at him, her entire face glowing. I watched with interest. Was this the someone Arphaia had found? 'Your mother sent me to fetch you. The Dying God will soon be here.'

Arphaia jumped to her feet. 'I'm ready, Zeno.' Suddenly remembering me, she turned and said, 'Are you finished eating?'

Without waiting for my answer, she and Zeno started for the door.

'Yes.' I stood and followed the laughing couple. I'd never thought of Arphaia as a pretty girl who would be of interest to a young man, but she clearly had something I didn't see.

By the time we reached the main road, puffs of dust from the oncoming procession were visible. The wooden bull's head came into view first, the horns rising high above the post that elevated it. Then the priest who held the standard, his long robes flapping, appeared. Behind him was another priest playing a flute. The thin sound of the music could barely be heard above the excited shouts of the farmers gathered along the road.

Finally, Tinos appeared, riding a goat. Instead of a long robe, he wore a rather ragged lion's skin to show his mastery of all the animals. His black hair hung loose underneath a circlet of ivy, and the mask of the Dying God's face covered Tinos's entire head. Other priests surrounded him, and as the farmers rushed forward holding baskets of grapes and figs, pomegranates and more, the priests accepted the offerings. More priests followed, bearing a palanquin, piled high with the offerings, on their shoulders. The fruits would be sacrificed to the God tomorrow.

Tinos dismounted from the goat. He did not seem aware of the hands reaching out to touch the lion skin and perhaps gain some of the God's favor for the coming year. He paused by the vineyard that edged the road. Arphaia's aunt handed him a beaker of wine. Calling on Dionysus, the God of the Harvest and Master of Animals, Tinos poured the red liquid on the ground. It was probably recently made, and as harsh-tasting as flint, but the expectation was that the God Who Dies would appreciate the offering. His favor would ensure a good grape harvest next year, as well as plentiful yields of olives, wheat and barley in the spring.

I wondered how many times Tinos had already performed this ceremony today.

My mother had told me when I was younger that this ritual had once been performed with the sacrifice of the wanax and it was his blood sprinkled on the soil instead of wine. I shuddered at the thought, glad that we no longer practiced that.

When the beaker was empty, Tinos returned to the road and

remounted the goat. The procession started forward once again. I was aware of the exact moment when he saw me. The eyes framed by the mask's eyeholes widened and he shook his head. Although he could not reprove me now, I knew I would suffer a scolding about this later.

The farmers thronging the road began to drift away. I turned and looked around for Arphaia, but she was nowhere to be seen. And neither was the young man she had sparkled at. I did not doubt they had taken the opportunity, when everyone's attention was elsewhere, to sneak away together.

Since even Arphaia's aunt was also returning to the villa, I started down the road toward Knossos. I would have to hurry if I wanted to reach the city before the procession did.

I almost made it. Tinos and the string of priests had stopped in front of the Priestess House. Tinos himself was out of sight in the vineyard that served the women. All the priestesses, including my mother, stood silently by the road. I sidled past the empty palanquin – the full one had been swapped out – and slipped into the Sacred Grove. I expected the trees would screen me as I positioned myself at the back of the crowd of onlookers. My mother would know I'd left the apartments – she would have found an empty room when she went to wake me – but I hoped I could keep her from knowing exactly where I'd been. She would not want me investigating Duzi's death. I wished Tinos didn't know either, but it was too late to fix that.

When Tinos stepped out of the vineyards, I shifted myself so I was closer to the front so my mother would see me from across the road. As the palanquin turned around, she crossed. 'Where were you this morning?' she asked.

'I was too excited to sleep,' I said truthfully.

She eyed me suspiciously but did not question me further.

'Where's Telemon?' I asked, trying to distract her. She pointed with her chin. When I turned, I saw Telemon with another, shorter boy.

'They'll be going into the agoge at the same time,' my mother said. She sighed, shaking her head.

'We should rescue the boy's mother,' I said, threading my way through the crowd. Besides Telemon's friend, the poor woman had two smaller children with her and a babe in her arms. Smiling at the woman, I called to Telemon. He threw a mutinous glance in my direction and did not move.

'Thank you so much for watching him,' my mother said from behind me.

The woman nodded. I eyed her more closely. I knew her slightly; she was only six or seven years older than I was but she looked older. Harried and tired, she seemed far too exhausted to speak or even smile.

'Telemon has had such a good time with your son. Why don't you let him visit with us for a little while,' my mother said warmly.

The young woman – I couldn't remember her name – brightened. 'Thank you. Thank you so much,' she said.

'Come, Telemon,' Mother said. 'Bring your friend.'

We walked together down the path. I looked behind once at the young woman. She was trying to gather up the other three without much success. I shook my head, promising myself I would never allow my life to diminish into that.

NINE

Tinos arrived at the apartment after my mother and I had eaten supper. By then the sun was beginning to set and my mother lit the lamps. Telemon was in his room; I could hear him humming and the clicking of his new wooden toys as he played with them.

Tinos, bathed and changed from the lion skin into a robe, was once more the fashionable man I knew. Feathers danced in his hair and on his left arm he wore several glittering bangles.

'What did Arphaia tell you?' he asked me without preamble.

'Arphaia? Your friend?' my mother asked me. I nodded.

'Arphaia was present when Duzi's body was found,' Tinos said without removing his gaze from me. 'And Martis was out of the city this morning, visiting Arphaia at the villa where she lives.'

My mother stared at me, shock becoming anger. 'I knew

something was off,' she said. 'You never leave home without eating. But you did this morning.' She stopped and bit her lip.

'What did Arphaia tell you?' Tinos repeated, glaring at me.

'Not very much that you don't already know,' I said. 'Duzi lived somewhere near the docks.'

Tinos nodded. 'Yes, I knew that.'

'If he was a pirate, plucked from the water after a battle, why was he allowed to roam around Knossos at will?' my mother interjected.

'He asked for asylum.' Tinos shrugged. 'We were keeping an eye on him. Geos said he was doing well.' He looked at me. 'So . . . Arphaia?'

'As I told you, I don't think Arphaia and Duzi talked very much.' I thought of the young man she'd been so captivated by. 'In fact, Arphaia and Duzi were no longer seeing one another. She'd cooled toward him.' I thought of something else I felt comfortable sharing with Tinos. 'She said he wanted to marry a girl who owned a farm or a business. That's what changed her feelings.'

'Ah,' Tinos said in comprehension. 'Do we know how Duzi felt?'

I shrugged. I didn't. 'I didn't see any obvious jealousy,' I said.

'Does Arphaia have any other jealous discarded boyfriends?'

'Not that I know of.' I paused. She might have and I just hadn't noticed. I was beginning to wonder if I'd paid sufficient attention to the rest of the team. Maybe there'd been something, and I'd been blind to it.

'What about the other girl? Could Duzi—'

'Obelix? Forget her. Duzi called her Fish Guts. No romance there. But there's Nub—'

'Hmm. How old is she?'

'Twelve, I think.'

'Forget her for now,' Tinos said. 'She's probably too young. Let's concentrate on the men.'

'Without Duzi, there are four others. Elemon, Tryphone, Thaos and Curgis. As far as I saw, Elemon ignored Arphaia, although she might be interested in him – he's wealthy and famous. Thaos and Curgis are in the final year of their agoge so they live in the dorms.'

Tinos shook his head. 'It's possible but it would be difficult for either of them to slip out. They are kept busy.'

'Tryphone?' I suggested. 'Maybe. He is a surly fellow, though.' I paused and thought for a moment. 'There is a young man on the farm – Zeno his name is' I considered him. 'Why would he be jealous? Arphaia is still too interested in him.' Unless Duzi had been the jealous one. But he had been the victim, and I knew I hadn't seen the handsome farm youth hanging around the practice ring. I would have remembered that.

'What about the boy that jumped last?' Tinos persisted.

'Costi? He's only thirteen. Arphaia treated him like a child.' I pictured Costi in my mind. He was short and scrawny and seemed to fly over a bull's back. 'Anyway, I can't imagine him possessing the strength necessary to drag Duzi into the bull pen.'

'Why are you dissecting the death?' my mother demanded. 'I thought Duzi's death was an accident, but you're discussing it as though it was a murder.'

I looked at Tinos, my mind going blank. He was staring at me. The silence expanded until it became awkwardly obvious that Tinos and I were hiding the truth. 'Another murder?' my mother said unhappily. 'And you are investigating it, aren't you, Martis?'

'No,' I said quickly. 'Not really. It's just that, well, I thought Arphaia would be more willing to talk to me than to Tinos.'

'She doesn't find me charming,' he put in dryly.

'Please don't involve her in this,' my mother said to Tinos. 'Last time, she was almost killed.' Sudden tears filled her eyes. 'I couldn't bear it if I lost another child.'

'I told her not to question Arphaia or anyone else, Nephele,' Tinos said defensively. 'She didn't listen. I couldn't believe it when I saw her on the road standing next to that other girl.'

My mother turned her reproachful gaze on me.

'It wasn't dangerous,' I said quickly. 'Arphaia is my friend. I ate breakfast at the villa. She is not the killer.' But she knew something; I was sure of it. I turned an innocent look on Tinos. 'You can talk to her again if you want. But I think you'll see she knows nothing.'

Tinos sighed. 'So, we are no further ahead than we were.'

'*You* are no further ahead,' Mother said, emphasizing the pronoun. 'I don't want Martis involved.'

Tinos said nothing but he glanced at me. He knew – he and my mother both knew – that no one could forbid me to investigate if I chose to do so. Not even the High Priestess herself could make me obey.

My mother woke me early, very early, on the third day of the week-long ceremony. Stars still twinkled in the dark sky. I dressed in my newest jacket and skirt and fastened the tight gold and silver belt around my waist. I instantly felt as though I couldn't breathe. But I did not remove it. Today everyone would wear their best.

When I went into the main room, Telemon and Pylas were already there. Pylas glanced at me with bleary eyes, and I wondered where he'd been the night before. Not here; that I knew.

'Eat something, Martis,' my mother said. 'And be quick about it. It is a long walk to the Dying God's Sanctuary.'

Because this was a festival honoring Dionysus, the ceremony did not take place in the Sacred Grove but at a distant forest spot in the foothills of the mountains. The Dying God is not a God of towns and cities but of woods and fields. Although my mother preferred the more restrained worship of the Goddess, I enjoyed the harvest festivals far more. The morning began with declamations by poets and segued into plays depicting stories involving Gods and Goddesses, monsters and heroes. Dionysus was usually the star, recognizable in his lion skin tunic and the ivy wreath on his horned brow. The poets and the masked actors would continue presenting their works for the remainder of the week in the Knossos theater.

After the conclusion of the plays and the poetry in the Sanctuary, the first fruits were sent to the God on a wave of flame and smoke. Then a bull and several goats were sacrificed, their hide and bones delivered to the fire. His meat was distributed to his worshippers in a grand feast. Tinos and the High Priestess consummated their union at the conclusion of the festival; I planned to slip away before then and hurry back to Knossos. I couldn't watch Tinos with the High Priestess; I just couldn't.

Anyway, I needed some time away from my mother's watchful gaze to visit the docks, find Duzi's room and search it. I wouldn't have more than a few hours. My mother never stayed all day at the festival. Since Dionysus was also the God of wine, it flowed freely, and as the day turned into night, the behavior of his worshippers grew more and more unrestrained. She did not approve.

'Are you planning on remaining at the festival all day?' I asked her. I wanted to be sure I could escape when the time came.

'No.' She glanced at me suspiciously. 'I'll leave long before dark, as I always do. It becomes . . . dangerous.'

'He is the God of harvest and of wine,' I said as though I did not understand what she meant. But I did. Drunkenness was the least of it. My older sister Opis had spoken admiringly of couples copulating behind every bush and tree. As someone who followed the virginal aspect of the Goddess, and who planned to remain untouched, I was just as happy to agree with my mother in this case.

'He is an old God. Some of his devoted followers engage in rituals.' My mother shook her head. 'The Goddess I serve does not approve.' Again, she went silent. But I was satisfied. I knew now how much time I could expect to have for my search.

TEN

The forest clearing was thronged with people in bright clothing. Despite our early departure, we were among the last to arrive. I could smell woodsmoke: the bonfire that would consume the offerings had been lit. My mother and I both gravitated toward the center of the cleared space. A man in a dirty robe was declaiming the story of Zeus-Dionysus's birth in a cave, nursed by goats. I recognized the poet; he regularly presented his works in Knossos. Since he always returned to the stories of the past, I found his poetry uninteresting. I preferred the younger, newer poets.

I glanced around to see if I recognized anyone.

'Nephele,' said a voice nearby. 'And this must be your family.'

'Lavra,' my mother said with a certain cautious reserve. I turned.

The white-haired older woman smiled at me. Although she wore a jacket and skirt, they were plain, without the woven pattern and flounces that made clothing fashionable. Her hair went down her back in two long braids. She glanced at Telemon but she stared at me with such great interest I shifted uncomfortably.

'So this is Martis,' she murmured. 'Are you interested in joining the priestesses, as your sisters Opis and Arge did?'

'I am a bull dancer,' I replied. I did not want to become a priestess, ever. Although powerful, their lives were governed by endless rituals. I thought again of the healer's offer. That profession also required numerous prayers, and the healers were also frequently priestesses too, since their craft involved invoking the Goddess and magic as well as knowledge of herbs and wound care. Still, the healer who'd asked me about apprenticing was not a priestess but a woman from far away. And, as a healer, I would still have more freedom than a priestess.

'Surely you worship the Goddess?' Lavra challenged me.

'I do,' I looked at my mother for help.

'She follows the virgin aspect of the Lady,' she put in quickly.

'The Lady of childbirth and animals,' Lavra said approvingly. 'Perhaps someday you will become a healer.'

I started and tried to smile, my lips stiff. I wasn't sure what to say to that. How odd that Lavra suggested such a path. Was becoming a healer my destiny?

'It is time for the ceremony,' my mother said, glancing over her shoulder. Lavra followed her gaze.

'Yes, it is. It was nice to finally meet you, Martis.' Lavra inclined her head and joined the throng.

'Who is that?' I asked my mother when Lavra was out of earshot.

'One of the oldest of the priestesses. Very powerful.'

'And?' I glanced at my mother. 'I can hear your hesitation.'

Nephele looked at me. 'She is a follower of Dionysus. As Opis was. Even I do not know all those rituals.' She shuddered. 'I hope you do not follow in your sister's footsteps, Martis.'

I thought of Opis who had died a horrible death and shivered involuntarily.

We joined the throng climbing the slope up to the ledge above. I saw several priestesses in the crowd but not on the rock platform; this part of the ceremony belonged to Tinos and the priests.

The path that led up climbed over rocks and tree roots and sometimes bare dirt. In some places, the combination of the incline and the loose stones made the footing treacherous, especially for those of us in long skirts. Telemon leaped over the rocks and darted up the hill like a young goat. *His pumping arms and legs wrote an ode to the Goddess*, I thought. I would have to add that line to one of my poems.

I followed Telemon slowly, envying him the freedom of movement afforded by his loincloth. I had to assist my mother who was struggling even more than I was. If I clung to a sapling and extended my hand to help her, she could pull herself over the rocks. Although the air was much cooler than it was during the hot dry summer, the combination of the bright sun and the strenuous exercise bathed me in perspiration.

After about twenty or so minutes of climbing, we reached the flat sheet of bedrock in front of a small cliff. A wide ledge protruded from the rock face and on it was piled a mountain of first fruits heaped on logs and tinder. The fire had been set at one end; it was just a modest blaze so far, but after the necessary prayers and salutations were proclaimed to the heavens above, the priests would light long thin sticks and bring the flames to the wood underneath the offerings. The entire mound would catch on fire, and the inferno would stretch all the way to the heavens.

Tinos, in his role as Dionysus, sat on a stone throne a distance away. He once again wore the bedraggled lion skin and a fresh wreath upon his head but not the mask of the grinning horned God. Grim and unsmiling, he looked quite different from the tired man who had visited me the previous night.

Several of the younger priests carried baskets of grapes and figs and other fruit to lay at Tinos's feet. He waved his hands over them. As the young men tossed these offerings on the pile, an old priest, his hair glittering silver in the dappled sunlight, lifted his arms and began to pray in a loud and sonorous voice.

As the priests began to shout invocations to both Dionysus and to the Goddess, my attention wandered. I looked around to see if I could spot any other bull dancers among the crowd. There was Nub, with a mother and young sister who looked enough like her to recognize as family. Obelix slouched against a tree to one side. Arphaia stood at the back with someone I thought was her aunt. No headscarf today, so she appeared quite different. But I recognized the young man she stood arm in arm with as the handsome Zeno I'd seen at the farm.

Tryphone stood to one side, alone and scowling ferociously. Over what, I wondered. Costi and the twins were racing around apparently with no parent or minder. They'd stolen fruit and were eating it with great gusto.

Finally, I saw Elemon. As usual, young women surrounded him. I eyed him critically; I did not think he was that handsome. His thin lips turned down like a reversed crescent moon and made him look mean. I turned my gaze to the women vying for his attention. Some of those faces I recognized as part of Opis's set. Weren't they all married now? It didn't seem to matter. They were clustered around Elemon like bees around honey, smiling up at him and trying to gain his attention.

Hmm. I wondered if Tinos could see them. Once he'd been in Elemon's boots, surrounded by young women who'd lavished gifts upon him. Tryphone was beginning to attract interest, although not to the degree Elemon did. Would Duzi have become as popular? He had not been unattractive.

'Pay attention,' my mother scolded me, shaking my arm. 'Sometimes you are as difficult as Telemon. Worse, because you should know better.' I dragged my gaze back to the ledge and the interminable prayers.

Finally, as the sun reached the zenith, the invocations and entreaties came to a stop. Tinos rose from the throne and walked to the front of the pyre. A priest brought a lighted brand and Tinos held it to the tinder. As the flame caught, other priests ran forward with more burning splints. The fire took hold, the tinder catching with a shower of sparks.

As smoke rose into the sky, the smell of charring fruit poured into the Grove.

> Fireflies glowing on the wings of the smoke
> The sparks rise to the sky, carrying the sweet scents
> Grapes and figs, pomegranates to nourish
> The God who dies and is reborn every spring—

My mother shook my arm and I realized I was muttering the lines of my poem to myself. When I glanced at her, she frowned reprovingly.

Tinos returned to his throne to await the High Priestess. Trailed by three attendants, she walked across the ledge. She wore a long robe like the one Tinos wore sometimes, but open in the front. She too carried a basket brimming with fruit but also seed wheat and barley. Tinos stood up. If possible, his expression was even grimmer than before, almost as though he expected to be sacrificed and his blood sprinkled on the ground. But he was not afraid, only angry.

I couldn't watch. It was time for me to go. 'Will you be all right?' I asked my mother. 'I'm going to the back.' I gestured in the general direction of Arphaia. My mother directed a compassionate glance at me and nodded.

'Go,' she said. I began to move away from her, but she caught me by the arm. 'Wait for me down below,' she said. 'We'll sit together. After the feast, we'll go home.'

I gave her a half-nod that could have meant anything and turned away. She would not find me in the clearing below; I would be in Knossos by the docks, and – as was my plan – searching Duzi's room. I hoped she did not look for me too hard but instead assumed I'd returned to the apartments.

I started down the slope. Curiously, the image I carried in my thoughts was the sympathy on my mother's face. It was as though she knew of my affection for Tinos. I didn't want anyone to know, and the thought that she did was the most unsettling feeling of all.

ELEVEN

The long walk back to the city was not quick, and it was almost mid-afternoon by the time I reached the outskirts of Knossos. The streets were quiet since most of the inhabitants were at the ceremony. I went directly to the docks. Although busier with foreign sailors than the rest of Knossos, it did not bustle with incoming and outgoing ships as it usually did.

I found Tetis at a tavern eating olives. She looked at me in surprise. 'What are you doing here? Does your mother know you're visiting me at the docks?'

'I hope you might know something that will help me,' I said, ignoring her questions. Of course my mother didn't know.

'I see,' she said drily. 'You need my help. What is it this time?'

'I'm looking for the room where Duzi lived?'

'Who?'

'The pirate. We were both here on the docks when he was brought ashore.'

'Of course. I didn't know his name was Duzi. He became a bull dancer?'

'Yes.'

'And that is how you know him?'

'Yes.' I bit my lip and willed my emotion back. 'He was found dead in the bull's pen two days ago.'

'I heard. But the story is the bull gored him.' Tetis eyed me sharply with those strange blue eyes. I made the sign of the horns behind my back and retreated a step. I didn't believe she had powers but there was no harm in being careful.

'He was found trampled,' I agreed cautiously.

This time Tetis stared at me for several unnerving seconds. Finally, she said, 'I know you are keeping something back. There's more to this story.' Although she paused, I did not respond. 'I expect you to tell me all about it someday.'

'I will.' That was an easy promise to make. 'Do you know where Duzi lived?'

'In the general area. Why?'

I struggled to think of a plausible lie, but nothing came to mind, and I blurted out the truth. 'I want to search his place.'

'What do you expect to find? He was poor. Very poor.'

I shrugged; I didn't know. 'I just thought there might be something there,' I said.

'I see.' Again, she shot me a glance from those light eyes. 'You suspect he was murdered. Does the wanax know you think that?'

'He does,' I said uncomfortably. 'But he doesn't know I'm here.'

Tetis shook her head at me. 'Someday your recklessness will get you into trouble,' she said. 'Come on.' Popping the last olive in her mouth, she stepped away from the counter.

'Are you coming with me?'

'Of course. You'll never find it by yourself.'

She led me from the street into a warren of back alleys. Strewn with rubbish and pungent with the smells of urine and rotting garbage, these narrow lanes appeared to belong to a different city than the one I knew.

I quickly lost my bearings. I tried but I couldn't keep track of all the turns. If Tetis abandoned me, I would not be able to find my way out. Even she seemed uncertain a few times, hesitating at the junction of two passageways before deciding on one.

At last, she came to a stop in front of a small dark tavern. The shutters were up, but she hammered on them until one of them swung back and a face peered out. A heavy-set man with thick eyebrows, a large fleshy nose and a mole right beside it looked out at us. 'Did I wake you?' Tetis asked, but not as though she cared.

'No. I would be opening soon anyway,' he said. His speech was heavily accented, and I could barely understand him. He looked at Tetis and then at me, his gaze running up and down my body. I stepped behind Tetis, suddenly frightened. 'What are you doing here?' he asked.

'Do you know Duzi?' Tetis asked. She did not seem frightened, just wary, and I wondered if she knew him.

'Of course. What do you want with him?'

Tetis stepped to one side and gestured to me. 'Duzi is dead,' I said.

'Dead?' His heavy eyebrows rose. 'I knew he was not around . . . How did he die?'

'He was found in the bull's pen,' Tetis said.

'I warned him. I told him jumping over a bull would kill him.'

'She found him.' Tetis pointed at me. His gaze moved to me once again, but this time he was only curious.

'You're one of those bull leapers?'

I nodded. 'We were friends, Duzi and me.'

'He told me he had a good friend.' He leered at me.

'That was not me,' I said stiffly, wondering if he was talking about Arphaia or someone else. 'Duzi and I were just friends. Did you ever see his woman friend?'

'No. She never came here. He told me she had an elegant home. He always visited her there.'

Elegant? Could the farm where Arphaia lived be described as elegant? I doubted it. Arphaia told me Duzi had found someone else. At the time, I hadn't believed her but now I wondered. Could that someone be one of the fashionable ladies who swarmed around the bull dancers? 'Do you know where that elegant house was?' I asked.

'In Knossos, I suppose.' He shrugged a beefy shoulder.

'Did Duzi ever describe her?'

'No.'

'Did he tell you anything about her?' Tetis asked.

'Why would he? We weren't friends.'

'Did he have any friends?' I asked.

'He didn't spend much time here. Why?'

Struck by inspiration, I said, 'I am trying to find his girlfriend, to give Duzi's things to her. She was closest to him. That is why we're here.'

'Duzi didn't own anything,' he said discouragingly.

'You seem to know him well, even if you weren't friends.' I leaned forward. He shrugged.

'He was my countryman. I gave him a room for a small rent.'

'Can I see that room?' I asked.

He eyed us both again and finally nodded 'Very well. At the top of the stairs.' He disappeared briefly to unbar and open the door.

Inside, it stank powerfully of beer and unwashed people.

I started up the rickety wooden flight, but Tetis lingered behind me. 'I haven't seen you for a few weeks,' she said to the man as she leaned enticingly toward him.

I did not hear his response. I knew now how she'd known of him and this tavern. But I wasn't here to judge. I continued to the second level on my own.

The door at the top of the stairs stood open as though someone had already gone inside. It was a tiny room, barely bigger than a closet, and with only one small window. The stench from the alley filled the chamber and I put my arm over my nose. The scant furnishings consisted of a pallet on the floor and two ragged cushions. The rug he used to cover himself at night lay between the wall and the pallet, thrust aside as though he'd jumped hurriedly to his feet to leave. There were no eating utensils that I could see, not even a spoon. Unless they'd been stolen. Considering the neighborhood, that was possible. I shook my head, a wave of pity sweeping over me, followed by shame. This was truly terrible.

No wonder Duzi spent so much time with the bull dancers. There was nothing for him here. I wished I had paid more attention to Duzi, especially since it was now clear to me he could have used a friend. I hoped the woman the tavern keeper had spoken of, if she were not Arphaia, who clearly had already moved on to someone else, was another, nicer woman, who had treated Duzi kindly.

I took a few steps further into the tiny room. I picked up the cushions, not only ragged but quite dirty, and just as quickly dropped them. I took a few more steps and kicked the pallet with my foot. It skidded across the floor, leaving a streak mark in the dust. Then I shook out the tattered rug. Along with several insects that skittered away, something metal pinged on the floor. I picked up a small dragonfly hair clip. I knew it did not and never had belonged to Duzi. It was far too valuable. The dragonfly's body was gold, the eyes, lapis lazuli. Jeweled chips, all different colors, spattered the wings so they seemed to flicker with the movement of the light.

Where had Duzi come by such a costly piece of jewelry?

'Did you check the cushions?' Tetis asked, coming to the door behind me. I quickly stuffed the hair clip underneath my tight belt. I didn't doubt I would have a bruise there by the end of the day, but I did not want Tetis to know I had the piece. Her first instinct would be to trade it for something.

'No,' I said, turning with a smile. 'They are too filthy.'

Nodding, she gingerly picked up the pillows and shook them.

I touched my belt thoughtfully. I was sure this clip was connected to Duzi's death. I needed to know exactly how and where he had acquired it.

TWELVE

'You must be disappointed,' Tetis said as we descended the steps and walked away from the tavern.

'Why do you think so?' I asked.

'You didn't learn anything that would help you,' she said, raising her eyebrows. 'There wasn't a thing in that mean little room. And if there had been,' she added under her breath, 'it would have been stolen long ago.'

I shook my head. 'I did learn something.' And I found something; the hair ornament pressed into my skin underneath the belt. 'I did,' I repeated when she looked at me in surprise. 'I learned Duzi was struggling. And he had no one to help him. Now I understand why he spent so much time at the ring with the bull dancers.' Duzi and I had frequently arrived early at the practice ring, earlier than the others, and he was always still there when I left. 'He was so afraid of the bull,' I muttered as tears pricked my eyes. 'I wish I had treated him better.'

Tetis's expression softened. 'I know. But you weren't cruel to him. I know you. And Duzi must have felt welcome among you bull worshippers.'

'That's true,' I agreed, feeling a little happier.

I thought again of Arphaia. Had the split been a mutual one? Or had he moved on first, despite what she'd said? Although I planned to ask her about the dragonfly clip, I could not imagine how she would have come by it. It was a costly piece. Obelix? I shook my head. Even if Duzi hadn't named her Fish Guts, her family were only fishermen. She was even less likely to own it than Arphaia. And then the question became, if not her, who? The lady in the elegant home? And who was she?

Tetis and I separated once she'd guided me to the docks once again, and I started home. Although it was now late afternoon, almost evening, the main street seemed sunnier than the alleys through which I'd just walked. This road smelled better too. At this time of the day, the aroma of roasting meat was predominant; families had begun returning home before the end of the festivities to put their sleepy children to bed.

I passed fathers carrying mewling babies in their arms as their wives and older children trailed behind them. I increased my pace. My mother and brother would be home soon as well, and I didn't want to answer any inconvenient questions.

I made it home just minutes before they came through the door. Since our cook still hadn't returned, I'd found olives and stale flatbread to snack on. 'How was the ritual?' I asked my mother, my mouth full. She bit her lip and shook her head at me.

'Let me see Telemon to his room first.' She followed him down the hall and wished him goodnight. She stopped in and spoke to the wet nurse. I did not care for the woman, who I found surly and unpleasant. After a few minutes, the wet nurse joined me in the main room.

'Goodnight,' I said. She glanced at me and went out the door without speaking.

Now that baby Ria was sleeping, and hopefully down for the night, the nurse was going home to her own children. Her youngest had been weaned to soft foods and so was no longer dependent on his mother's milk.

I'd emptied my bowl by the time my mother returned to the main room. By then the sun was setting, and long golden rays stretched through the windows. The sounds of drunken hilarity outside were so loud it sounded almost like the revelers were in the room with us.

Nephele went to the kitchen and helped herself to a beaker of beer. She carried it into the main room and collapsed on to the cushions with an exhausted sigh.

'What happened?' I asked. Usually, my mother was happier than this.

'It did not go well,' she said, glancing at me. 'Tinos had difficulty performing. I knew they have been quarreling, he and the High Priestess, but I didn't know it had come to such a pass.' She darted a glance at me. Although I could not repress a flare of excited hope, I tried to keep my face blank.

'Maybe Tinos will look elsewhere,' I said. For a brief moment, I pictured myself in Tinos's arms, but even my imagination couldn't carry me further than that.

My mother stared at me disbelievingly. 'It is necessary they consummate their union. Would you have the entire country starve so that he might turn his attentions to you?'

I gasped, stung. 'Of course not.'

'Besides, the Lady is a jealous woman. Even if she doesn't want Tinos any longer, she will not allow him to find another love. A competitor.' She paused for several seconds. 'I suppose it's possible she'll look for another consort, though.'

'Can she do that?' I asked in surprise. Tinos had successfully passed his nine-year trial just this past spring. 'The Goddess accepted Tinos . . .'

My mother nodded. 'I know. Changing a consort has been done, in the past, but it is not a common thing. Usually, the consort was ill, too ill to perform his duties. He would be quickly inducted into the priesthood and be nursed, either back to health or until he died. Then the High Priestess would choose another consort. But in this case . . . I don't know. I just don't know.' She eyed me with a mixture of sternness and compassion. 'Do not believe Tinos would turn to you. Even if he wanted to. For one thing, the High Priestess still wants him. She isn't prepared to surrender him. For another, Tinos has known you a long time. He still thinks of you as a child. No, you will marry some young man after your agoge – a young man your age.'

'I don't ever want to marry,' I said. 'Not even Tinos.' I did not want to continue discussing this. There were many things I kept from my mother, and I'd wanted my desire for Tinos to be one of them. I was angry at myself for so openly displaying my feelings. 'What happened then? After the problem?'

'Well, he finally succeeded.' She paused and blew out a breath. 'Thank the Goddess. In a few days, the farmers will go into the fields to plant wheat and barley. We won't know until next spring whether or not the consummation was successful.' Chewing her lower lip, she shook her head with worry.

'I'm sure it will be fine—' I began, my words interrupted by a yawn. The day had been both stressful and physically active, and I was suddenly so tired I could barely think.

'Please, bathe before you retire,' my mother said. 'I can't imagine what you've been doing, but you are both dirty and sweaty.'

'Very well.' I rose to my feet, but before I'd taken more than two or three steps, someone tapped on the door. I changed direction and went to the entrance to the apartment instead.

To my surprise, Costi stood outside the door. Instead of the grubby loincloth he usually wore, this one was brand new. His hair, even the short strands now growing in, had been combed back, and he'd been recently bathed.

'Who is it?' my mother asked from behind me.

'One of the bull dancers,' I said over my shoulder. I turned back to the front. 'What are you doing here?' I asked him.

'Geos sent me. I wanted to help. Duzi's funeral—' Costi stopped short, his eyes moistening. Looking away, he gulped. I waited patiently until he could pull himself together. 'We will send Duzi home tomorrow morning,' Costi said formally.

'All right. Where will the procession leave from?' Usually, it left from the deceased's home, but right now, I was the only one who knew where Duzi had lived. I did not think any of us wished to meet in those dangerous alleys.

'We will meet at the arena and leave from there.'

'I will be there,' I said.

Costi nodded and stepped back. 'I've other stops to make . . .'

'I'll see you tomorrow,' I said. I watched him march determinedly away. He looked so small.

Sighing, I closed the door and went down the hall to my bedchamber.

Thankfully, I removed the tight belt, catching the gold dragonfly before it fell. Since wasp waists were all the fashion, everyone wore a belt that pinched in the midriff. I went without the belt whenever I could, but today I'd worn it – to be as fashionable as everyone else. I was glad now of my vanity. I held up the gold and bejeweled ornament and examined it. The gem flakes that dusted the wings caught the light, sparkling with the same nacreous color of a living dragonfly. Small rings attached to the body offered a way to secure the piece to a gold necklace or a rope of pearls that twined through the hair. Only the wealthiest among us would own such an exquisite ornament, and that was not Duzi.

I dropped the dragonfly into my jewel box and piled a few of my own ornaments over it. Then, with a sigh of relief, I removed the tight jacket.

By the time I reached the bathroom, the bathtub had been filled with hot water. It steamed faintly; I lowered myself into it with a groan of pleasure. My mother was right; I was dirty. I could see lines of tan skin interrupting the gray where the straps of my sandals had cut across my feet. I lay back until my head rested on the rear lip of the tub.

So, how had that beautiful dragonfly come into Duzi's possession? Had the woman mentioned by the tavern keeper given it to Duzi? Perhaps he'd stolen it? From where? As far as I knew, he did not travel in those circles. Besides, Duzi had never struck me as a thief. I tried to remember if any of the other bull dancers had complained about losing jewelry or other items. Nothing sprang to mind. That wasn't surprising. Although we might wear something sparkly during a performance, usually we wore only loincloths and boots. Bull dancing is dangerous enough without catching a necklace on a bull's horn. I shuddered at the thought of a dancer, unable to free himself, being dragged around the ring and tossed randomly into the air.

I knew nothing had been stolen from me, but then most of my jewelry – and I wore little of it – was only moderately valuable. I yawned. Tomorrow I would go to the practice ring and ask around.

'Martis. Martis.'

I opened my eyes. The bathroom was dark, except for the dish lamp in my mother's hand. The water in which I reclined had cooled around me. I sat up. 'What happened?'

'You fell asleep.' She held up a thin wool rug. 'Get out and dry off.'

I clambered out of the tub, and my mother wrapped me in the towel. Staggering a little and yawning, I followed her from the bathroom.

THIRTEEN

I awoke suddenly, groggy with fatigue, wondering what had awakened me. Sleep had proven elusive last night, despite my weariness. The noise from the celebrants outside had kept me awake until quite late. I saw what my mother meant about the worship of the Dying God; it was rowdy and uncontrolled. The rites for the Goddess tended to be more restrained. Still, they had sounded as though they were having fun. The hilarity had not faded until the rain blew in a few hours before dawn.

'Martis.' Arge moved into my line of sight. Murdered at her wedding the previous spring, she visited me often. Back then, she'd offered suggestions that helped me investigate and solve her own murder.

'I'm sorry I haven't visited you at the tomb.' I burst into speech. Paying due respect to the dead was very important, especially if they were family. Arge inclined her head.

'I understand,' she said. She was always the sweetest and most forgiving of my sisters.

'And now you are looking into another murder.'

'Yes,' I said. 'One of the bull dancers.' I hesitated a moment. 'If you see Duzi, will you watch out for him? We are sending him on this morning.'

'Of course. You feel guilty about him now, don't you?'

'I wish I'd been kinder.'

'Your actions would not have changed his fate. You know that, don't you?'

'Yes,' I said with a sigh. 'But I wouldn't feel so bad now if I'd been nicer to him.'

Arge nodded. 'And finding his murderer will ease that guilt.'

'It will help.'

'I see. Well, the dragonfly you found is costly.'

'I could see that.'

'It is something that would be worn by a young person,

probably a young woman. I suggest you look among those Opis and I called friends.'

I thought about that for a few seconds. I could imagine both Opis and Arge wearing such a beautiful piece, and that was even truer of their fashionable friends. 'That's a good idea,' I said. Arge smiled.

'Begin with Anesdura and Ynna. They were the wealthiest among us and the most likely to own something like that dragonfly.'

I nodded. And Eile too. I should have thought of them myself. They'd been fast friends with my sisters, particularly Opis. I knew all three women still lived in Knossos, but it would be awkward visiting them. When my sisters were alive, their friends had treated me with the disdain reserved for younger siblings. After Arge's murder, I'd lost touch with them, although I still saw them occasionally at the rituals. All were, or had been, married, and I thought at least one had children. I'd paid so little attention to them that I wasn't sure. Now, I would have to think of a handy pretext for visiting them and asking awkward questions. My first query: did any of the women know Duzi?

I opened my eyes, surprised to see gray light streaming through the window. There was no sign of Arge. She never stayed with me long.

'If you want some breakfast before you leave, you should rise now,' my mother said from the door. I jumped to my feet and hastened to join her.

After breakfast, I dressed carefully. One must show respect for the dead. At the last moment, I slipped the dragonfly ornament under my belt. As I left the apartment, my mother, with a sympathetic look, handed me a square of oiled canvas to protect me from the drizzle outside.

The rain stopped as I walked to the arena, although the air remained heavy with moisture. I was very early, but Geos and several other bull dancers were already in the ring. Duzi's coffin, a very simple pottery container, had been placed to one side.

Geos had spread a rug over the damp ground and on it he'd spread food: strips of roasted goat, almonds, grapes and figs. It was customary for the family to offer such refreshments, and I was both surprised and touched that Geos had made the effort for Duzi.

'Have something to eat,' he said, gesturing to the feast laid out on the rug.

'Thank you.' I took a grape and nibbled it. I wasn't very hungry. Grief and guilt had twisted my stomach into knots.

Costi, Nub and the twins were already here. Costi, planted on the edge of the rug, had arranged large portions of everything in front of him. He was eating with single-minded concentration, paying no attention to the rest of us. Elemon and Thaos had arrived and were walking around the ring, but I did not see the others yet.

There were no professional mourners, and when I asked Geos, he looked at me in surprise. 'Isn't this enough?' he said with a gesture at the food. 'Duzi didn't know anyone else but us.'

'That is why we should make as much effort as we can,' I muttered. Geos nodded.

'Did you bring a ship to speed Duzi's soul on to the under-world?' he asked. Guilt swept over me. I hadn't even thought of it. 'Nobody did,' he continued.

Poor Duzi. None of us had paid him enough attention.

Arphaia hurried into the arena, panting, her face flushed. Gold glittered at her throat and wrists. I crossed the ring to meet her. 'I left late,' she explained, fanning her face with a hand. 'I ran all the way.'

'You arrived before Tryphone and Obelix,' I reassured her.

'Here comes Obelix now,' Arphaia said, pointing with her chin. I turned and saw the other girl hurrying toward us. She too had dressed in her best and arranged her hair in the latest fashion. I realized with a start that she was actually quite pretty, prettier than Arphaia, although the long skirt and jacket with tight short sleeves did not flatter her lanky build.

'You look very nice,' I said.

'Don't sound so surprised,' Obelix replied, raising an eyebrow.

'Finally. Tryphone,' Arphaia murmured as the young man sprinted toward us. He too was hurrying and appeared flustered. I stared at him in amazement. Instead of a loincloth, he wore a robe – and a nice one too. Purple bands decorated the sleeves and the bottom hem.

'I lost track of time,' he apologized to Geos.

With a nod, Geos wrapped up the remains of the food in the rug and tucked it inside the wheeled cart with the attached bull's horns that we used for practice.

Elemon, Curgis, Thaos and Tryphone picked up the coffin, one to a corner. Geos went to the front, the closest thing to a family member Duzi had here. We began walking to the cemetery.

Without a flute player, we walked in silence. I had never done so before. It felt strange to march without music or the loud wailing of professional mourners.

The tholos for the bull dancers was tucked into a corner of the cemetery. It was quite small, especially compared to the family tombs around it. When Geos rolled the stone away from the entrance, I saw that the interior was also quite modest. But then there were only a few coffins inside.

As the men carried Duzi's body into the gloom, the rain began again, lashing down in a sudden heavy downpour. It was hard to hear over the roar of the deluge. Arphaia and Obelix huddled under the canvas square with me. We were all crying and clinging to each other for support. Duzi had not deserved such a terrible end.

The coffin was placed on a ledge inside. Each of us went inside to say a final goodbye to our comrade. I could barely force myself to enter the dark space, and then all I could think of to say was 'I'm sorry. I should have been a better friend.'

Arphaia went last. She was the only one to think of bringing a grave good; she placed a handful of copper rings on Duzi's shrouded chest inside the coffin. 'For your journey,' she whispered.

For a moment, we all stood outside in the rain. Then Geos and Elemon rolled the stone back into place.

I did not realize another mourner had joined us until I turned to leave.

'Who is that?' Arphaia asked at the same moment I saw the lone woman standing at the back.

'I don't know,' I said. Was this Duzi's elegant lady?

She was fashionably dressed in a striped skirt. Her wrists

sparkled with jewelry. But she also held a piece of canvas over her as a shield against the rain so I couldn't see her face.

She turned abruptly and walked away, hurrying as though she did not want anyone to identify her.

'All of you, go home,' Geos said. 'Change your clothes and return to the arena. The rain is ending. I want to fit in some practice time—'

'What if the rain doesn't stop?' Elemon asked.

'We will practice in the caves.' Geos paused and added, 'It is difficult to find practice time. Let's take this opportunity. Remember, the Harvest Festival concludes with a ceremonial bull dance and the sacrifice of the chosen sacred bull. I don't want anyone to get gored or trampled at that performance.'

FOURTEEN

As Geos predicted, the rain stopped again. Although the ground remained dark with moisture, the clouds began to disperse. Shafts of sunlight dappled the ground with light.

After changing my clothes, I returned to the ring. I was one of the first to arrive, after Costi. He still wore his new loincloth, so I assumed he'd come directly from the funeral.

I was surprised by Arphaia's absence. She lived a distance away, so I'd expected she would go straight to the ring from the cemetery, as Costi had, and so would be one of the earliest arrivals. 'Arphaia's not here,' I commented to Geos.

'No.' His bristly gray brows went up and down a few times. 'It is not unexpected.'

'What? What do you mean?'

'She won't stay,' he said. 'I see the signs. She'll marry and—'

'But she hasn't even gone through her agoge,' I objected. 'Arphaia is only fifteen. And she told me she doesn't want to marry.'

'She doesn't want to marry that man her uncle chose for her,' he corrected me. 'That doesn't mean she doesn't want to marry anyone.'

I recalled the handsome young man at the villa and nodded slowly. 'I think you might be right,' I agreed. 'Then we will be short two dancers. What will we do?'

'Duzi is a loss,' Geos said. 'But Arphaia? I've had – um – comments.'

'I'm sure you have. She was described to me as jumping like a sick cow,' I said. Geos chuckled. 'Maybe she just needs more practice.'

'I doubt more practice will help,' he said even more drily than before. He blew out his breath and shook his head. 'We'll have to bring Costi and the twins along more rapidly than I'd planned.'

I thought of Costi and the other children. They all seemed far too young, even Costi, to make that kind of life-altering decision. 'My grandfather used to say that someday there would not be enough volunteers for bull dancing,' I said.

'He was correct,' Geos said with a nod. 'There are fewer and fewer young people each year who want to honor the Goddess in this way.'

'What happens when there are none?' I asked. Geos shot a glance at me.

'Duzi is the future,' he said. 'Captives will be asked if they prefer bull dancing to prison or execution.'

I swallowed a sudden lump in my throat. A team of Duzis, poorly trained and most of them probably afraid of the bull. 'What if they all jump like sick cows?' I asked.

Geos shrugged. 'We'll cope. We'll have to. Besides, there will be some Elemons among them, youths trained as acrobats or who are otherwise athletic. There always are.' He glanced at Costi, who had helped himself to the remains of the food. He was eating as though the food might be taken away at any moment. A small, scrawny boy, he looked as though he'd missed more than a few meals. 'For now, we must work with the kids and make sure they are ready to leap as soon as possible. By next spring, at the latest.'

'Next spring?' I repeated incredulously. Only six or so months away.

He nodded. 'I want you to work with them.'

'What? Me? You want me to babysit them?' I was horrified.

'Not babysit. Train.'

'What if I don't do it properly? Their lives—'

'You'll do fine. Take the practice bull. You remember how I taught you?'

I nodded. I was both resentful and scared. Training the kids seemed like too much of a responsibility. What if I taught them badly and someone was hurt?

'Costi is the best of that lot. After he warms up, Elemon will take him aside and work with him. He's almost ready to join the rest of you and jump before an audience. He just needs a little more practice.' He paused and added drily, 'He is already more graceful than Arphaia.'

I smiled although I felt a little disloyal to my friend.

As I wheeled out the cart with the bull's horns, Nub and the twins arrived. I put the practice bull outside the ring and arranged rocks behind the wheels. The back was only a hide-wrapped cylinder, much smaller than a real bull. I could hardly believe I'd struggled with the jumps over this. Now that I'd danced with a real bull, this mock-up appeared tiny and pathetically easy.

The children lined up without me reminding them. Costi made sure he was first. 'Are you going to be able to run after eating all that food,' I asked, only partially teasing. He threw me a scornful look. 'Didn't you eat yesterday?'

'That was yesterday,' he replied.

I laid one hand on the vehicle to steady it. 'Get ready,' I said. Costi nodded, but before I was completely ready, he broke into a run. I experienced an odd sensation being on this side of the practice bull; it seemed unnatural. I felt Costi's weight on the horns, the shift as he rose into the air and flipped over. From this angle, I could see that he pulled left, just a little but noticeably.

'I know,' he said in exasperation when I corrected him. 'Geos told me already. You don't need to tell me again.' He sighed audibly as though I was tormenting him just for pleasure.

'And after you've done this a few times and warmed up, you can go to Elemon,' I snapped in annoyance. 'Next?'

The first of the twins moved into position. I knew them slightly. Originally studying boxing with Geos, they'd decided they wanted to bull dance instead. The first twin flew over the practice bull, his flip awkward but competent. I nodded at him, and he ran back in line. His twin moved into position. A pudgier boy, he was fleet of foot, but his jump did not carry him into the air. 'Try it again,' I instructed him. He returned to the line, to Costi's displeasure.

'Hurry up, fatty,' he called.

'Costi,' I scolded. 'Don't be cruel.' He sniffed.

The twin ran forward. Grunting, he managed to flip over the horns and land astride the imitation bull's back.

I did not see how Geos would manage to prepare these children to jump in time for the spring festivities.

'Pathetic,' Costi muttered.

'Costi!'

'I don't have to listen to you,' Costi retorted defiantly.

I wanted to slap the little brat.

'Martis is just trying to help,' Elemon said, coming up behind me. Then, to my surprise, he added gently, 'I know you and Duzi were friends. You must miss him.'

'More than anyone,' Costi admitted, his voice trembling. I stared at the boy. I hadn't realized. 'Sometimes he let me stay in his room when I didn't have any place else. And if he had food, he shared with me.'

'We all miss him,' Elemon said. I nodded, my eyes filling.

'Not like me,' Costi said. He broke out of line and ran, but not before I saw the tears streaking his face. I started after him, but Elemon caught my arm.

'Let him go. He'll come back when he's ready.'

I nodded, staring after the boy. Shame at my earlier snappishness swept over me. Costi was grieving. And although I didn't appreciate his rudeness, I was glad someone cared about Duzi enough to sincerely mourn him.

FIFTEEN

The other bull dancers began to trickle in. Obelix arrived first, her eyes still swollen. She offered me a faint smile, and I smiled in return. For the first time, I wondered why she'd joined the bull dancers. It was an unlikely choice for a fisherman's daughter, but I had no time to ask her. It was Nub's turn to jump. Like Costi, she was small and scrawny. I'd seen her with both a young man and a young woman; I didn't know if they were her parents or older siblings. But I knew Nub had family, so I assumed she was fed and had shelter, unlike Costi. Although the connection between Costi and Duzi had surprised me at first, it now made sense. Both outsiders, they had drawn together and become their own family.

The girl jumped and somersaulted easily over the practice bull, landing on the hide-covered bench. 'Very nice,' I said as I helped her down. Nub might be ready by spring, I thought as I examined her more closely. Although she looked skinny, her arms and legs were muscular and strong.

As the first twin took his place in line, I saw Thaos enter the ring with Tryphone, still in his new robe, and Curgis. I stared at Tryphone; he was flushed and smiling and looked happy. How odd. Where was the surly man I knew? 'I'm ready,' the twin said impatiently. I returned my attention to the children. As the youngest boy prepared to run, Costi quietly moved into the line behind Nub. I said nothing to him and pretended not to notice the tear-stains on his cheeks.

Now all the dancers were here, except for Arphaia. Geos threw me an 'I told you so' glance.

'I'm sorry I'm late,' Tryphone said as he removed his robe. 'I stopped in the square . . .' I nodded in understanding. The poets and playwrights would be performing there now. I planned to stop and listen before I went home. 'I saw Tinos,' he continued as he carefully folded his new clothing and put it down.

'Doing what?' Geos asked.

'Going into the tunnel to the caves. I peeked inside. I think he's investigating the pen where Duzi was found—' He stopped abruptly, and we all shared a moment of silence.

I thought of the dragonfly folded inside my street clothes. I knew I should show it to Tinos, although I didn't want to answer his questions about how it had come into my possession. But he needed to know I'd found it. 'I'll return in a few minutes,' I said, hurrying to the side of the ring. I quickly pulled on my skirt and jacket and clipped on the tight belt. I pushed the dragonfly underneath.

'Martis, wait!' Geos shouted as I left the arena. I ignored him as I broke into a run.

It was still quite early when I reached the square, but the large space was already crowded with people listening to the poets.

Although I would have liked to pause and listen, I hurried on to the cave entrance nearby. I heard the low thrum of voices, and even from the entrance I could see torchlight reflected from the stone walls. I stepped into the tunnel and followed the sound of voices to the center of the cave.

Tinos and another man were inside the pen where I'd found Duzi's body. I did not quite have the courage to join them, but I stepped up to the entrance. I went down on one knee to examine the floor. Against the stone were several darker, dull streaks that I guessed were dried blood. Swallowing, I closed my eyes and pushed away the picture of Duzi crawling across the floor.

'Duzi met someone in the cave,' Tinos said from the interior of the cage. 'They got into a fight and the other person stabbed him.'

'There isn't a lot of blood outside,' the other man pointed out. 'It is mostly on the floor in here.'

'I know. Duzi was weakened by the stab wounds. The other fellow unbarred the pen gate and pushed Duzi inside. He fell. See the blood here?'

'So the stains around the fence mean Duzi was still alive . . .'

'And trying to get away from the bull. I think so. See the blood on the floor here, by the entrance, as he tried to escape.'

'I saw scratch marks on the inside of the pen's gate too,' said the other man.

I couldn't help imagining Duzi, wounded and covered with blood, crawling desperately around the pen to escape the bull, and I felt sick. It would have been kinder to kill him outright. I gagged and fought my unruly stomach.

Tinos turned. 'What are you doing here, Martis?'

'I found something—'

'Go home. This is no place for you right now.'

The other man eyed me in amusement. 'I guess your charms are such that they lure this bedraggled lily to a crime scene.' Tinos's cheeks went red.

Humiliation swept over me in a burning flood. 'That isn't it,' I retorted angrily.

'Go home,' Tinos repeated, exasperated. 'This is no place for a little girl.'

Little girl? Blinded by fury, I turned on my heel and ran. I slowed down only when I exited the cave and bright daylight hit me. Tears of rage and mortification streaked my face as I stormed back to the ring. Fine, if Tinos didn't want my help, I wouldn't tell him about the jeweled dragonfly under my belt. I would make it my mission to speak to Opis's friends as well as to the bull dancers and would begin today by calling on Anesdura. She'd been more Arge's friend than Opis's and had always treated me well. Like a human being. The other two had either ignored me or spoken to me like I was a worm. Not unlike how Tinos had just treated me. And he was supposed to be my friend.

Spurred by anger, I broke into a run. I'd been gone less than half an hour. How I hoped Arphaia had arrived so I could share my humiliation and anger with her.

Obelix had been assigned the role of working with the children in my place and she greeted my arrival with relief. 'Thank the Goddess you've come back,' she said. Then, looking at my expression, she added in concern, 'Are you all right?'

'Fine,' I replied stiffly. Obelix didn't know how I felt about Tinos, and I intended to keep it that way.

She did not appear convinced but nodded. 'Good,' she murmured, abandoning her post.

Perhaps guessing my mood, the kids behaved unexpectedly well, jumping with all their concentration. Geos soon removed Costi from me to begin practicing with the adults.

I fell into a routine, automatically correcting positions and assisting where needed.

Although still angry when Geos finally called a halt, I'd calmed down.

'Martis,' Geos said, 'I need to speak to you.' I looked at his angry expression. 'Come here.' Reluctantly, I crossed the ring. 'Don't do that again,' he said to me. 'Don't run off. Do you hear me?'

'It won't happen again,' I promised, heat rising into my face. Geos stared at me for a few seconds and then finally nodded.

'Very well.'

'Has anyone seen my robe?' Tryphone asked. 'I put it right here.' A chorus of noes answered him.

'Was it you, maggot?' Tryphone asked Costi.

'Why would I take your robe?' Costi asked.

'To sell.'

'Do I look like I have it?'

I hurried to catch up with Obelix, the conversation among the other bull dancers fading behind me.

'I can't go to market today,' she said over her shoulder. Her skirt belled out around her legs as she trotted. 'The fishing boats brought in a large catch early this morning. I promised my mother I'd go straight to the docks.'

'Oh, yes?' I glanced at her, suddenly shy about asking her why she'd joined the bull leapers. 'I have a friend who used to be a dancer. Kryse. She's married to a fisherman—'

'I know her. Your friend, you say? I've never seen you visiting her.'

I could feel my face flaming. It was true. I hadn't seen Kryse for months. Guilt prompted me to say, 'Yes, it's been too long. I'll go with you now.' Obelix's eyebrows went up in surprise and then she smiled.

'Keep up, then. I've got to hurry.' Obelix set off, almost running. Despite my height and long legs, I had trouble keeping up and she quickly pulled far ahead. I soon lost sight of her.

The fishing boats docked on one side of the wharf, and as I approached that area, the smell of fish intensified. I pinched my nostrils together, but it didn't help. I walked slowly through the area. One of the boats had brought in baby octopuses, another a catch of silvery seabream.

Then I saw Kryse, almost not recognizing her at first. A lithe, slim bull dancer when I first knew her, she was pregnant now. The canvas apron that covered her belly was liberally sprinkled with blood and scales, and it made her appear even larger. The injury that had ended her career as a bull dancer had left her with a severe limp. Only her face looked the same.

She was busy cleaning fish, her sharp, thin knife easily slicing off the heads and slitting open the belly so the offal slid into the basket at her feet in one motion. And she was fast – so quick her table was already almost empty.

'Kryse,' I said.

She paused and brushed her forehead with the back of her hand.

'Martis. What are you doing here?'

'I came to visit you. See how you are faring?'

'Well, I'm doing well. My husband and I are expecting our first.' She gestured to her belly, and I nodded. I could see that.

'Did you buy that fishing boat you and your husband wanted?' I asked, casting my mind back to our previous conversations.

She nodded. 'We did. He is captain of his own craft now.' She looked around, smiling proudly.

'Another fisherman's daughter is bull dancing now,' I said after a moment's silence.

'I know. I suggested Obelix try it.' Kryse glanced over at another table. I followed her gaze to the other woman. Obelix had changed clothes and donned a canvas apron identical to the one Kryse wore. Obelix was also cleaning fish, scowling ferociously as she did so, but she was nowhere near as fast as Kryse. 'She doesn't want to be among us, the fishermen,' Kryse said. 'I'm not sure what she wants to do. But at least she may win enough prizes to do something else.'

'She isn't as talented a dancer as you were,' I said.

Kryse grinned and nodded in acknowledgment. 'I'm not sure she enjoys that either. I always liked it. Until this.' She gestured to her damaged leg. I said nothing. Kryse seemed happy enough and at peace with the injury.

'I'd better go,' I said after an awkward silence. 'I just wanted to say hello.' I started to back away.

'Martis,' she called after me. 'I heard about Opis. I'm sorry.' I turned.

'Thank you.'

'She had a baby?'

'Yes.'

'If you need a nursemaid, consider my sister. She doesn't want to wed a fisherman either.'

I thought of Ria's current nursemaid, Miss Surly. It would be nice to have someone pleasant caring for my niece. 'Thank you. I'll suggest it to my mother.' With a final wave, I walked quickly from the wharf. I realized I no longer noticed the smell of fish.

SIXTEEN

'What is that smell?' my mother asked when I entered the apartment. I sniffed my skirt. Now I could smell a faint odor of mingled perspiration and fish. 'I walked Obelix home,' I said, not altogether truthfully. 'I'll change my clothes.'

I went straight to my bedchamber. By the time my mother poked in her head, I'd changed my clothing and washed my face and hands. I still felt as though the smells of the fish market had soaked into my skin, so I added a dash of Opis's perfume. I carefully drew a line of kohl around my eyes. It was a little crooked but passable, I thought.

'What are you doing?' my mother asked in surprise. My dislike of kohl was well known.

'I plan to call on Anesdura today,' I said.

'You what?' She gaped at me. I glanced at her and nodded.

'I thought it was time to reconnect with some of my sister's friends.' It wasn't completely true but it wasn't a lie either. I wanted to ask Anesdura if she recognized the dragonfly ornament.

She stared at me suspiciously as though she thought I might be lying. I gave her my best innocent smile. 'Here, let me help you,' she said at last as she stepped into my room. 'Your hair is a mess.'

An hour later, made up so I did not look like myself at all in the bronze mirror, my hair festooned with pearls and jeweled ornaments, and wearing my newest and best jacket and flounced skirt, I started out for Anesdura's villa. As a girl, she'd lived in apartments in the large complex but now, a married woman, she lived on the outskirts of Knossos. I walked through the city, feeling uncomfortable in my finery. But no one gave me a second glance. I looked exactly like most young women. Like the set of young women my sisters had been among. I sighed, nostalgic for those more innocent times. Not only had Opis and Arge been home but Nuia and my father as well. I didn't know if my father and Nuia were still alive.

I shook away the memories as I walked up the slope to the fine villa above. Anesdura had done well for herself. I hesitated before I climbed the steps. Maybe she wasn't home and all this finery was for nothing. What if she didn't remember me?

Realizing I was searching for an excuse not to speak with her, I stiffened my spine and climbed the remaining steps.

A servant opened the door. When I gave my name, I heard Anesdura's voice from the back. 'Martis. Oh, Martis, I am so happy to see you.' She hurried into the hall. Except for her obvious pregnancy, she looked exactly as I remembered. 'My goodness, Martis, you are quite grown up now. And you resemble your sister Opis so much.' Tears flooded her eyes as she threw her arms around me and hugged me. I smiled awkwardly, not quite sure what to say. Opis had been considered a great beauty, and I knew that was not me. 'Surely you aren't married yet.'

'No.' My voice squeaked, and I cleared my throat. 'I still have my agoge ahead of me.'

'Come, talk to me.' She linked arms and pulled me inexorably toward the back. We stepped into a courtyard, pleasantly shaded by trees and plants. A dark-skinned woman wrapped in many layers of cloth tended to a small child. The little girl looked up at me and smiled, her teeth like little pearls. She was an extremely pretty child with gold-flecked eyes and curly fair hair. A ringlet almost covered a small mole on the left side of her forehead. 'My goodness,' Anesdura continued, 'I haven't seen you since Arge . . .' She sniffed audibly as the tears began running down her cheeks.

I nodded. I'd seen her, as well as Arge's other friends, when my sister had been placed in the family tomb. I'd paid little attention then, but now I saw how grief-stricken Anesdura was still. My eyes prickled; Arge's funeral had been an emotional day. 'How are you?' I gestured toward her belly.

She smiled through her tears. 'This is my second. You've met my first.' She gestured to the child.

'She's beautiful. How old is she?'

'Almost eight months.'

'My mother is raising Opis's daughter . . .' My voice trailed away. I did not want to discuss either of my sisters. Gossip about Arge and Opis had lasted long enough. Anesdura bit her lip and looked down at her hands. I hurried into speech, choosing another more neutral topic. 'Do you see much of Eile and Ynna?'

'I see something of Eile,' she said, raising her head with a smile. 'You know she became a priestess?' I shook my head. No, I hadn't known. 'Yes. She is quite devoted, I understand. And she's quite friendly with Hele, the High Priestess's daughter.' I nodded. It was widely expected Hele would become High Priestess when her mother stepped down. 'I lost touch with Ynna.' She pressed her lips together, and I knew there was some scandal there.

'Why is that?' I smiled innocently.

'I prefer not to say.' Turning her head, she clapped her hands. When the young maid appeared, Anesdura called for refreshments. As the maid bowed and left, Anesdura added, 'If you wish to call on Eile, she may be at the Priestess House. I understand she spends quite a bit of time there.'

'Thank you.'

'But let's not talk of them. I want to tell you about my daughter. She is such a funny little bug.' She chuckled. 'Yesterday, she tried to catch the sunlight. She couldn't understand why it wouldn't stay in her hands.' Anesdura launched into a rambling story about her daughter. Now I remembered how much of a talker she'd been, and that obviously hadn't changed.

I pasted a smile on my face and fingered the dragonfly ornament as I waited for a break in the monologue. I thought I would find a chance to interrupt when the tea and the honey pastries arrived. But Anesdura never ended a sentence, scarcely taking a breath as she moved from one topic to another.

I could feel my eyes glazing and my mind beginning to wander. Finally, I stood up. 'I'm sorry,' I said, breaking into an account of a journey she'd taken with her husband. 'My mother is expecting me home.'

'Of course, of course.' Anesdura did not seem put out. I suspected she was used to visitors leaving mid-word. Putting aside her bowl, she struggled to her feet. 'I'll accompany you to the door.' Still talking, she took my arm.

I did not have a chance to show her the dragonfly until I was outside. Then I turned, as though I'd forgotten something, and pulled the ornament from my belt. 'Is this yours?'

She took the trinket and turned it over in her fingers. The jewels sparkled enticingly in the sunlight. The wings especially shimmered with garnet, sapphire and emerald. A flicker of recognition crossed her face and was quickly masked. 'What a beautiful piece. No. It isn't mine. I've seen it, or something like it, before. Where did you get it?'

'I found it.' That was true, up to a point. 'I'm trying to find the owner.'

'I'm sorry to say it is not mine. I wish it were; it's beautiful.' She rubbed one thumb over the sparkling jewels.

'Thank you. And thank you for the refreshments,' I said as I turned away.

'Will you visit me again?' she called after me. 'Please.'

'Of course,' I said, glancing at her over my shoulder. Someday, when I had hours to spare.

'I don't go out much . . .'

Hearing the loneliness in her voice, I turned around. 'I'll visit you again in a few days,' I promised.

My mother was waiting for me when I returned. 'What happened?' she asked, taking my arm. 'How is she?'

'I'll tell you everything after I change my clothes,' I said, hurrying to my room. Off came the tight belt, jacket and skirt. I slipped on older, softer clothing and hid the dragonfly ornament in my jewelry box once again.

Once I was redressed, I joined my mother in the main room. It was almost time for supper, and I could smell roasting meat from the courtyard outside. I felt slightly nauseous from the combination of tea, figs and honey pastries and wasn't sure I could eat anything more.

'So, how is Anesdura?' Nephele asked.

'She's fine. Pregnant with her second child. She already has a little girl.'

'How sweet,' my mother said, her tone a combination of sadness and envy.

'I told her about Ria,' I said. 'And she told me Eile is a priestess.'

'So she is. I'd forgotten that. And she's Lavra's granddaughter.'

'Anesdura also said something odd. She told me she'd lost touch with Ynna, and I sensed there was some scandal. Do you know what that was?'

My mother's brow furrowed. 'I did hear there was some problem with her husband but I'm not sure what that was. Anesdura didn't know?'

'She wouldn't tell me.'

'Opis and Arge would have known everything, down to the final detail,' my mother said with a sigh. 'I'm the wrong genera-tion, and I don't hear all the gossip anymore. Eile might know.' She smiled slightly. 'If she's willing to tell you.'

'I'll visit her tonight, after supper,' I said.

'I'm not even sure I know where she is living now,' my mother murmured. 'She was widowed, you know.'

'No, I didn't know,' I admitted, startled and guilty. 'Did you tell me?'

'I thought I did. But, Martis, you've always been so involved in your own interests.'

Although she did not sound angry, I felt the sting of her disapproval. 'Anesdura suggested I look for Eile at the Priestess House.'

'That is probably the best solution,' she agreed.

'Did Eile have any children?'

'Not that I know of. But she is still a young woman and I have no doubt she'll remarry—'

At that moment, Pylas and Telemon entered the apartment, putting an end to the conversation. Both males appeared tired, sunburned and windblown.

'Where have you been?' I asked.

'We visited the boys' dorm,' Pylas replied, collapsing into the cushions. He began rubbing his lame leg. 'It was a lot of walking.'

My mother suppressed a sob. Telemon would turn seven soon. The induction of all seven-year-old boys into the dorms would be held tomorrow, and with his birthday so close, Telemon would be among them. Since our father was gone, vanished we knew not where, and my mother's brother was still at sea, Pylas had volunteered to step in as the male relative. Telemon would disappear into the dorms and the world of men. I felt tears prickle my eyes as well.

'I saw where we'll eat,' Telemon said.

'That can't be all,' my mother said, trying to smile.

'No. We saw the—' Pylas began.

'I'm going to learn how to shoot a bow,' Telemon interrupted. 'And sail a boat.'

'I know some boys in the dorms,' I said, raising my eyes to my mother's. 'I'll ask them to look out for him.'

'I don't need anyone looking out for me,' Telemon said in annoyance. 'I am not a baby anymore.'

We wouldn't know him in a few years.

SEVENTEEN

Before I finished eating supper, the rain began to fall again. I did not relish walking through the rain to the Priestess House but did not want to lose the last few hours of daylight either. Since I did not think a priestess would care about my appearance, I didn't bother changing to fancier clothing. I also refused to refresh the kohl around my eyes, fearing it would run in the rain and leave black streaks on my cheeks.

I did put on the tight belt, though, with the dragonfly tucked underneath.

My mother handed me the canvas square and I set out, going down the front steps into the wet. Everything was slick with moisture. After the dry summer, we needed the rain. I just wished it had waited a day or two.

I walked to the path that ran alongside the Sacred Grove. The shower did not reach the ground here, underneath the trees, although the wet, dark soil told me the earlier heavier rain had. I folded the canvas under my arm until I reached the main road. Small puddles were beginning to form in the ruts left by cart wheels. I started across the thoroughfare just as the skies opened up again. The sudden downpour screened the Priestess House in a silvery curtain. I quickly put the canvas shield above my head and sprinted through the mud to the other side.

A young woman opened the door. I recognized her but didn't know her name. When I told her I wanted to speak to Eile, the young novice gestured me inside, into the hall. There were snakes everywhere, lying in the corners, coiling down the steps to the lower level and draped around the pithoi. Although most homes kept snakes to control the rodent population, I had never seen so many in one place in my life. The air stank of snakes.

The young novice guided me down a long hall to a large eating area beyond. A lighted brazier sat by the back door, the glowing coals inside sending warm perfumed air into the space. An older woman, Lavra, the priestess I'd met at the Harvest Festival, was engaged in conversation with Eile. Just a few years older than I was, Eile wore her hair as I did, in curls down her back save for the three locks over her shoulders. Both her jacket and skirt were dyed a deep royal purple, and when she turned toward me, I saw an amethyst necklace glittering around her throat.

'Martis,' Lavra said warmly. 'Do you know my granddaughter, Eile?'

'Yes. She was once friendly with my sisters. Opis and Arge? I'd like to speak to her, if I could,' I said.

'Of course.' Lavra touched her granddaughter's arm in farewell and disappeared down the long hall that led to the front.

'Martis,' Eile said, looking at me in surprise. 'I haven't spoken to you in months.' She did not suggest I sit down or offer refreshment, unlike Anesdura. It was surprising that a priestess felt comfortable ignoring the rules of hospitality.

'Not since Arge's funeral . . .' My throat involuntarily closed up. The grief still hit me, as fresh as if Arge's death had just occurred.

'I'm sorry,' Eile said, taking my hands. 'I regret now that Arge and I were not such good friends at the end.'

'You weren't? I hadn't known that.'

'No. I warned her about marrying that barbarian. She refused to listen.'

'Saurus had nothing to do with her death,' I said in annoyance, pulling my hands free. Although I disliked the man, Arge had loved him. And her belief in his character had been borne out by later events.

'I heard that,' Eile said. 'But I am still not persuaded. He brought his weapons to the wedding. He betrayed his uncivilized origins with every action.'

I took a deep breath and struggled to refrain from contradicting her. I did not want this conversation to dissolve into an argument, especially about something long past. 'I found this ornament.' I pulled the dragonfly from my belt. 'Do you recognize it? I am trying to find its owner.'

Eile took the piece of jewelry and turned it over and over in her fingers. 'It is beautiful and so carefully done. I have seen it, or something like it, before, but I don't remember where. Have you asked the jewelry maker, Dombus? His shop specializes in fine jewelry, especially gold set with gems such as this. Most of the palace ladies wear the pieces made in his shop.' She handed the dragonfly back to me.

I had not spoken to Dombus; I hadn't even thought of it. Since my mother had given me all the jewelry I wore, what little there was, I had never chosen or commissioned anything of my own. 'Thank you,' I said, tucking the dragonfly under my belt. 'That is a good suggestion.'

'How are you, Martis?' Eile asked. 'You look quite grown up. Are you preparing for your agoge?'

'Yes, I enter the women's dorm next spring,' I said.

'I look forward to attending your wedding,' Eile said with a smile.

'I don't plan to marry,' I said. 'I follow the virgin aspect of the Goddess.'

'Do you? I will be interested to see if you maintain your commitment.' Eile did not sound convinced. 'Neither Opis nor Arge could manage celibacy.'

I bit back an angry retort. Instead, I asked, 'Do you see Anesdura or Ynna much?'

'I meet Anesdura once in a while. She is quite a devoted mother. But Ynna . . .?' Shaking her head, Eile looked away from me. Again, I sensed a reluctance to speak about Ynna. I was growing more curious about her with every person I spoke to.

'What happened with Ynna?'

Eile hesitated, and I hoped for a moment she would tell me. Finally, she spoke. 'She and her husband divorced. I don't know if you knew that.' I shook my head. Divorce was unusual but not unheard of. 'Hmm. The rest of her story is her own. I suggest you visit her and ask her yourself.'

'Where is she living now?'

'She returned to the apartments she lived in with her parents. They are both gone now, of course, and her siblings scattered, so she lives there alone.'

'All right.' I knew where that apartment was. 'Thank you.'

'I'll walk you to the door.' Eile gestured to the hall. Since there seemed to be nothing else to say, I preceded her to the front door and back out into the rain. Well, Eile had not been very helpful. But if I hurried, I should reach the jewelry shop before it closed for the night.

The downpour had eased to a faint mist. I ran across the road and darted into the trees. As I stepped on the path, my sandals made damp footprints on the stone. I took the dragonfly from my belt and rolled it through my fingers. The goldsmiths, like the potters, the weavers and the other craftspeople, lived in the same area of the city complex as I did, but not on the same street. I did not turn right at the end of the slope. Instead, I turned left and descended the hill that ran all the way down to the sea. The mist rising from the water shrouded the bottom of the street in white, cloaking the docks and the boats tied up there in invisibility.

Dombus's shop was located close to the wharves. In the heavy fog, I walked past the door twice before I saw it. But my little trip along the lane also showed me there were other goldsmiths here, so if Dombus did not recognize this ornament, I had additional places to visit.

Inside Dombus's shop, the clang of hammers beating gold into delicate sheets was deafening. Holding one hand over my left ear, I approached a young man working with thread-like gold wire. 'Excuse me,' I said, pitching my voice so he could hear me. 'I found a hair clip and I am trying to identify the owner.'

The man put down the wire. He was dressed in a loincloth with a shawl over his shoulders. A large nose dominated his face. Instead of the long locks draped down his chest, his hair was

caught back with a gold chain. 'Let me see,' he said, holding
out his hand. I dropped the piece into his palm. He glanced at
it once before turning and shouting over his shoulder for someone
else. After a few seconds, an older man with scarred hands and
wrists from sparks and hot metal approached us. 'Did we make
this?' the young man asked. He resembled the older man so
strongly that I was sure they were father and son.

Dombus took the dragonfly and examined it. 'Yes,' he said
briefly. 'It is your sister's design.'

'Do you know who this was made for?' I asked.

He glanced at the clip again and shook his head. 'Come with
me, please. We'll ask her – she might remember.'

I followed Dombus to a smaller, quieter chamber at the
back. It was quite warm here. Through the open door on
the other side, I saw a kiln and an apprentice pouring a river of
molten gold into a mold.

A young woman just slightly older than I was stood before a
long table. Baskets of gems, gold wire and other items were laid
out on the table.

Dombus showed her the dragonfly. 'Do you remember making
this?'

'Of course. I made two, exactly alike.' The young woman
straightened up. Taller than average, she was almost my height.
Like her father and brother, she had a large nose, but I barely
noticed it after seeing her large, lustrous brown eyes. 'It is a year
ago now. Maybe more.'

'Who did you make this for?' I asked.

'A young woman. Very beautiful, very fashionable.'

'What was her name? Do you remember it?'

She hesitated, pressing her right hand to her lips. 'I am not
sure. It was a long time ago.'

'Please try,' I said. 'I want to return this beautiful piece to
her.'

The jeweler nodded, her gaze floating over my scanty jewelry.
'If you like it, I can make something as beautiful for you,' she
offered.

'Maybe,' I said. The dragonfly was beautiful. 'I will have to
ask my mother.' I paused a moment. 'Please try to remember her
name. It is very important.'

'Her name. She came in with a group of other women. What did they call her?' She closed her eyes. 'Ah, yes. I don't remember her name. But one of her companions, yes, I remember her. They called her Opis.'

'Opis!' I repeated, shocked. Opis, my sister. That meant one of her close friends had purchased the dragonfly ornaments. Since Anesdura and Eile recognized the clip but claimed it did not belong to them – if they'd told me the truth – I guessed the woman in question was Ynna. All paths led to Ynna.

EIGHTEEN

I left the shop tired but pleased that I'd accomplished so much today. Once I returned the dragonfly to safety under my belt, I began trudging up the steep hill. It was growing late, and because of the heavy cloud cover, the sky was already dark. Although the rain had stopped, the air remained cool and moist.

I fingered the dragonfly thoughtfully. Had Anesdura and Eile truly not known who it belonged to or had they lied to protect their old friend? More importantly, how had that dragonfly ended up with Duzi? I knew that many women, especially some of the wealthy, fashionable ladies, invited the bull dancers into their beds. For all that I thought Elemon was homely, he had his choice of partners. We all knew it, although he didn't flaunt it. Had Ynna been attracted to Duzi and given him the dragonfly as a love gift? That would explain the tavern keeper's description of the lady with the elegant home. Except, if Duzi had been receiving valuables, why did he live in such squalid conditions? Perhaps the relationship was a new one? But Duzi had jumped in the ring only once, and since he'd been stiff with fright, he had not distinguished himself. Would Ynna be attracted to a new and very clumsy bull dancer? And a foreigner to boot? Without knowing her, I had to believe it was possible.

Stopping at the top of the hill to catch my breath, I looked around. I'd reached the market square. The shops were beginning to close for the night. A shaft of ruddy light from the setting sun broke through the clouds, brightening the darkness. For a few seconds, we were in daylight again. The brief glimpse of the red sky gave me hope tomorrow would be fair. We bull leapers were supposed to practice in the morning, and I expected Arphaia to be present. I wanted to show her the dragonfly and see if she recognized it. Ynna made more sense as the stylish lady than Arphaia, and anyway she claimed her connection with Duzi had been short. But I wouldn't know for certain until I spoke to both.

Pylas and Telemon were still out when I returned to the apartment. To my surprise, my mother had Ria in the main room, cuddling her and playing with her. This was unusual. My mother had had a hard time accepting the little girl. Ria reminded all of us too much of Opis and the events of the preceding spring.

'You have Ria out here,' I said in surprise.

'It is not her fault Opis died,' my mother replied, almost defensively. 'It is so silent here . . .' I nodded in understanding. An active baby would help fill the emptiness left by Telemon's absence. 'Besides, that silly nursemaid isn't here. She told me she had an emergency, and she ran out very suddenly.'

I remembered Kryse suggesting her sister for the post. 'I know someone else who might want the job,' I said.

'Can she breastfeed?'

I considered that for a moment. I suspected Kryse's sister was younger than she was and probably childless. 'I doubt it,' I admitted.

My mother looked at Ria. She was approaching her six-month birthday. 'Ria has begun eating some solid food, but I think she still needs breast milk. Maybe in another month or so? Would the woman you know be willing to work for me then?'

'Probably,' I said, although I had no idea if that was true.

I glanced at the baby. As she sat in my mother's lap, she waved Telemon's carved goat around. One of the hind legs was dark with moisture; Ria had been chewing it.

'She will keep you busy,' I said.

My mother nodded. 'I think we will be glad we have her.' She looked up at me. 'Where have you been?'

'I called on Eile. And I saw Lavra.' I hesitated. 'Eile was not very friendly.'

'I understand she is quite devoted to the worship of the Goddess,' my mother said. 'Although I have heard rumors that she is fonder of Dionysus.'

I thought of Eile and shook my head in bemusement. She seemed too stiff, too controlled to be an acolyte of the Dying God.

'It's time for this little one to go to bed,' my mother said, rising to her feet. As she carried Ria into one of the other rooms, I slipped out of the apartment again. Ynna lived inside the complex, not far away from my home. I hoped she could answer all my questions.

In a matter of minutes, I reached Ynna's apartment. But when I knocked on the door, no one answered. Could she already be in bed for the night? I knocked again, more loudly. Still nothing. I was just about to turn away when I heard halting footsteps on the other side. The door opened a crack. 'Yes?' the shadowy figure said hoarsely.

The stink of stale wine rolled over me and I involuntarily stepped back. 'I'm looking for Ynna,' I said.

The door swung a little wider. 'Who are you?'

'Martis. Sister of Opis and Arge and daughter of Nephele the weaver.'

'Martis.' Her voice lifted in surprise. 'Come in.'

I stepped inside the hallway. It took me several seconds to realize the half-dressed, raddled creature in front of me was Ynna. Both skirt and jacket were dirty, soiled by food and wine stains. The kohl around her eyes wandered across her cheeks in a wavering black line.

'You were at the funeral,' I said in surprise. 'Did you know Duzi?'

'What do you want?' she asked, ignoring my question.

'Just to talk to you,' I said.

'About what?' She turned her back and reeled toward the shadowy room beyond.

Although I hadn't been invited, I followed her inside.

The apartment stank of wine, rotting food and perspiration. When we reached the front room, she collapsed, loose-limbed, into a heap of cushions. Only one dish lamp had been lighted to beat back the gloom, and it was in danger of expiring. 'Have some wine.' She gestured to the open jar at the same time as she drained her cup.

'Thanks, but no,' I said, gingerly sitting on a cushion across the room.

'What are you doing here again?'

'I thought I'd call on you—' My words were interrupted by Ynna's rough laughter.

'Did Anesdura send you?'

'Uh, no. Where are your servants?' I looked around at the squalor surrounding us.

'My maid ran off. Bitch took some of my jewelry with her.'

'Your jewelry? What did you lose?' My voice sharpened, but she didn't seem to notice.

'What does it matter? Everyone is gone.'

'Your husband . . .' I began before remembering my mother had told me Ynna was divorced.

'He's gone too. No one loves me.' Tears began rolling down her cheeks. 'Not even that damned barbarian.'

'Did you know Duzi?'

'What's it to you?' She took another swallow of wine, spilling most of it down her chest. Horrified, I stared at her in an appalled silence. What had happened to her? I remembered her as a giggly fun-loving girl, flirtatious with all the men.

Swallowing down my disgust, I took the dragonfly from my belt and held it out. 'I found this—'

''S mine.' She made an ineffectual grab at it and lost her balance, almost toppling on the floor.

She had never paid me any attention but hadn't been unkind either. What should I do?

'Maybe you should eat something,' I suggested, returning the jewelry to my belt. I stood up and picked my way through the mess on the floor to the kitchen. Gray light filtered through the window. If possible, this room was even messier than the other. Flies rose in a cloud when I entered, their buzzing deafening. From the look of this space, it had been a long time since anyone had cleaned here or prepared any food.

Using my jacket-covered arm to shift some of the dirty bowls and cups – the thought of touching them sent shivers of disgust through me – I searched for something Ynna could eat. Although there were still a few sealed pithoi, I didn't want to open them and risk spoiling whatever provisions were inside. Finally, I found a few shriveled olives and a handful of soft but still edible grapes. I put them on a serving plate and brought them into the other room.

Ynna lay sprawled on the cushions, snoring loudly. 'Ynna,' I said. 'Wake up.' She turned over. I bent down and touched her shoulder. She did not react. Realizing that she was out cold and would not respond to me, I put the plate down a little distance from her.

I turned to look at her one last time before I left. But she was unconscious. I continued down the hall and left.

The air in the large hall outside smelled fresh and sweet. Shaking my head, I started home. Although Ynna said the dragonfly was hers, I couldn't be sure that was true. Maybe it had belonged to her at one time, but I recognized the possibility that she saw a pretty ornament and wanted it. Then the question was, if it were hers, had she given it to Duzi? I didn't see any other way he might have obtained it.

And what had happened to Ynna? I shook my head in dismay. From the condition of her apartment, I guessed she'd been alone and drunk for some time. Was this the shame? Or was she one of the women who made a practice of sleeping with the bull dancers and that was the scandal?

I would have to make good on my promise to visit Anesdura again, but this time I would press her for the truth about Ynna.

NINETEEN

As I'd hoped, the rain ended overnight. I rose early and the skies were already flushed with sunlight. As soon as I ate – the cook was already up and making flatbread – I left for the practice ring. Tomorrow was the final day of the Harvest Festival and Geos wanted us to practice – with a live bull – beforehand. I was one of the first to arrive, following Geos into the ring. The practice bull was also already there. Although

I couldn't see him, I could hear him trotting around the pen nearby.

'I hope you're wearing a loincloth underneath that skirt,' Geos said, looking at my clothing.

I nodded as I shed my skirt and jacket and piled them carefully on a stone. I put the dragonfly underneath the belt so no one could see it.

As I made my third nervous circuit of the ring, Geos asked me to help him position the wheeled practice cart with the bull's horns and place the hide over the back. Costi might be ready for a living, breathing animal, and maybe Nub, but the twins and the other child certainly were not. 'You are not going to ask me to help train them today, are you?' I asked.

Geos grinned at me and did not reply.

Costi arrived next. He looked around hopefully, as though he thought there might be food served again. I saw Geos offer the boy something. When Costi glanced at me, I behaved as though I was very interested in the cart's horns and pretended I'd noticed nothing. Nub and the three boys reached the ring a few minutes later, the twins arguing as they came down the slope. The quarrel rapidly intensified until they began punching one another.

'Hey, hey,' Geos cried as he hurried to separate them.

Today, a few onlookers gathered in the seats. A handful of fashionable women and two young men. I eyed them once and ignored them after that. I knew they were here for Elemon.

At last, the other dancers drifted in, Arphaia last. Like me, she wore a shabby skirt and jacket. She dropped them and the linen under-blouse next to my clothing. I crossed the ring toward her, so I could show her the dragonfly, but Geos called to us. It was time to begin our practice.

The handler released the bull into the ring. Like many of the aurochs we trained with, this was an older bull. I could see the white hairs on his muzzle, but he still seemed dangerously lively. I turned and glanced at Costi doubtfully, not sure he was prepared for a bull like this. Costi saw me staring at him. He straightened his shoulders and threw me a defiant look.

'Tryphone and Elemon, go first,' Geos instructed. I understood; he was attempting to tire the bull so that Costi – and the rest of us – would have an easier time.

We all queued up. I was behind Curgis with Obelix behind me. Arphaia was behind her, right in front of Costi and the kids. As usual, when I was preparing to leap over the bull, my heart speeded up.

Tryphone's first jump was routine. As we all moved forward, someone stuck out a foot and I almost sprawled face first in the dirt. When I regained my balance and looked around, Elemon was smiling at me. Obelix, who'd been behind me, had begun crossing the dirt toward the ring to serve as catcher. 'Who tripped me?' I demanded. Arphaia blinked at me in surprise.

'No one.'

I looked around again and took a large step to the side, away from Elemon. He was paying me no attention now, already focused on the bull pawing the dirt in the center of the ring.

Elemon's leap was perfect, and when I took my turn, I understood why. This bull did not run very fast. Trained as a bullock, he knew what he should do, and he lowered his head to the exact level where grasping his horns was easy. When he tossed his head, he lifted us effortlessly and we flew over his back, landing without a problem on the ground.

Then it was Arphaia's turn. She cleared the bull's horns and attempted a clumsy somersault. Instead of landing on her feet on the bull's back, she landed astride, in a sitting position. When she slid off, Geos put her back in the line ahead of both me and Thaos. She jumped again, and her landing was just as awkward.

'Again,' Geos shouted. Angry and embarrassed, Arphaia ran to the front of the line once again. This time, her flip was smoother, and she landed on her feet. Geos nodded and allowed her to go to the end of the queue.

Geos sent Elemon to work with Nub and the twins while Costi moved to the front. I put my hand to my mouth, worrying that the boy would not be able to do this. But the bull was tiring as well. His trot had become a fast walk and he could not throw the bull leapers as high. The skinny Costi went up into the air and performed a graceful turn. He landed well, on the bull's back, and jumped off with a cocky grin.

Geos nodded approvingly at him.

I overheard Arphaia swear under her breath. I glanced at her. 'It's not fair,' she muttered, her eyes sliding away from mine.

We practiced a few more times before Geos called a halt. By

then, despite the cool air, we were all perspiring, Arphaia especially. While Elemon joined the young women waiting for him, I joined Arphaia and Obelix. We walked together to the outside of the ring, where our street clothing waited.

'I hate him,' Arphaia muttered. 'And he doesn't like me either.' When I glanced at her, she continued. 'Geos. Did you see what he made me do? I had to jump, over and over. It's not fair.'

'Geos just wants to make sure you can do this,' I murmured. 'He doesn't want you to get hurt.'

'That's not true,' Arphaia argued. 'Elemon is the best of us. The best of the best. And he was gored.'

'That's the point,' I said. 'If even the best of the best can be injured, what happens to those of us who are struggling?' Although no one now was struggling as much as Arphaia, not even Costi. I pulled on my skirt and fastened the belt around my waist. But I did not tuck away the dragonfly. Instead, I held it in my hand, waiting for an opportunity to show it to her.

'Huh! Well, bull dancing is stupid anyway. Pretty soon I'll be married, with a home of my own, and I won't be doing this anymore.' I looked at her in surprise.

'I thought you didn't want to marry,' I said.

'I changed my mind. And so will you, eventually.' She tugged on her jacket and turned away.

'Wait,' I said. 'I want to show you something.'

As she turned back to me, I held out the dragonfly. 'Have you ever seen this before?'

'No. It's so pretty.' She stared at it covetously. 'Can I have it?'

'No. I'm looking for the owner—'

'It's mine.' Tryphone leaned over my shoulder and reached out his hand.

'Yours?' I closed my fingers tightly around the ornament.

'Yes.'

'Where did you get it?'

'Someone gave it to me.'

I stared at him for several seconds. Could Ynna have given this to him? Tryphone, despite his surly nature, wasn't bad-looking. Like all bull dancers, he was lithe and muscular, and I could see that he might appeal to Ynna. As an accomplished bull dancer, he would certainly be a step up from Duzi.

But I didn't have proof and no way of obtaining it until I could speak with Ynna again. 'I'll tell Tinos that when I give this to him,' I said.

'That's mine,' Tryphone repeated, grabbing angrily at me.

'Here, here, what's going on?' Geos said, putting one brawny arm in front of Tryphone's and knocking it out of the way.

Although I hadn't planned on revealing the dragonfly to everyone, now I had no choice. I held it up. 'I found it,' I said, 'and now I'm trying to locate the owner. Tryphone says it's his, but how do I know that's true?' My eyes swept over the group.

'How would you obtain something so costly?' Geos asked Tryphone disbelievingly.

'None of your business,' Tryphone snapped.

Everyone stared at the clip, some with more interest than others. 'I'll give it to Tinos and then Tryphone can explain how it came into his possession,' I said, tucking the jewelry into my belt.

He growled under his breath but did not try to stop me from leaving. Arphaia and Obelix followed me, their heads together as they whispered. I saw Obelix hand Arphaia something gleaming gold. Tryphone fell into step behind them.

I sped up, glancing over my shoulder every now and then, just to make sure he was not pursuing me. Arphaia and Obelix trailed behind me, a buffer.

But the picture that kept replaying in my mind was not of Tryphone or his angry expression as he tried to grab the dragonfly from me. It was of Costi and his scarlet cheeks as he stared at the piece. He'd recognized the dragonfly as soon as I held it out. Recognized it and knew something about it; I was sure of it.

TWENTY

I'd planned to visit Ynna once again after the noon meal. But my mother insisted I go to the weaving room and weave until it was time for Telemon's induction – in fact, the induction into the dorms of all the seven-year-old boys. Since she spoke to me with tears in her eyes, I felt I couldn't say no. I knew she already felt Telemon's imminent absence keenly. Besides, I'd begun to realize how right she'd been when she pointed out that bull dancing was not a long-term profession. I could see for myself there were few dancers older than twenty. At least, not older and still jumping the bull. I still wished to become a poet. But I couldn't envision myself wandering the roads, sleeping rough and never knowing where the next meal was coming from either. Although I did not want to weave for a living, or marry, I wasn't sure what I wanted to do. I thought once again of the healer's offer. That drew me. It seemed much more interesting than weaving.

But today I did not pass into the weaving room too reluctantly. I needed to think, and the tedium of passing a yarn-wrapped stick through a warped loom provided a great opportunity for doing so.

I could see my mother's surprise when I went willingly. 'You are growing up, Martis,' she murmured.

Once I'd found my rhythm and no longer needed to think about my hands, I began considering Duzi's murder and Tryphone's possible involvement in it. I'd theorized that Duzi and Ynna were lovers and that she had given the dragonfly to him. Perhaps Tryphone was first, before Duzi, and now was a jealous lover, enraged by Ynna's preference for Duzi? That sounded plausible and explained why Tryphone had claimed the dragonfly as his own. Plausible until one considered the people involved. From what I'd seen of Ynna, she might have a hard time attracting a man. Duzi, I could understand; he had nothing and might be desperate enough to accept Ynna. But Tryphone? Would he be interested? He'd claimed the dragonfly as his, but I could not imagine him demonstrating interest in Ynna. Or was I just blind to an attraction I didn't understand?

But wait. Ynna herself claimed she didn't have anyone; that was borne out by her sad wail that no one loved her.

Then another thought struck me. If the dragonfly truly belonged to Tryphone, how did it find its way into Duzi's mean little room? And even there, it was hidden. The surly Tryphone had treated Duzi with rude indifference, so I could not imagine a friendship between them. Had Tryphone murdered Duzi and then searched the room? What did I know about Tryphone, anyway?

None of it made sense. Despite my anger, it was time to turn over the dragonfly to Tinos and trust that he would uncover the truth. Besides, I could not resist a sneaking hope he would appreciate my efforts and be grateful. I imagined him thanking me – bending forward for a grateful kiss, with his hands on my arms – and fire surged through my body.

'Martis,' said my mother sternly. 'Stop dreaming. Weave.'

I doubted I would find an opportunity to speak to the wanax this afternoon, even though I expected to see him. This was the fifth festival day, and everyone would be at the grand ceremony in which the seven-year-old boys were initiated into adulthood. Telemon, too. It was supposed to be a time of rejoicing, but most of the mothers I saw walking to the square were weeping, Nephele among them.

A brisk wind blew off the sea, a stiff, salty breeze that caught at the women's flared bell-shaped skirts and pulled at them. I used one hand to hold my jacket closed and the other to press my heavy skirt down.

We were all dressed in our best. Pylas wore a fine white woolen robe with colored bands around the bottom. Telemon, although normally dressed in a loincloth or short robe, was clad in a skirt and jacket. Kohl circled his eyes. His head was still shaved, except for the braided lock at the back, and my mother had wound a strand of carnelian beads through it. Like all the inductees, he appeared to be a little girl.

He kept tugging at the jacket and trying to move the skirt from his legs. I understood. After the freedom of a short kilt, the heavy fabric in one of these garments felt like weights hanging around one's body. I was used to the heaviness now, but a year ago I'd found it hard to walk in one, let alone run.

My mother reached out for Telemon's hand, but he refused to hold it, instead slowing down so he could walk side by side with Pylas. My uncle walked slowly, lamed as a young man in the bull capture. The final piece of a young man's initiation into adulthood required the bagging of a wild bull with no weapon but a rope. Injury was common. My mother glanced at Pylas's scarred leg and sniffed audibly. But she didn't protest. Telemon was already lost to us and the world of women.

Brightly dressed people crowded the square; most of the inhabitants of Knossos were here to witness the ritual. Tinos, and
several other priests, stood to one side on a dais surrounded by
carved limestone horns – the Horns of Consecration. In the center
of the dais stood a tall stone pillar with a bonfire blazing before
it. Boys had already begun to form a line. Without even saying
goodbye to us, Telemon pelted away, taking his place in the
queue. My mother sobbed, and Pylas put a hand on her shoulder
to comfort her.

I'd attended such a ceremony every year since I'd been
small. It had always seemed quite exciting – but this was the
first time I had a brother joining the mass of boys. When I saw
Telemon disappear into the mob of bright skirts and bald heads,
tears began running down my cheeks. Yes, he frequently annoyed
me, but I was used to having him around and I hated the thought
he would change and become someone different from the child
I knew and loved.

Some boys elected not to participate. They usually chose to
live as women or they went directly into the priesthood. But that
was not our Telemon. He wanted to be a merchant sailor like
my mother's brother.

The line of boys began to move forward. As each boy stepped
up to the stage, two or three priests stepped forward to stand at
the child's back.

'How can you become a man in this?' Tinos asked each boy,
gesturing to the embellished jacket.

'I cannot,' responded the boy, removing the jacket and tossing
it aside.

'How can you run, fight, honor the Goddess in this? How can
you take your place in the world in this?'

'I cannot,' each boy responded, sliding the skirt past his hips
to the floor. 'Take this skirt from me.'

'How can you grow up with this?' Tinos gestured to the jewelry
twining through their braided locks of hair.

'I cannot,' each boy chorused as he stripped the ornaments
from his hair. The sound of beads hitting the stone floor of the
dais was clearly audible, each one a small explosion marking a
boy's steps toward becoming a man.

As the priests took the feminine clothing from the boys, the skirts and jackets sailed into the fire while the boy was redressed in a loincloth. They were led away to the other side of the dais where young men and older boys waited to accompany them to the dorms. I saw Thaos and Curgis among them and resolved to ask them to keep an eye on my brother.

Some of the seven-year-olds looked back at their mothers, but not Telemon. He went forward eagerly, vanishing into the crowd of boys. These children would not be seen again until the next Harvest Festival in March. And by then the families would hardly recognize them.

Loud sobbing erupted all around me as the mothers saw their sons disappear into the mass of males.

They would live in the dorms until they grew into men and left at eighteen. After their ritual attempts to capture the wild bull, they would choose their own paths. Some would opt for the navy; others would pick the military. The sons of the craftspeople would rejoin their fathers in the shops or sail out as fishermen.

But they would never again be their mother's baby.

Blessed are the boys who have two mothers and a father –
the mother who bore you and the father who offered her
his seed; and the Lady above us all who exults in the joyous
Arrival of a child. Blessed are the boys who begin as girls
    but
Become boys and initiates into the world of men
Despite their mother's grief.

Despite my pride in my poem, an involuntary loud wail burst out of my mouth, embarrassing me. I looked around. No one even glanced my way. Most of the mothers wept; the fathers held themselves immobile, stoically staring straight ahead.

The bonfire roared higher and higher. I could feel the warmth of the flames even from where I stood. The smell of burning cloth permeated the air. Now Telemon stepped on the stage. Nephele clutched at my hand, so tightly I grunted in protest. We both began weeping as his jacket and skirt were consigned to the flames.

When all the boys had shed their female clothing and joined the older boys, the fathers, older brothers and uncles, such as Pylas, crossed the stone floor to join their charges. Tonight, they too would sleep in the dorm, just to settle the boys. I did not doubt a lot of the children would miss their mothers and cry during the night. I was much older than Telemon and I already dreaded leaving home for my agoge.

I saw Costi running around the edges of the crowd and wondered for the first time why he did not live in the dorms. It was not because Costi wanted to leap the bulls. The twins and the younger boy had been released from the dorms to learn bull dancing. It was a special dispensation from the High Priestess. If they opted not to continue, they would return to the residences and take up archery or something. I would have to ask Costi why. I suspected, though, that he was one of those who refused to settle and ran away so many times no one bothered to recapture him anymore. I'd never understood why some children chose to surrender a comfortable bed and regular food to run wild, but there were always some.

'Why do you think some boys run away from the dorms?' I asked my mother. Her eyebrows rose. She wiped the tears from her cheeks.

'I don't know,' she said. 'Maybe they can't adjust to the rules. My brother, your uncle, was such a one. He stuck it out until he was sixteen but then ran away.'

'I didn't know that,' I murmured.

'He signed on to a merchant ship and worked his way up to captain.' My mother smiled slightly. 'He's better at giving orders than taking them.'

'I haven't seen him for so long I'm not sure I would recognize him now. He likely wouldn't know me.'

My mother sighed. 'Sadly true. Come, Martis, let's go home.'

'In a minute.' This might be my best chance to speak to Tinos. 'I'll see you at home,' I said over my shoulder. I was already heading toward the dais. If he was too busy to speak with me now, perhaps I could arrange a time tomorrow.

I stepped carefully around the stage. Tinos stood among the priests, talking. Before I reached him, one of the palace guards came sprinting across the square. He leaped over the Horns of Consecration and, calling Tinos's name, ran to him.

'What's the matter?' Tinos asked. I edged closer. He saw me and said brusquely, 'Not now, Martis.'

'I found something that relates to Duzi's murder,' I said. 'Something important.'

'Not now,' he repeated impatiently.

'There's a dead woman,' the guard panted. 'You need to come.'

Tinos took two long strides forward and jumped to the ground. 'Show me.'

'Who?' I called out. 'Who is the victim?'

The guard threw me a brief glance. 'Ynna.'

'Ynna!' I screeched as Tinos and the guard rushed away. 'Ynna!' I must have been one of the last people to see her alive.

TWENTY-ONE

I accompanied my mother home but did not waste time changing out of my finery. Desperate to see what had happened, I intended to leave my mother and hurry to Ynna's apartment. Had Ynna died from natural causes? Or had she, like Duzi, been murdered?

I started out the door but found I couldn't abandon my weeping parent. The house was too silent without Telemon. Sighing in frustration, I went back inside and sat beside her on the cushions. 'Telemon is my only son,' she wailed. 'I miss him already.' I nodded and put my arm around her to comfort her. Telemon was not only her sole son but also the last of her children. He'd been a surprise, arriving after my mother thought her childbearing days were over.

After a few minutes, I brought wine and honey pastries to her, hoping the food would ease her sorrow. When that failed, I brought in Ria and put her on the floor. After a few minutes, my mother lifted the baby into her lap.

Breathing a sigh of relief – my mother's emotional outburst was a surprise since she usually kept life calm – I slipped out the door. I ran through the halls to the other side of the complex. I could hear the crowd outside Ynna's apartments before I could see them, a rumble of conversation and shocked excitement.

There were so many people that when I approached her door, I couldn't even see it.

'What's happening?' I asked, pretending I didn't know.

'The woman who lives here was found dead,' said the lady in front of me.

'It's no wonder,' said the woman standing in the open door across the hall. 'Ynna was . . . not a bad woman. But she couldn't resist the bull dancers.'

'It's no wonder her husband divorced her,' the woman in front of me said acidly. 'What her poor husband had to put up with. I pitied him.'

'What did he have to put up with?' I asked.

The woman in front turned to stare. 'Are you married?'

I shook my head. 'I haven't finished my agoge yet.'

'Then you are too young to hear this,' she said, wrinkling her nose.

'What happened to Ynna?' No one answered me.

I moved closer to the wall and tried to squeeze past the bodies blocking my path to the door. It was quite a struggle, but I finally reached it. A young guard stood in the opening. When I looked over his shoulder, I saw a canvas-wrapped bundle blocking the hall inside. I gulped.

'Make sure you look in the . . .' Tinos's voice faded to a mumble as he moved away from the open door.

I tried to creep past the guard to look at the victim's face, just to make sure it was truly Ynna, but the young man grabbed my arm.

'Tinos said no visitors,' he growled.

'I'm not a visitor. I need to see Tinos,' I said.

'Does he want to see you?' The guard guffawed at his own joke.

'Why don't you ask him?' I said in my mother's sharpest offended tone.

'He's busy.'

I glared at the young man. Like most of the guards, he wore the customary dagger at his waist but not a sword. He had painted kohl around his eyes. Although his long locks had been tied back with a cord, I could just imagine him dressing his hair in the most fashionable style and sprinkling it with hair ornaments.

'I'm Martis,' I said. 'I'm a bull dancer. Tinos knows me.'

His skeptical expression changed slightly as I continued talking. 'A bull dancer? I think I've seen you. But you still can't come in.'

At that moment, I saw Tinos through the open door. 'Tinos,' I called. 'Tinos.'

'Martis,' he said, glancing at me. 'What are you doing here?'

'I need to talk to you.'

'I'm very busy now,' he said in exasperation, turning his back on me.

'I visited Ynna yesterday,' I said loudly.

For the first time, he looked directly at me. 'You did? Why?'

'I had to.'

'You had to,' he repeated disbelievingly. With a sigh, he said to the guard, 'Let her in.'

I threw a triumphant look at the guard. He dropped his arm.

When I stepped into the hall, I knelt by the body to turn back a corner of the canvas.

'What are you doing?' Tinos demanded as he watched me.

'I want to make sure this is Ynna,' I said.

'It is. And you don't need to see her,' Tinos said, his voice sharp. 'Come inside.'

I ignored him. After seeing Ynna yesterday, I was finding it hard to believe she was dead. I flipped back the canvas. It was Ynna all right – very pale, her lips bluish. Slowly I replaced the shroud over her face. But I did not join Tinos immediately. Instead, I spent a moment grieving for the bright-eyed girl I remembered.

'Martis,' Tinos said gently.

'I'm coming.' Rising to my feet, I followed the hall into the main room. I glanced around. Something was different. I couldn't quite identify what that was, and before I had a chance to think about it, Tinos spoke in an impatient tone of voice.

'Why were you visiting her yesterday? Did you know her? Or was it curiosity?' He looked tired and I noticed a few silver threads glittering in his black hair.

'I knew her slightly. She was a good friend to Opis and Arge.'

Tinos's expression softened. 'I see. You called on her.'

'Yes.'

'Why yesterday? Have you visited her before?'

'No. I was told the dragonfly belonged to her . . .' I still wasn't sure I wanted to tell Tinos where I'd found the jeweled piece.

'The what?'

'The dragonfly. A piece of jewelry. I've tried to speak to you about it over and over, but you've sent me away every time.' I stopped. My voice had risen with grievance. It was Tinos's own fault he didn't know about it. He stared at me.

'Maybe you'd better start at the beginning.'

'I wanted to show this piece to her and see if she recognized it.' I glanced around at Tinos's men. Although no one was paying any attention to me, I stepped as close to the wall, and as far away from them, as I could and lowered my voice. 'I found this.' I removed the dragonfly from my belt. His eyes widened and he held out his hand.

'Where? Where did you find this?' I hesitated and Tinos eyed me suspiciously. 'I can see you were somewhere you shouldn't have been. Tell me.'

'I found it in Duzi's room.'

'What in the name of the Goddess were you doing at Duzi's? And how did you even find it? I've been looking for it for days. Were you closer friends than you claimed? Did you lie to me?'

'Of course I didn't lie.' I glared at him. 'And Duzi and I weren't that close. I asked Tetis to help me. She knew where it was. Anyway, I found the dragonfly. Dombus's daughter said she made it for Ynna.' I stopped and corrected myself. 'For one of Opis's friends. I think that friend might have been Ynna.'

'I understand. And then you hurried over here to question her as fast as you could. Not even thinking it could be dangerous.'

I squirmed but said defiantly, 'I was right, wasn't I? Ynna told me it was hers.' Not exactly, but I was pretty sure that was what she meant. I knew she might have lied and after a few seconds, I added honestly, 'Tryphone also said it belonged to him.'

'Tryphone? The bull dancer?' Tinos examined the dragonfly. 'This is quite a valuable piece,' he murmured as he examined it. 'Far too costly for all but the most successful bull dancers.'

'I know. Dombus's daughter said it was a special order.'

Lifting his head, Tinos eyed me. 'You have been busy.' He did not sound either grateful or approving.

'I tried to tell you I found it,' I said defensively. 'But you wouldn't listen.' Tinos glanced at me, his expression unreadable.

'You are like a biting fly, Martis.' He turned the clip over and stared at it once again. 'Did you show this to Tryphone?' he asked.

'Yes— No, not exactly. I showed it to Arphaia. But Tryphone was there. He said it belonged to him now.' I paused and then added thoughtfully, 'I am not sure I believe him either, though.'

'Martis, this is dangerous. You know Duzi was murdered—'

'Yes, I do. I discovered his body, remember?' I hesitated, remembering Duzi's battered body. Shoving the horrible scene out of my thoughts, I continued, 'And I think the murderer might be Tryphone. I mean, what do we know about him?'

Tinos's eyebrows rose. 'Just why do you suspect Tryphone?'

'I suspect he might have been Ynna's lover, and she gave him the dragonfly as a love gift. Then her affections changed. She took the jewelry from Tryphone and gave it to Duzi instead.'

Tinos stared at me for several seconds. 'That sounds plausible,' he said at last, sounding surprised. 'I'll keep this. And I will consider Tryphone. But, Martis, I want you to stop looking into Duzi's murder. It is far too dangerous. Now Tryphone – and everyone else – knows you are investigating. What if he decides to go after you?'

'What do you mean?' I asked. To my shame, I sounded frightened. I knew I'd already angered Tryphone.

'I want you to tell Arphaia and Tryphone and everyone else you gave this dragonfly to me and that I am investigating the murders. Understand?'

'Yes,' I said with a nod. Would Tryphone threaten me? I thought of his surly nature and how angry he'd been when I refused to give him the dragonfly. It was not a reassuring thought.

'How was Ynna when you visited her yesterday?' Tinos asked.

'She was . . .' I hesitated. Somehow, it seemed disloyal to describe her drunkenness to Tinos.

'Everyone knows Ynna . . . had some problems,' he said. 'But she was alive?'

'Of course. I made her a plate of olives . . .' I looked over my shoulder. The plate had been kicked to the far wall. 'There was a struggle,' I said. 'There's the plate, there.'

Tinos nodded. 'Thank you,' he said sarcastically. 'We've figured that out.'

'She was still alive when I left. She was – um – sleeping. How did she die?'

Tinos hesitated for several seconds. I could see he did not want to tell me; it would be bad news. 'She was stabbed, just like Duzi,' he said at last.

I nodded without surprise. I'd expected the deaths to be connected. 'By the same knife?' I asked.

Tinos huffed an exasperated sigh. 'Maybe. Probably. But that is none of your business. Stay out of this, Martis.'

I glowered at him without speaking. He probably didn't even know for sure. But the healer might know. If so, she would tell me. I was almost certain of that.

'Ynna was murdered,' Tinos said in a sharp voice. 'That is why I don't want you meddling anymore. If you aren't careful, Martis, yours could be the next violent death I am looking into. And I don't want that.'

TWENTY-TWO

As I left the apartment, Tinos called after me. 'Wait, Martis.' I turned, my heart fluttering in my chest. 'Please tell your mother the ceremony planned for tomorrow has been postponed for one day. Out of respect for Ynna.'

I nodded over my shoulder and stepped into the corridor outside. Poor Duzi, the foreigner. None of the festivities had been postponed for him.

Members of the crowd surged forward, shouting questions at me as I pushed through them.

'What happened?'

'Is Ynna truly dead?'

'Who killed her?'

'Whoever she was arguing with.'

I stared around until I met the gaze of the woman standing at her door across the hall from Ynna's. She was older, probably older than my mother, and beautifully dressed. Neither of us spoke as she withdrew into her own home.

I did not realize until I was almost home that I had not told Tinos about my suspicions regarding Costi. But then, I did not really know if I had anything to tell. I was almost certain Costi did not murder Duzi; the boy had seemed too heartbroken by the death. Anyway, although his skinny body had a certain wiry strength, I doubted he could overpower a full-grown man and then push him into a bull's pen. On further consideration, I supposed it was possible Costi had employed a trick to maneuver Duzi into position in front of the pen's gate and then stabbed him. I could not imagine what trick that might be, though.

I was missing something; I knew it. Although I had a theory about the connection between Ynna and Duzi, it was just a guess. As far as I knew, no one had ever seen the two of them together. I had certainly never heard of it. But then, I had never heard of any relationship between Ynna and Tryphone either.

When I entered the apartment, my mother was waiting with a sour expression on her face. 'Where have you been?' she asked in annoyance. 'I turned around and you were gone.'

'I had an errand to run—'

'An errand that you never thought to mention to me,' she interrupted sharply. 'And where was this errand?'

'I had to find Tinos.'

Her expression went through several changes: anger, fear, suspicion. She finally settled on anger. 'You are involving yourself in Duzi's murder, aren't you? After I specifically told you not to. And you promised.'

'I found something – a piece of jewelry,' I explained quickly. 'I suspect it relates to Duzi's murder so I brought it to Tinos. And if it makes you feel any better,' I added unhappily, 'he told me to stay out of the investigation as well.'

Expelling her breath in a whoosh, she stared at me for several seconds. 'Is that the truth?'

'Yes,' I said. I hesitated, wondering how to tell her about Ynna.

'What?' she asked, shooting me a sharp glance. 'What are you not telling me?'

'The Harvest Festival, the final festivities, have been postponed for one day.'

'What?' she repeated, her voice rising in astonishment. 'Why? I've never heard of such a thing.'

There was no help for it; I would have to just jump in. 'Ynna is dead, murdered.'

My mother stared at me disbelievingly.

I nodded. 'It's true. That's why Tinos left the ceremony so hurriedly this morning.'

'And why you ran out as soon as you had the chance,' my mother said. I swallowed and did not reply. She sighed. 'Oh, that poor young woman. She just never grew up.' Then her eyes widened. 'Martis. You were just there, visiting her. What if you'd been in Ynna's apartment then? You might have been attacked as well.' I shivered suddenly and gulped. But I had seen no one lurking around Ynna's apartment, either when I'd arrived or when I'd left.

'Oh. I'm sure the murderer would have waited until I was gone,' I assured her with a confidence I didn't feel. 'He would not have wanted to fight off two of us.' Although Ynna, lying there in a drunken stupor, would not have been any help at all. But my mother did not need to know that.

Nephele inspected me skeptically for several seconds and finally relaxed. 'I hope you listen to both of us, to Tinos and me. We are only looking out for your safety.'

I bit my lip, holding myself back from arguing. Instead, I went past her to the main room. Both my mother and Tinos had told me not to interfere. And Tinos, it was becoming obvious, was trying to keep me at arm's length and purposely excluding me from the investigation. Without knowing what Tinos knew, it would be difficult for me to continue even if I wanted to flout his direct order. Other than speaking to Costi, of course, and I doubted he knew much.

'Are you hungry?' my mother called from the other room. I nodded even though my appetite had disappeared. Too much excitement. 'We'll eat something, and then maybe you can finish the rug you're weaving. You're almost done.'

I sighed. Was this to be my future? Days, months and years of unutterable boredom? I could hardly bear to think about it. I thought once more of the healer's offer. Every time I thought about it, I became more interested. But what would my mother think?

*   *   *

I awoke suddenly. It was still quite dark, but when I sat up, I clearly saw my dead sister Arge sitting beside my couch. I never knew when she would visit me, but when she did, she usually offered me good advice. Suggestions I should have thought of myself but hadn't.

'Ynna is dead,' I said to the shade.

'I know,' Arge said. 'Murdered. Stabbed, just as Duzi was.'

'I'm afraid it might be my fault,' I burst out. I'd barely allowed myself to think this, and I certainly had not shared it with anyone. Arge bowed her head, her eyes cast to the floor.

'Your investigation may have frightened someone,' she murmured in agreement.

'The murderer could have been following me,' I said. 'He might have seen me visit Anesdura and Eile and finally Ynna. If I hadn't gone—'

'She might still have been murdered,' Arge pointed out in a practical tone.

'Now Tinos is angry with me. He says I've put myself in danger.'

'Then the best solution for protecting yourself is identifying the murderer.'

That was exactly what I thought. 'Except for talking to Costi, I don't know where else to look,' I said.

'You already wished to speak to Anesdura again,' Arge said. 'You're curious about the scandal surrounding Ynna. But Anesdura might have additional information, besides that. Don't you remember how competitive she, Ynna and Opis were? Always trying to outdo one another. The most fashionable clothing, the prettiest and most expensive jewelry, the most suitors. They even competed for the most attractive bull dancers.'

I cast my mind back and after a moment I nodded. Although Opis had already been wed to Pylas, she'd continued to behave as though she were a young and unmarried girl. 'But you and Eile stood apart from the rivalry – you especially,' I said to Arge. 'That's why Opis was so angry when you captured Saurus's heart. She wanted him and she never expected to lose to you.'

'Yes. I was the homely one. How dare I win the prize?'

'She was nasty to you.' I remembered how Opis's remarks

became even more cutting than usual; she'd begun calling Arge names – Mud Face and Buckteeth.

'The competition between Ynna and Opis was particularly fierce,' Arge continued. 'You must recall the quarrel between them when Ynna flaunted the bull dancer she was seeing and mocked Opis's old lame husband.'

'Yes,' I said. That fight was hard to forget. The two young women had resorted to slapping and hair pulling until my mother had intervened. I suspected Opis had begun approaching the bull leapers afterwards, so she too had something to boast about, but I didn't know for sure. I didn't want to know.

'I tried to stay out of it,' Arge said. 'Besides, I was seeing Saurus then, and soon after I began preparing for my wedding, so I paid less attention than I might have otherwise.'

I attempted to call that time to mind. Although we were discussing events of only a year or so ago, so much had happened that it felt like several years. And since I'd avoided my sharp-tongued sister Opis as much as I could, all the activities she and her friends had engaged in were hazy.

'Anesdura will remember. If you can persuade her to tell you.'

'I'll visit Anesdura tomorrow,' I said. 'After practice.'

'Don't allow her to change subject,' Arge warned me. 'She does that when she doesn't wish to talk about something uncomfortable.'

'I know,' I said. Every time I'd tried to raise questions about Ynna, Anesdura had shifted the conversation to her daughter. Eventually, I'd just given up trying to break in. I wouldn't do that next time.

Satisfied, Arge thinned to smoke and disappeared.

TWENTY-THREE

Although the performance and the sacrifice of the bull had been postponed, I went to the ring anyway. Some of the bull dancers might not have heard the news – I expected we would attract an audience of people who hadn't heard – and anyway I knew Geos would want to arrange another practice.

When I arrived at the ring, Tryphone was already there, standing on the sidelines and chewing his nails. As I approached, my heart sinking, he straightened up and headed for me with a scowl on his face. I tried to hurry, so that I would be at the ring with Geos, just in case Tryphone became physical when brow-beating me didn't work. But he cut me off, ensuring I was out of Geos's sight.

'I want my dragonfly ornament,' he said.

'I don't have it.'

'Yes, you do. Give it to me.' He grabbed my arm and reached for my belt.

I tried to wrench myself free but he was too strong. 'I told you, I don't have it. I gave it to Tinos. He will probably speak to you about it.'

'You are a liar.' He unclipped my belt and stared in shock as nothing fell from it.

'I told you, I gave it to Tinos,' I repeated.

'What is going on here?' Geos asked, running to my side.

I looked at Tryphone's furious expression. He was already livid with me. I did not want to anger him any further; we relied on one another too much during a performance. If he wanted to hurt me, he could push me into the path of the bull. Or, if he was catcher, he could step aside and allow me to fall into the ring. I'd already been tripped once, although, since I didn't remember him nearby, he might not have done it. I did not want to believe he would purposely hurt me, but right now I didn't trust him. 'Nothing,' I said.

Geos glanced at Tryphone and then at me. 'Go on, then,' he said. But worry furrowed his forehead. He knew something had happened, just not what.

When Arphaia and Obelix arrived, I quickly joined them. I glued myself to their sides, and when we lined up to begin prac-tice, I made sure I stood between them. Even then, although I tried to keep a sharp eye on Tryphone, someone pushed me when I began my run forward and I almost went sprawling in front of the bull. The live bull was thundering toward me; I could have been trampled before the galloping auroch even knew I was there.

Fortunately, I was able to regain my balance in time for the jump. But I slid off the bull's back, my legs trembling and almost boneless from fright.

Realizing something had happened, Geos sent me to work with the children. Today I was glad of it. I was far away from Tryphone – from all the adults, in fact. Here, with the kids, I felt safe.

After all the children had jumped at least once, Costi sneering the entire time at this babyish practice, I began to calm down. I remembered I'd planned to speak to him. 'Costi,' I said. He turned his head away, avoiding my gaze. 'Costi,' I repeated, more loudly this time. He turned and stared over the hills. As Nub flew over the model's back, I took two large steps toward the rear and grabbed Costi's arm before he realized I was there. 'I want to talk to you,' I said.

Costi glanced at me. Then his gaze shifted to a spot past my left shoulder. 'The wanax is coming,' he said.

I couldn't help it. I turned. Costi took the opportunity to wriggle out of my grasp and speed away. But he hadn't been lying. Tinos, his long robe flapping around his calves, walked up the slope to the ring. He carried his staff of office and was accompanied by three guards, so I knew this would be the formal visit. Tryphone threw me an angry look as though Tinos's arrival was my fault.

Geos motioned all of us bull dancers into a circle around him. Tinos joined Geos.

'I expect some of you are surprised by the change in plans,' the wanax said, glancing at each of us in turn.

'Yes,' said Arphaia. 'Why are we practicing instead of at the ceremony?'

Tinos nodded at her. 'A good question. Yesterday there was a . . . a death. The festivities were postponed as a gesture of respect.'

Arphaia's eyebrows rose in surprise. 'But—'

'Arphaia,' Geos said reprovingly. 'Be polite.' She bit her lip and stared down at her feet.

'Since you are not performing today, it is a good opportunity for me to ask a few more questions,' Tinos said. 'About Duzi.' He looked around the circle once again, but this time none of us spoke.

'All right,' Geos said at last. 'Which one of the team do you wish to speak to first?'

'Martis,' Tinos said.

Geos gestured at me. Confused, since I could not understand why he needed to question me, and anxious about it, I stepped forward. Tinos guided me to a spot out of earshot of the others. 'Don't look so frightened,' he said in a low voice. 'It would seem odd if I didn't speak to you.'

I looked at the other bull dancers. Most of them were sneaking covert glances at me. 'I see.'

'Are any of them missing?'

'Costi.'

'Ah. The boy who was talking to you. But we already know he is neither big enough nor strong enough to overpower the victims.'

I nodded hesitantly. I too doubted Costi could have physically subdued Duzi, but I was not prepared to believe he was entirely innocent. And Ynna? Costi might have been able to prevail over her, in her drunken condition. 'Do you know anything else?' I asked.

Tinos eyed me for a moment. 'Both your mother and I have told you to stay out of the investigation. Why aren't you listening to us?'

'I am. I am staying out of it.' Mostly. 'But surely it can't do any harm to tell me what you've discovered.'

He smiled slightly. 'Well, I spoke to Dombus's daughter once again. She confirmed your story.'

'I told you.' I did not apologize for my snappishness. Did Tinos think I would lie to him?

'I'm more interested now in how Duzi obtained such a valuable piece of jewelry.'

'Me too,' I agreed. 'There was nothing else in that awful room . . .'

'Which has been re-rented, so anything that might have been there has been taken by that slimy landlord,' Tinos said with a frown.

'It looked as though the room had been searched before Tetis and I got there,' I said, looking up at Tinos. 'There wasn't even a spoon . . .'

'I don't doubt that.'

'It sounds like you found the room?'

'I did.'

'How?'

'I asked Tetis. She remembered.' Tinos grinned at me.

Great, I thought. Now she would be angry with me too. 'I was trying to keep her out of it,' I grumbled.

'If Duzi's killer is to be found, no one is out of it,' Tinos said. 'Now, get along home. I'll talk to the others.'

'Can't I remain here and listen in?' I asked hopefully.

'No. You're supposed to be out of this, remember? Besides, I doubt any of them will tell me the truth with you eavesdropping.'

Since that was a fact, I nodded. 'Will you tell me what they say, then? Especially Tryphone? I don't trust him.'

'Go home, Martis,' Tinos said, his voice rising with frustration. 'Go home.'

Muttering under my breath – without my help, he wouldn't even know to ask about the jeweled dragonfly – I went to the side of the ring and pulled on my clothes. Well, I had other avenues to pursue. The healer could tell me if Ynna's wounds looked the same as Duzi's. And Tinos still did not know about Anesdura. I didn't plan to tell him either. Once again, I decided he didn't deserve my assistance.

TWENTY-FOUR

Once I'd scaled the rows of stone seats surrounding the ring and reached the top, I descended the slope to the square. I broke into a trot and went rapidly around to the southwestern end of the complex. Since I approached the healer's room from a different entrance, I had some trouble finding my way. I smelled it before I found the stairs: the sharp and spicy herbal scent I recalled from my previous visit.

As I descended the steps, I saw a young girl, her back to me. Two black braids went down a skinny back, the shoulder blades protruding like wings. She must have heard my footsteps; she turned to face me. 'The healer isn't here,' she said before returning to chopping greenery at a small side table.

'Where is she?' I asked.

She looked at me once again. Freckles spattered her nose, and she looked even younger than I'd thought. 'She's with a patient. She should be back soon.'

'Are you her apprentice?' As I approached the girl, I smelled the herb's sour tang.

'One of them.' She turned around and chopped at the green stems in front of her with several vicious strokes. 'But not for long.'

I looked at the leaves. 'Why not? Too boring?'

'I don't mind this. If it was just mixing herbs, I'd stay. But the blood!' She shuddered, her eyes widening with a memory. 'And other things. It makes me sick.'

I had a good idea what other things she spoke of, so I hesitated a moment before asking about Ynna. 'Did a body of a woman come in?'

Before the girl could answer, the healer said from behind me, 'Yes. It is in the back room. How are you, Martis?'

I turned and smiled at her. 'Well enough.'

'I assume, since you are here, that you wish to see the body?'

I nodded gravely. 'I want to look at the knife wounds. Do you believe they were made by the same knife as the wounds on Duzi?'

'I do. Come and look for yourself.'

As I passed the young girl, I caught her expression. She was gaping at me in absolute disbelieving horror.

Ynna's body lay on a long table in a small chamber off the main area. The healer pulled back the canvas sheet covering the body. The stink of stale alcohol wafted into the room. Ynna was even paler than she had been, but she looked very calm and peaceful. She still wore her blood-soaked jacket and bead necklace, but the linen chemise underneath had been cut away and the blood washed off. I glanced at the healer for permission to approach the body. When she nodded, I shifted away the canvas to study the punctures more closely.

'They look identical to those on Duzi's chest,' I suggested cautiously.

The healer nodded. 'I believe they are. I measured them against a dagger carried by one of the wanax's guards. These wounds, like Duzi's, were made by something extremely sharp and with a narrow blade. Much narrower than the usual dagger.'

Retching sounds came from the room outside. Both the healer and I peered around the door. The girl had stopped chopping and was staring at us, her skin a greenish color.

'Finish chopping those herbs,' the healer said sternly. 'You shouldn't be listening to us.' The sound of chopping started up once again.

'Ynna was murdered by the same person,' I murmured as I returned to the body.

'That would be my guess,' the healer agreed. 'He is still angry.' She pointed to the group of stab wounds over the heart. 'But not as angry as he was with Duzi.'

'If the weapon is not the usual dagger,' I said slowly as I thought it through, 'then what is it? An obsidian knife?'

'I doubt it.' The healer fingered the lapis beads at Ynna's throat and turned one over. 'See the scrape?' I nodded. The gash was difficult to miss. 'I think the murderer hit the necklace by mistake.'

'In the frenzy of killing,' I muttered. She glanced at me and inclined her head in agreement.

'An obsidian knife would have broken. No, this knife was metal. And striking the lapis bent the tip. See, here and here.' She pointed to two of the punctures. 'The wounds are torn.'

I inspected the gashes with the torn imperfection in the skin. For a moment, both the healer and I were silent.

'But why?' I muttered. 'Why kill Ynna? What did she and Duzi have in common?' I stared at the wall, so deep in thought I barely noticed the shelves stocked with jars. Duzi and Ynna must have been lovers; it was the only thing that made sense.

'Nothing, as far as I can tell,' the healer said as though I'd asked her the question. She drew up the canvas sheet and shrouded the body once again. 'It is fortunate you came today to examine the body; Ynna's brother is arriving later to collect it.' The healer looked at me to make sure I understood. 'The body will be prepared and interred in the family tomb the day after tomorrow.'

'Thank you.' I thought Anesdura would probably wish to attend the service, and I would ask my mother also. They'd both known Ynna well, once.

'Martis.' The healer broke into my thoughts. 'Have you thought any more about apprenticing to me?'

'Yes.' I offered her a shaky smile. 'It sounds interesting . . .'

'But?'

'I don't know what my mother would do without me.'

She gazed at me for a few seconds and then nodded. 'I understand. But if your mother wants you to be happy, she'll accept your decision.'

I hurried home to bathe and dress. After eating, I allowed my mother to draw the kohl around my eyes. What would she do if I chose the life of a healer? 'Don't bother arranging my hair. I'll just braid it.'

Today, Anesdura herself opened the door. Her eyes were red and swollen, and she flung herself into my arms. I patted her shoulder as I urged her inside. 'I suppose you've heard,' I said.

She nodded, sniffling. 'Do you know what happened?'

I murmured something. I wasn't sure Tinos wanted the manner of Ynna's death to become common knowledge. 'The funeral is scheduled for the day after tomorrow,' I said.

Once again, we walked to the back courtyard where the nursemaid and Anesdura's daughter were playing in the sunshine. As I looked at her fair hair, I thought it would be a shame if those curls darkened. Light hair was uncommon and quite striking.

The nursemaid, taking one look at Anesdura and her red eyes, scooped the child up and carried her away. As she passed me, I said, 'Will you ask the cook to bring wine and something for your mistress to eat?' The nursemaid nodded and disappeared through one of the doors.

I turned to Anesdura. 'How did you hear the terrible news?'

'One of the women I know. She heard about it and rushed over here to tell me Ynna was dead.'

'That's true,' I said, realizing there was no point hiding Ynna's fate from Anesdura – or anyone else. The news, via gossip, had probably spread through the entire city by now.

'Maybe murdered.' Anesdura sniffed. 'You know what she said to me as she left? That Ynna deserved it.'

'Nobody deserves that,' I said.

'What happened?' Anesdura asked, staring at me intently. 'Do you know? You planned to visit her, didn't you?'

'And I did,' I said. 'I did visit her. But I don't know what happened. Whoever did this called on her after I was there.'

I went quiet as the servant brought in wine, flatbreads stuffed with roasted meat and vegetables, and honey-soaked pastries. When I looked at the servant in surprise – this was much more food than I'd expected – she said, 'My mistress hasn't eaten anything since she heard.' I fixed a plate for Anesdura, and when she put it down, untasted, I put some food on the second plate and took a bite. The rules of hospitality demanded she eat with me. She took a bite and then another. Before long, she'd cleaned her plate. She sighed, her eyes still red, but her expression calmer.

I leaned forward and took hold of her sticky hands. 'We need to find out what happened,' I said. 'You must tell me about Ynna. Everything you know.'

TWENTY-FIVE

'But I don't know anything now,' Anesdura protested after a moment. 'We saw each other infrequently, especially after I married.'

'I know. You told me that,' I said. 'All right. Tell me, what was she like then?'

'You don't remember?'

'No.' I didn't want to admit I'd paid little attention to my sisters and their friends. Their interests – clothes, jewelry and men – bored me.

'We were so arrogant. We assumed everyone was watching us and interested in what we were doing.' She sighed. 'And that was true. There were many women, younger than we were, who copied our jewelry and clothes. If we added braid to our jackets, everyone added braid. Why, I remember—'

'You said Opis and Ynna were very competitive,' I said, interrupting her without compunction. 'Were you competing with them as well?'

A dull red flush stained her cheekbones. 'As much as I could,' she said, not meeting my eyes. 'Not while Opis was in Knossos. Your sister was so very beautiful. All the men wanted to bed her and all of us women wanted to be her.'

Not all the men, I thought, recalling Saurus, the barbarian engaged to Arge. He'd wanted nothing to do with Opis.

'She flaunted her beauty and sex appeal,' Anesdura continued. 'And she could be so cruel, oh yes—'

'What happened after Opis married Pylas?' I prompted, breaking into Anesdura's rambling conversation once again.

'Well, after her marriage, Opis wasn't in Knossos all the time. Instead, she lived at her villa. Oh my, how she hated that. She hated the animals and always said the entire farm smelled of manure, and she claimed there was never any adult conversation—'

'As fascinating as this is,' I said, interrupting her again, 'I am more interested in Ynna. Was she the leader of your group? I always thought Opis was.'

'Yes, it was mostly Opis, although they vied for the leadership,' Anesdura said. 'Opis usually won. She had a ruthlessness that Ynna simply did not possess.' I shuddered at that. I knew about Opis's ruthlessness and her determination to win at all costs. 'Once, when Opis put gold trim on her skirt and jacket, Ynna copied her with even more embellishment. Opis said Ynna resembled a hair ornament more than a person and then ripped off most of the gold. Neither Eile nor I knew what to say. Especially when Ynna began to cry and—'

'What about Arge and Eile?' I asked. 'Did they participate in the competition as well?'

'Eile was already turning her attention to the priesthood. She'd always been the most religious among us. But I think her decision to go beyond the rituals we all must learn was influenced by her grandmother. You know – Lavra?' I nodded. 'And then we didn't see Eile as much because she was busy. And when we did, she acted as though the competition between the rest of us was juvenile. In fact, she as good as said so. That did not please either Opis or Ynna, I can tell you. For a while, they aligned against her and called her the Goddess.'

'And Arge?' I asked, taking the opportunity to break in when Anesdura paused for a breath.

'It was about that time Saurus arrived, I think,' Anesdura said, staring at the ceiling as she thought. 'Both your sisters were captivated. Opis refused to visit the villa, or her husband, at all.' Anesdura looked at me, her eyebrows rising. 'Opis said you were the only one who didn't like Saurus.'

'I didn't,' I agreed, although I'd eventually learned to respect him. 'What about you? What did you think?'

'He was attractive but too rough for my tastes. Anyway, I thought then I might have a chance to win one of the contests with Ynna. She was not as beautiful as Opis and she didn't try as hard when Opis was out of town.'

'You and Ynna were competing?'

'Not for long. A few weeks at most. I became involved with someone, and I wanted to be with him.'

'Was that when you met her husband?' I asked.

Anesdura's cheeks went scarlet, and her eyes slid away from mine. 'About that time,' she murmured. I eyed her suspiciously, wondering what she was hiding. She glanced at me and hurried into speech. 'That was about the time Arge agreed to marry the barbarian. Opis began visiting more often, so Ynna competed with her instead of me. Anyway, I'd lost interest in spending all my time with them. I don't know exactly what they were involved in then.'

Although the last sentence may have been largely true, there were such gaping holes in her account that she may as well have lied to me. 'I have a pretty good idea what Opis was doing,' I said now. 'What about Ynna?'

'I told you, I don't know. Especially about Ynna. I was focused on my own concerns. Even your sisters didn't see Ynna much. They were busy with Arge's upcoming wedding—'

'You must have heard something,' I said curtly. I was rapidly losing patience with her clumsy attempts to divert me.

'There were rumors,' she agreed cautiously. 'But you know this city. There are always rumors. Always gossip. It's impossible to get at the truth sometimes. I remember once—'

'What were the rumors?'

'Well, that Ynna spent as much time as she could at the ring, watching the bull dancers.' Anesdura's face reddened once again and she averted her eyes.

'I see,' I said. I was not surprised. Ynna and yes, Opis, too, were exactly the kind of women I would expect to interest themselves in the bull dancers. 'Do you have any names? Of the bull dancers I mean.'

Anesdura's eyes widened. 'No. Well, she was linked with more than one.'

'Anyone I might know?'

'This was before you began bull leaping,' she said quickly. 'You might have heard the names, but I believe most of them are retired now.'

'Or dead,' I said, nodding in agreement. Most of the bull dancers I'd known when I first began training were dead. A few were retired. Only Elemon remained, and although he'd been badly injured, he was still jumping.

All the blood drained from Anesdura's cheeks. For once, she could think of nothing to say.

'It is a dangerous sport,' I added.

'I think that was part of the excitement,' Anesdura said. 'There could never be a permanent relationship. The dancers were always on the edge of injury or death. There was one among the bull dancers Ynna wanted, I remember. In fact, I suspect that connection grew into genuine feelings on both sides. She gave him many love gifts, and he dedicated his performances to her.'

I nodded. Such love gifts and dedications were common. I didn't know how many resulted from relationships; I felt uncomfortable even thinking about it. 'You seem to know a fair amount about it,' I said. 'Especially since you say you were estranged from Ynna then.'

She blinked and shifted in her seat. 'We weren't estranged,' she said. 'I just didn't see very much of her then. And what I just told you was common knowledge, discussed everywhere. Even Opis heard about it at the villa.'

'Hmm,' I said skeptically.

'Like I said, I'd met someone then. We spent a lot of time together . . .' She blinked again and began pleating her skirt between her fingers.

'Your husband?' I asked. 'I don't recall your wedding.' Surely, I would remember Opis and Arge discussing it. If it had happened before Arge's death, that is. Afterwards, I could think of nothing else but the tragedy that befell my sister.

'It was small,' she said quickly. 'A hurried affair.'

'Your husband spends a lot of time away from Knossos. Isn't that what you said?' I asked.

'He runs his sister's villa. He is there now, in fact.' A fleeting unhappiness crossed her face. I wondered if there was trouble in the marriage but did not want to ask. That wasn't my business.

'That must be hard for you,' I said instead. 'Especially now, after Ynna's death. And you expecting a child.'

'It is lonely,' she admitted. 'I miss him. But it is the way of things. And I appreciate the many fine wines and foods he brings home from the farm. Besides, he always buys me a lovely gift when he has been away so long.'

I tried to imagine Opis accepting such an arrangement and failed. Then I thought of the servant who lived at the villa – now my villa, I supposed – who was clearly keeping company with Pylas, and I couldn't help but wonder if there were other reasons for Anesdura's husband to stay away so much. Again, not my business.

I realized suddenly that she had begun talking about the latest gifts: a rhyton in the shape of a bull's head, a necklace of carnelian beads, a silver chain for her hair. They all sounded beautiful and expensive, but from her tone of voice, I knew she would rather enjoy his company.

'You wouldn't tell me before about the scandal surrounding Ynna,' I said, interposing my question between two of her words. 'Tell me now.'

She hesitated. I leaned forward and took her two hands in mine once again. 'Anesdura, two people are dead. Murdered. One of them your friend. It is no time to keep secrets.'

She blew out her breath. 'I know. And she went from bad to worse.' Tears filled her eyes. 'That bull dancer; I think she really loved him. After his death, it was like she didn't care anymore. She married a man chosen by her mother and went to live with him. But she didn't abandon her wild ways. Her husband came home one day and found her with another man. A bull dancer probably. And that was not the first or the last time.' She paused, and I gestured at her impatiently.

'Go on.'

'I am not entirely sure what happened. My husband and I were recently married, and I didn't see Ynna for a long time. But the gossip said the next time he caught her in bed with another man, he divorced her and she moved out. I believe he's married again now. Anyway, she—' Abruptly, Anesdura stopped. Tears slid down her cheeks. 'I saw her after that. She was drunk and singing at the top of her lungs. I pretended I didn't notice her. I turned my back and went home. I wish that wasn't the last time I saw my old friend.' She began sobbing, and I moved closer to put my arm around her heaving shoulders. 'I just wish I'd visited her after that. Maybe, if she knew she still had a friend . . . Oh, I'm so ashamed.'

I stayed with Anesdura until she was all cried out. Then I rose to my feet. But as I prepared to leave, Anesdura grabbed my hand. 'Thank you for visiting,' she said. 'I don't see Eile anymore, and anyway she's a different person now. Opis, Arge and Ynna are all gone. I feel . . . the world feels different. The end of my girlhood, I guess. So, thank you.'

I squeezed her hand. 'I'll visit again,' I promised.

'Don't forget,' she begged.

'I won't.' I was committed now.

TWENTY-SIX

As I walked home, I replayed the conversation in my head. Now that I knew for certain Ynna had a history of relationships with bull dancers, I wondered if both Duzi and Tryphone could be the latest in a long string of partners. That would explain the presence of the dragonfly clip in Duzi's room as well as Tryphone's insistence the jewelry belonged to him. But there were still so many unanswered questions. Were they sharing Ynna? Did that mean Tryphone murdered Ynna as well as Duzi? Although I could imagine Tryphone striking down Duzi out of jealousy, I could not see a motive for the murder of Ynna. Unless she'd broken off the relationship with Tryphone to begin one with Duzi.

That was unlikely; indeed, it was almost unbelievable. The bull dancers, especially the males, engaged in multiple romances with society ladies, frequently with several women at the same time. I found it hard to believe Tryphone had committed himself to Ynna.

And what about Anesdura? I couldn't rid myself of the conviction she had kept something back. Something she was ashamed of. Was it important? I didn't know. But I needed to learn what it was.

Drops of water spattered my hair and face. When I looked up, I realized gray clouds had swept across the sky. The falling drizzle rapidly increased in intensity and soon it was raining heavily. I began to run, the leather soles of my sandals slipping on the stones.

The summer world of dry golden grass was turning green. The gray-green olive leaves were unfurling, the irrigation trenches around the grape vines running with muddy water. Soon, the wheat and barley would be planted – but first would come the sacrifice of the bull. His blood would nourish the soil and guarantee a good harvest next year.

I burst into the apartments, breathing hard, and with my braid dripping wet down my back. 'My goodness,' my mother said. She came forward with Ria on her hip.

'Where is the nursemaid?' I asked.

My mother raised her shoulders in a shrug. 'Gone again. And how is Anesdura?'

'Sad. Grieving for Ynna. Her funeral is scheduled for the day after tomorrow.'

'I heard.' My mother deposited the baby on the rug. 'I never understood why Anesdura and Ynna lost touch.'

'Did you know about Ynna?' I asked. And when Nephele looked at me in confusion, I added bluntly, 'She had a reputation for taking bull dancers into her bed.'

My mother looked away for a few seconds, and I could see her trying to decide how to respond. Finally, she said, 'All those girls were . . . lively. Not Arge, of course. And Eile became more and more detached as she became interested in becoming a priestess. But Opis, until she married Pylas and moved to the villa, and the other two lived for clothes and men.' Her voice soured and I knew Nephele had not approved.

'That is your answer,' I said. 'Anesdura married and had a child. She lost interest in bull dancers. Ynna did not.'

'Most people grow up. Ynna got stuck somewhere.'

I thought of the woman I'd seen: her kohl poorly applied and running down her cheeks, her messy uncombed hair and soiled skirt. She'd looked far older than her years, her youthful beauty and zest for life crushed out of her. 'How sad,' I murmured as I went into my bedchamber to change.

When I came out once again, my mother was just returning from the baby's bedchamber. When my mother saw me, she disappeared into the kitchen. She brought out fruit, flatbread and some roasted meat, cold now since it was from breakfast. I hadn't eaten much at Anesdura's so I was hungry. I sat down with my mother, and we ate without speaking. The only sound was the patter of rain in the courtyard outside. A cool breeze swept into the house through the open windows.

While I was wiping my plate with the last of my bread, I said, 'I hope the rain stops before tomorrow.'

'I do too.' My mother's gaze went to the storm outside. Although we needed the water, as we always did after a dry, hot summer, attending the ceremonies in the rain was unpleasant.

'It is a perfect day to spend inside,' my mother said. 'In the weaving room. A few more hours and you will finish the rug that has taken you many months. More than it should have.'

I grimaced rebelliously and tried to eat the remainder of my food very slowly.

I was not yet able to weave the complicated patterns so beloved of my mother, and I probably never would be. But this rug, striped with bands of bright colors, was well woven and my mother planned to add it to those she would sell. It would not be expensive, but I hoped to barter it for something of value – my mother said I could keep the profit.

Because I'd been compelled to weave since I was a child, I could pass the weaving stick back and forth without thinking about it. I wanted to reflect upon Anesdura's confidences. She'd no doubt told me more than she wished, but not everything. I needed to consider what she'd confided – and everything she hadn't. Surely Anesdura had been more involved in the competition she'd mentioned – especially after Opis had married – than she'd admitted. The battle for supremacy would have moved from Ynna and Opis to Ynna and Anesdura. I tried to cast my mind back. With Opis living most of the time at the villa, and not at the Knossos apartments, I hadn't seen her friends as much. Arge had been busy with Saurus, and so rather indifferent to her female friends. I'd heard about some of the gossip about Ynna's escapades and now, with what I'd recently learned, I thought I knew most of her history. But there was some mystery surrounding Anesdura. Or maybe it was only a mystery to me. One of my most enduring memories was of my sisters whispering together, only to stop as soon as I approached. I wondered now if they'd been sharing scandalous rumors they did not want me to hear. I hadn't cared then. Now I wished I'd been more interested.

I saw no point in questioning the current bull dancers. They were all new, and the gossip I was curious to hear was ancient history. The only dancer from that time still performing was Elemon, and he had been absent for months as he tried to recover from the wound that had almost killed him. Even most of those I'd begun training with were gone; injured, dead or, like Kryse, involved in other lives. Tinos was too old by about ten years, almost a different generation. I doubted he would know – or care – about such old gossip.

Besides, I couldn't be sure if these old scandals had anything to do with either Duzi's or Ynna's murder. Maybe nothing. But I knew Anesdura was hiding something and I was curious.

TWENTY-SEVEN

To my relief, the skies cleared overnight and, by morning, patches of blue shone through the clouds. Rainwater still puddled on the roads, but when I left for the arena first thing, the streets were beginning to dry. Bull dancing in the rain was both difficult and unpleasant.

Today, the final day of the Harvest Festival would begin with a bull dance. I expected most of the city inhabitants would attend. Then everyone, or almost everyone, would go to the Sacred Grove for the sacrifice of the bull. Once his blood seeped into the ground and infused it with strength, the farmers could begin planting their fields.

After the bull's sacrifice, everyone would walk to the Sanctuary in the foothills of the Sacred Mountain where the hide and the bones would be burned on the altar, the perfumed smoke sent to the heavens for the Goddess. The roasted beef would be served to all the celebrants in a grand feast.

I joined the other bull dancers in the cave. This was the final bull dance for some time – and an important one – so we were all subdued. I wondered if the others were remembering the discovery of Duzi's body. I certainly was. I peered into the empty pen, the floor still stained with his blood. The enclosure hadn't been purified yet and was therefore unusable; the primary bull, and his back-up, had been put into different cages. I could hear them grunting and galloping around, their hooves ringing on the stone floor.

I found my place in the line. No one was missing today – not for a performance and a chance at valuable trinkets that might be offered us, as well as fame and glory. Arphaia turned around and gave me a weak smile. I nodded back.

A cool breeze blew through the tunnel from the cave entrance, and I shivered. Geos appeared, looming out of the darkness and stepping into the dim light cast by the dish lamps. He held up a hand. I could hear the roar of the crowd outside, but Geos could hear something else as well; he cocked his head and listened with one finger held up. He nodded. Costi pushed the twins forward and the entire line began to move.

We stepped into the sunshine outside. While we'd been inside the cave, all the clouds had blown away and the sun was bright. The people around us, mostly artisans showing off their wares, began cheering. To Geos's gratification, the twins turned cartwheels and walked on their hands. Arphaia executed a clumsy flip. Obelix jumped up into a handstand on Thaos's hands. When I turned, I saw to my dismay that Tryphone was behind me. He grinned, showing all his teeth.

'Handstand, Martis,' Geos shouted.

I hesitated a few seconds and then ran to Tryphone, putting my foot in his cupped hands. I jumped up and balanced on his shoulders. All I could hear were the shouts and cries of the crowd around me. Tryphone extended his arms up, palms out. Did I trust him enough to balance on his hands? What if he shook me off? What if he dropped me on the ground? Could I trust that his pride in his acrobatics would outweigh his anger at me?

'Come on, Martis,' Tryphone said sharply. 'Stop dawdling.'

Gulping, I leaned forward and placed my hands on his. I rose into the air, my toes pointed to the sky, balancing on his palms. I'd performed this move so many times it was almost effortless.

After a few seconds, Tryphone pushed me higher and I flipped over, landing with a solid thud on the ground.

Beginning to enjoy myself, I performed a few cartwheels and a few flips. I no longer felt the cold. Elemon, grinning with pleasure, gestured to me. We both wiped our perspiring hands on our loincloths and then he grabbed me and spun me through the air.

I could hear the bull behind us. The handlers were moving the beast to the pen by the arena.

We circled the ring twice and then lined up in preparation for the jumps. Geos assigned Arphaia as catcher and shifted the positions of the rest of us so Elemon and Tryphone would jump first. The children were lined up at the end. Except for Costi, none of them would jump today. They weren't ready, not even Nub.

I glanced at Tinos and the High Priestess. He stared to one side, his face averted. His lack of interest surprised me. As a former bull dancer, I would assume he'd be totally attentive, totally focused on us. The High Priestess was paying more attention, in between her comments to her daughter.

To an excited roar from the crowd, the bull trotted into the ring.

This was the same auroch we'd danced with at the start of the Harvest Festival. He was young and aggressive and, after a few days' rest, very energetic. It would take some time to tire him. I jumped third, after the two men, and the bull seemed as fresh then as he had been at the beginning.

Geos held Costi back until after the rest of us had jumped three or four times. By then, sweat was pouring off me in rivulets.

I could scarcely believe I'd been cold just an hour earlier. And I was tiring; all of us who'd already danced several times were. We appreciated the rest that came from the addition of another jumper.

I watched Costi take up his position at the front of the queue with my heart in my mouth. He turned with a grin, seemingly unafraid. He started his run, his hands outstretched for the horns. He grasped them, the bull tossed his head, and Costi's short skinny body flew up and over. He looked so fragile suspended in the air. But he landed perfectly, his feet as solid on the bull's back as if it were a table.

Elemon, Tryphone and I broke into spontaneous applause. The audience roared its approval.

Then it was my turn. Still distracted by Costi's jump, I wasn't ready. I started running before I was lined up with the bull's large cranium and when I reached out for the ivory spikes my sweaty hands slipped on the bone. The bull tossed his head, and I flew up into the air. I tried to correct but misjudged it. Instead of landing squarely on the bull's back, I twisted right and landed on the ground instead. Pain shot through my ankle and up my calf. Arphaia tried to catch me and we both fell, me landing on top of her. She grunted underneath me.

The bull's tail lashed the air above us, sending a cool bull-scented breeze across us. The shouting of the crowd eddied around me and for a moment I wondered if I'd lost consciousness.

Obelix ran forward, shouting. After a moment, Tryphone joined her. They both ran toward the bull. He hesitated, snorted and ran in their direction. I rolled away from Arphaia and tried to stand. She got to her feet first and reached out to help me up. Then, since she had to run to the rear of the bull and be there for Tryphone who was preparing to leap the bull, Arphaia left me balancing on my left foot.

I inspected my ankle. It was already swollen, but I did not think it was broken.

I put my foot down. It would take my weight, but it was painful. By the Goddess, it was painful.

I limped to the side and looked at Geos for instruction. He had one hand clapped to his forehead.

'Hey, girl.' I looked at the man leaning toward me from his seat. He flipped a lapis bead at me. 'Good try.' I smiled and nodded and bent to pick up the bead.

The bronze gong chimed; to my relief, the first half was over.

Geos gathered us together as the handlers drew the bull away. 'Let me look,' he said. I lowered myself to the ground. Geos's blunt fingers probed my sore ankle, drawing a gasp of pain from me. 'It isn't broken,' he said in relief. 'What happened?'

'I don't know,' I mumbled, embarrassed to admit I'd been distracted by Costi's jump.

'Can you stand?'

'Yes.'

He stared into space for several seconds, his mouth moving in and out. 'You'll have to be the catcher, Martis. I need the others to dance with the bull. And Nub and the twins aren't big enough or strong enough. Do you think you can do it?'

I pushed myself to my feet and tried to put my weight on my ankle. It held. 'I can do it,' I said bravely. If no one fell on me as I'd done to Arphaia.

After a short rest and some water, the second half began. Arphaia, as the freshest dancer among us, took up her position. As the bull snorted and pawed the ground, I limped to the bull's rear. Arphaia began her run. I limped after the bull as he ran at her. I just barely made it to my spot before she came sailing over the horns. Her jumps were clumsy, her landings on the bull's back as graceful as a sack of barley hitting the floor, but she made it without incident. She jumped off the bull's back with only a touch to my shoulder for balance.

Most of the other bull leapers jumped effortlessly over the bull without requiring my help. I was grateful.

At last, the bull began to tire. His gallop dropped to a trot and the head tosses that lifted the dancers into the air shortened and lost their punch. Tryphone barely cleared the tips of the horns. The gong reverberated through the ring. I was tired, and my ankle throbbed so painfully that I did not know if I could make it to the front of the arena where the others congregated.

The rest of the team looked no better. We were all sweating, dirty and staggering with fatigue. But the audience was thrilled. Almost all of us, even Arphaia and Costi, were called to the side for tokens of admiration. Obelix, her face glowing, accepted a gold necklace and a handful of smaller prizes – rings, I think. She handed the necklace and a ring to Arphaia.

Besides my lapis bead, I was given a string of pearls for my hair and a gold bull charm. Elemon, Tryphone and Costi, the surprise hero of the performance, returned to the caves with their hands full.

Despite my injury, it was a good day.

TWENTY-EIGHT

I would not have succeeded in leaving the cave without the help of Arphaia and Obelix. They each took a side and helped me down the tunnel and out into the light. A shaft of sunlight illuminated my mother, standing by a litter. 'I didn't think you would mind today,' she said. 'Considering your injury.'

I smiled at her gratefully as Arphaia and Obelix supported me to her side. I lowered myself to the litter with a groan. 'Thank you,' I said to Arphaia and Obelix. 'I could not have made it without you.'

'You're welcome.' Obelix said gravely.

'Will we see you at the Sacred Grove?' Arphaia asked.

'I hope so,' I said as the bearers lifted the litter. After all, although painful, a sprained ankle wasn't much of an injury. Not compared to the risks of trampling and goring.

The bearers broke into a rapid trot. They arrived at the complex far sooner than I usually would and paused by the steps. When I looked through the curtains, I saw my mother hurrying to catch up. When she reached us, the bearers lowered the palanquin to the ground and I sat up. I pushed myself to my feet. Although my ankle still throbbed, it was no longer as painful as it had been. I managed to walk to the foot of the stairs, but although my injured ankle allowed me to walk, it would not support my weight ascending the steps. My mother put her shoulder under mine, and with her support, I climbed to the top.

Once we reached the apartment, she examined my injury. 'Geos said it isn't broken,' I told her.

She nodded. 'It will be painful for a few days.' She looked up and met my eyes. 'After a little rest, I expect you can walk to the Sacred Grove. But not to the Sanctuary.'

I thought about the walk over rough terrain and the time it took to walk that far and nodded in agreement. 'I'll miss the feast,' I agreed. I did not mind much. Like many bull dancers, I looked upon the bull as an honored adversary. The thought of eating him filled me with aversion.

I bathed before changing my clothing. The cool water soothed my ankle and it felt better when I clambered out of the tub. I changed into my newer skirt and jacket, woven in purple and yellow. My mother dressed my hair with the locks over my shoulders and wove the new strand of pearls through it. I allowed her to outline my eyes with kohl.

When we sat down in the main room, the cook brought out tea, flatbread with meat and olives, and another plate of honey pastries. Suddenly realizing how hungry I was, I ate my way through the food until only crumbs remained. I drank the last of my tea and sat back with a sigh of contentment.

'Here is the baby.' The nursemaid came out into the main room and shoved Ria at my mother. 'I'm leaving now for the Sanctuary.'

'Wait,' my mother protested, trying to rise to her feet at the same time she clutched the baby to her.

'She's been fed,' the woman threw over her shoulder as she left the apartment.

'What will we do with her this afternoon?' I asked.

My mother glanced at me. 'I'll have to bring her with me to the ceremony.' I stared at her without speaking. My mother sighed. 'And I'll begin searching for another woman. This can't go on.'

It was just past mid-afternoon when my mother and I, and baby Ria, began walking to the Sacred Grove. We'd started early for the Grove since we knew we would be walking slowly. My mother was weighed down by the baby, and my sore ankle kept me to a slow limp. Despite our early start, though, the path was already crowded.

The small slice of forest smelled of wet earth and growing things. From the white Horns of Consecration marking the entry into the Sacred Grove, I could hear the rumble of many voices. Although I'd hoped to reach the consecrated ground early and find a good vantage point to watch the ceremony, I was already too late for that. I found a space in the middle of the crowd. My mother handed me the baby and disappeared. She had a part to play in the ritual.

The High Priestess and her ladies would act out the birth of the Dying God first. Dionysus would be presented to us, the worshippers, as a baby in a basket. He was born and grew to manhood as we mortals did. Then, as the fields went fallow, he died, only to be born once again.

I looked around. To the side, I saw Telemon, standing in a crowd of boys. Despite the gravity of this occasion, all of them, including my brother, were fooling around, play-fighting and pushing one another. As I watched, Thaos and Curgis grabbed several of the boys and shook them. Although I couldn't hear them over the noisy throng standing around me, I guessed they were scolding the worst offenders.

On the opposite side, I spotted Arphaia. To my surprise, Tryphone, dressed formally in a new long robe, had joined her and her family. Fisher folk, including Obelix, stood in a tight group at the back. I did not see Elemon.

A solitary drum began to pound a beat, drawing my attention to the altar at the front. My mother, the senior priestess, brought out a woven mat and laid it on the floor. Surrounded by priestesses, the High Priestess reclined on it and pretended to suffer the pains of labor. My mother held up a basket filled with fruit and nuts to represent the newly born God.

A young boy chosen from the dorms walked across the stone slab. He wore a mask of the God's grinning face, with horns on the brow, and a circlet of ivy on his head. After he disappeared into the trees on the other side, another, older boy, identically garbed, appeared. He too walked across the stage.

Finally, Tinos emerged. Wearing his lion skin costume, Dionysus mask and ivy wreath, he took his place next to the High Priestess. They did not look at one another. I was beginning to wonder if she *would* choose another consort. In years past, she had turned to him with a smile, but this time he might have been invisible.

Now the priestesses reappeared with large baskets. The lids were removed to reveal hefty snakes. The High Priestess held one aloft, its body as thick as my arm. The drumbeat increased in speed. She lowered the snake and wound it around her waist. My mother – as Nephele, Priestess – came forward and placed a headdress on the High Priestess's black hair. This one was of gold, with spokes radiating out from it like rays from the sun. It glittered in the light, throwing reflections on to the trees and into our faces.

The High Priestess began to chant.

Oh, great Goddess, mother of all,
Nourisher of wheat who rejoices as we sow and reap
The grain. It was you who first yoked the ox to the plow.
I call on your son, bull-horned.
Wrapped in skins and wearing an ivy wreath.
Draped in grapes and baskets brimming with summer bounty
The master of the wine press. We offer thanks
For the vines, heavy with fruit,
And pray for the harvest next year.
Take this blood from the brave bull.
An offering of thanks.

My mother had once told me that long ago, even before she was a child, they sacrificed not the bull but the wanax, so that his strength would go into the land and make it fertile. I shuddered and looked at Tinos. Did he know of that story? Since his face was covered by the mask, I could not tell what he was thinking.

I'd expected to stand apart from the ceremony and think my own thoughts. After all, I'd seen this ritual performed every year of my life. But with the drum mirroring my heartbeat, the smell of sweet, herbal smoke, and the chanting all around me, I found myself shouting the responses with everyone else. Ria whimpered, alarmed by the noise and chaos around us.

A large black bull was led out by one of the priestesses. He staggered a little, and I guessed he'd been drugged to make him easier to handle. I looked at him closely and was relieved to see he was not the brave adversary we'd met in the ring this morning.

The High Priestess strode forward, holding the double axe. He did not seem to realize the danger and stood there, patiently, head hanging low. She struck him hard with the golden axe and his legs buckled, sending him to the ground. Then the High Priestess stepped back and handed the double axe to one of the other priestesses.

Tinos, still masked and in his role as the Dying God and the Master of Animals, came forward with the silver knife and a bowl. Usually, in most of the ceremonies, the High Priestess performed this part, but during the Harvest Festival Tinos collected the blood. He held the knife high; it glittered in the sun. Then he nicked the bull's neck, just a small wound, and caught the resulting flow of blood in the bowl. The thick meaty smell rose into the air.

The bull could heal from this wound. It was but a small puncture. I wished just then that the auroch would rise to his feet, break the rope that held him and run. Of course, I knew he wouldn't. And he didn't.

For a moment, I watched Tinos's fluid movements, but then I noticed the High Priestess. Her behavior was so unusual that I stared. She stood to one side, her mouth pinched tight with impatience. She was almost trembling with the desire to step forward and pluck the knife and bowl from Tinos's hands.

Tinos carried the full bowl to the western side of the paved floor. He sprinkled the blood on the ground.

> Here is my blood. Let the earth open up
> And drink, offering up in return
> The grain that sustains us.

When all the blood had been distributed over the soil, still dry despite the recent rains, Tinos brought the empty bowl back to the front of the platform. This time, he pierced the bull's artery. Blood spurted out in a red fountain, easing to a trickle as it washed across the stones. The grooves cut into the floor directed the life-giving liquid to the same patch of soil where Tinos had sprinkled the blood from the bowl. As the bull's blood drained from him and into the furrows, it washed to the dry ground where it formed a lake of blood. Insects of all kinds descended upon the red pool in a cloud of wings.

At least the bull didn't suffer, I said to myself as I did every year. I thought the Goddess's requirement of a death so that we might live was a harsh one.

The High Priestess nodded at her attendants. They brought forward baskets of fruits and nuts and small trinkets and began to distribute them among the crowd. All of it – the food, the rings set with semi-precious stones, the beaded bracelets of lapis and topaz – were gifts from the Goddess and represented prosperity for the coming year.

Screaming and shoving, some of the people vied for the best, most valuable favors. I selected a handful of grapes but then I hung back, watching the insects and even a few birds settle on the surface of the blood. The shimmer of dragonfly wings caught my eye, and I thought of the hair clip I'd found. What had Tryphone and the other bull dancers told Tinos? Did it belong to Tryphone? And had Tinos asked him about Ynna?

TWENTY-NINE

As the crowd began to disperse, I stood to one side, waiting for my mother. I could see her among the other priestesses. They stuffed the snakes into their baskets and collected the other props. When the women finished, they formed a procession with the High Priestess at the head and paraded back to the Priestess House, singing and dancing as they went. I hoped my mother remembered her grandchild and came for her.

I had another purpose for waiting, and I didn't want the distraction of a baby. Since I knew where Tinos was at this moment – not with the priestesses since men were not allowed in the Priestess House – but still here at the Sacred Grove, I wanted to catch him and ask my questions.

Some of the priests came in to gather up the bull and transport the body to the Sanctuary. The meat would be roasted for tonight's feast, his bones and hide set upon the altar of ashes and burned.

The Sacred Grove was almost empty of people when my mother finally appeared. Her eyes sparkled and her cheeks were still flushed with excitement. 'I thought you might have already started home,' she said.

'No. I have some questions for Tinos.' I handed her the baby.

'He is still here somewhere . . .' My mother looked around. 'Oh, Martis, I wish you weren't so fond of him. He would not be so foolish as to choose another and humiliate the High Priestess. She would destroy him.'

I flushed fiery hot, and for a moment I thought I would throw up. I could not speak for several seconds. Then I said stiffly, my voice trembling, 'You are mistaken. I wish to speak to him about something else.'

She eyed me for several seconds. 'The murders. I hoped you were not still meddling in the murders,' she said disapprovingly.

I refused to respond.

'Oh, Martis,' she said sadly, 'Tinos will not thank you . . .' As Ria fussed, my mother began jiggling her. 'I must get her home.'

I nodded, still angry and embarrassed.

Soon I was alone in the Grove. The large stone blocks had dried, and even the lake of blood was disappearing as the liquid soaked into the earth. Finally, Tinos, who had retreated to the trees screening the back of the stone floor, appeared. He'd removed his mask, revealing his sweat-soaked hair, but still wore the lion skin. 'Tinos,' I said loudly, starting toward him.

'Martis.' He did not sound overjoyed to see me. 'Why are you still here?'

'Just a quick question,' I said as I approached him.

'Nothing with you is ever quick,' he said sourly.

'What did you find out? Did the jeweled dragonfly belong to Tryphone?'

'No.' Tinos smiled at my dismay. I took several steps closer.

'No?' Then I retreated. 'Phew,' I said. 'What is that smell?'

'The lion skin is old, and I don't think it was properly cured, to begin with,' Tinos said, grinning. 'I'm used to it now.' He sniffed. 'I barely smell it anymore. But when I first put it on, I thought I would vomit.'

I nodded, shielding my nose with my hand. 'So – Tryphone?'

'The dragonfly does not belong to Tryphone.'

'Why did he tell me it did?'

'I don't know – unless he planned to take it and barter it.'

'He sounded so certain.' So passionate.

'I asked around. Tryphone grew up to the west of here, on the coast somewhere, and moved to Knossos when pirates destroyed his village. Several captains in the navy recalled the attack. He arrived here with almost nothing, just a few pieces of jewelry. Not the dragonfly.'

'Nobody thought he brought it with him. I think the dragonfly might have been a prize given to him at one of the performances,' I said. 'Or as a love token.'

'That dragonfly is extremely valuable,' Tinos said. 'I doubt it was given to Tryphone as a prize. He's a competent bull leaper, nothing more.'

I considered that and nodded reluctantly. Although Tinos sounded slightly sneery, he wasn't wrong. 'Then it was a love token from a fashionable lady.'

'From whom? Have you seen him with anyone?'

I thought of Ynna and then Arphaia but shook my head. I didn't *know* anything. 'Who does that dragonfly belong to then, if not to Tryphone?' I asked, sounding grumpy.

'Elemon said it belonged to him.'

'Elemon?' My voice rose in shocked disbelief. Elemon had said nothing when I'd shown the ornament to Arphaia.

'He showed me the mate.'

I recalled the jeweler telling me she'd made a set of two. 'He owns the other dragonfly?' I asked in amazement.

'Yes. I saw it. It is almost identical.'

I nodded slowly, realizing that Elemon, who'd been a popular bull dancer for over a year, must own a chest full of such love gifts. Although not handsome, he was charming, unlike the gruff Tryphone. It made sense that Elemon would own the dragonfly.

'Thank you,' I said, looking up.

'Thank you for bringing the dragonfly to me. But it was a

dead end. Please do not keep poking into the murders. Whoever killed Duzi has already murdered once, maybe twice. I don't want you to be the next victim. Understand?'

As a surge of happiness swept through me – he did care about me! – I nodded. Tinos turned and began walking quickly away. 'Wait,' I called, stepping forward so quickly pain shot through my ankle. 'I have another question.' But Tinos did not hear me, or he pretended he didn't. He quickly disappeared down the path. By the time I righted myself, he was out of sight, leaving me to limp back to town by myself.

I started my slow journey, carefully avoiding puddles and slick patches. Alone, and in the quiet, I began to think. Had Tinos thought to ask Elemon what woman had given him the dragonfly ornaments? And if he had, what did Elemon tell him? Now, additional questions were presenting themselves. Was the gift giver Ynna, as I'd originally thought? That would imply Ynna and Elemon were or had been lovers. Why would he choose Ynna? Elemon had his choice of women. She may have been a beauty once, but hard drinking had taken a toll. Tryphone – or Duzi – as her bedmate made sense to me, more sense than Elemon. Both were too poor – and Tryphone too bad-tempered – to be choosy. I remembered Ynna's bitter assertion that no one loved her. She'd sounded desperate, willing to accept what she could get. That was a pairing that made a certain amount of sense.

But Elemon? I sighed. If he owned the dragonfly I'd found in Duzi's room, then Tryphone, who might be a poor liar and a thief, probably had nothing to do with either Ynna's or Duzi's murders. I reluctantly pushed him aside for now.

As I left the Sacred Grove and turned on to the path to town, however, I thought of something else that was odd. Usually, when one lover gave a gift to the other, especially such a valuable gift, she kept one. Each partner owned one of the pair. It was supposed to symbolize eternal love. Why did Elemon own both? That did not make sense.

And I still did not know how the ornament had ended up in Duzi's mean little room.

THIRTY

I arrived at the practice ring very early the next morning. My ankle was much better but still painful, and I knew I couldn't jump the bull. But I could help training the kids. While I assisted Geos in carrying out the equipment, I kept watch for both Costi and Elemon. Neither would escape my questions today.

Costi arrived first. As he approached Geos, I hobbled to his side and grabbed his arm.

'Ow,' he said, struggling to pull away.

'You know something about that dragonfly ornament,' I said sternly. 'I want to know what it is.'

'I don't know anything,' he protested, pulling even harder in his attempt to be free.

Now certain he knew something, I grasped his arm with both hands and dragged him to the side. There, I shook him. 'Yes, you do. And I'm not letting you go until you tell me what it is.' I hoped I could follow through on my threat; I couldn't hold him for long and I certainly couldn't run after him. Although Costi was younger than I was and he looked skinny, he possessed a wiry strength that taxed my ability to control him. 'Where did Duzi get the dragonfly? Who gave it to him?' I shook him again for good measure.

He squirmed. 'Duzi didn't even know – I brought it to his room.' Costi spoke quickly, in a rush.

'What do you mean, you brought it to his room? Where did you get it?'

'Don't tell Geos,' Costi pleaded, looking up at me with wide eyes.

I sighed. I wanted to refuse to promise anything so foolish, but instead I nodded. I didn't want Geos to know about a lot of silly things I'd done either.

'All right, I promise.'

'I stole it. Someone had it here. I saw it and thought I could barter it for food.'

'Why was it at Duzi's if you stole it?' I asked.

'Duzi allowed me to stay with him and fed me whenever he had food. I wanted to pay him back. I would have shared whatever I got with him.'

I stared at Costi for several seconds. 'Why didn't you go back to the dorms?' I asked at last, mystified. 'You would have been fed there. And could sleep in a bed of your own.'

'Too many rules. Too many people telling me what to do. Duzi never ordered me around. He treated me like an equal.'

I blinked and nodded. I could understand that. 'But you didn't barter the dragonfly away. Why not?'

'Duzi was—' Costi gulped and his eyes filled with tears. 'You found him in the bull pen the next morning. I never got a chance to show the hair clip to him.' The last few words ended on a sob. He looked away from me. Since my own eyes were burning, I did not mock his tears.

'Who owned the dragonfly then?' I asked. 'Who did you steal it from?'

'I don't know. I saw the sparkle mixed in with some clothes. A rug.' He inhaled a deep breath. 'It was wrapped in a rug. When I looked to see what it was, well, I just took it – I didn't even think. I just took it. Then I ran away.' He paused for several seconds before continuing. 'No one mentioned it the next morning. And then Duzi's body was found . . .'

I nodded. I remembered all too clearly what had happened that morning. I shuddered, the image of Duzi's bloody body popping into my head. Costi, taking advantage of my momentary inattention, wrenched his arm free and fled. Now that I had learned how the valuable dragonfly had ended up in Duzi's room, I let him go.

But I was no farther along now than I had been. In fact, now there were more questions than before. I still did not know for certain who the jeweled piece belonged to. Both Tryphone and Elemon claimed it. I wasn't sure I believed either of them. Neither one had reported the theft; an innocent man would have done so, right?

I followed that thought to its logical conclusion. Now that I knew it had been stolen once, what was to say someone else – one of the other bull dancers – had not stolen it before? Without a reason for owning it, and no way of explaining why he had it, he might not raise a fuss at its disappearance.

But then, why would Tryphone and Elemon both claim to own the dragonfly?

Because they each saw an opportunity to acquire it. It was a valuable piece. I nodded slowly. Both men merited further investigation.

Geos assigned me to the children again, as expected, but I kept watch for Elemon's arrival as I helped Nub and the twins. Tryphone, Thaos and Curgis arrived together, but although I remained at practice until Geos dismissed us, neither Elemon nor Arphaia made an appearance. Not unsurprising since yesterday's performance was the last important ceremony for a little while. They probably didn't see the point in practicing.

But Geos threw me a significant look, and I knew he was thinking of his prediction: that Arphaia would marry and leave.

As I pulled on my old skirt, Tryphone came up to me suddenly and grabbed my arm. 'I told you that dragonfly belonged to me,' he said, almost spitting in my face with his fury.

'And I told you I would give it to the wanax and allow him to sort it out,' I said, my heart rate speeding up. I was taller than average, so Tryphone and I were almost eye to eye. But his arms were muscular and sinewy. I could feel the strength in his hand as it clenched my upper arm. I knew I would see bruises there later today.

'Yes, and he gave my dragonfly to Elemon.' Tryphone said the name with a sneer. 'Everyone loves Elemon, especially the women. Taken in by his looks and that surface charm.'

Several responses ran through my head, ranging from 'You might be more successful if you were more pleasant' to 'What is your quarrel with Elemon?' Since I also had questions about Elemon's claim to the dragonfly, I said none of them. Finally, I settled on, 'But I did not give the dragonfly to Elemon. I gave it to the wanax.'

'He made a poor decision. You should have given me the jewelry when I told you it was mine.' He shook my arm angrily.

'Ow,' I protested. He loosened his grip slightly but did not release me.

'That jewelry was mine.'

'You said. But how did I know you were telling me the truth?' I looked him straight in the face. 'I found it with no idea who might own it.' I thought of Costi and added, 'Where did you obtain such a valuable piece? And where did you lose it?'

Suddenly self-conscious, Tryphone dropped my arm. 'Someone gave it to me, not that that is any of your business. I'm not sure where I lost it. It might even be here. Elemon could have taken it.'

'You think he might be a thief?' I asked, shocked.

'Why not? He takes what he wants. Even the adulation of the crowd. We all work hard, but the women throw flowers at him and give him valuable trinkets.' Grievance colored his voice. I stared at him.

'He's been a popular bull dancer for over a year,' I said. 'And he's good at it.'

'Looks and charm,' Tryphone muttered. 'Looks and charm. I don't trust him. And if you're smart, you won't either.'

'That sounds as if you think he might throw one of us in front of a bull,' I said. Could Tryphone be correct or was this just jealousy talking?

'You remember Kryse?' he asked, astonishing me once again. I nodded.

'I visited her recently,' I said.

'Elemon wanted to sleep with her, but she wouldn't.'

'She was getting married,' I said. Had I noticed any tension between Elemon and Kryse? Not that I recalled, but I had been so focused on my own concerns then that I might not have noticed.

'She was badly injured, wasn't she?'

Yes, she had been and still walked with a limp. 'She wasn't paying attention,' I said quickly. 'And how do you know? You weren't even in Knossos then.'

'I heard about it,' he said. 'You women are entirely taken in by Elemon, but the other men aren't. I've heard stories . . .'

Stunned again, I had no answer. I had never imagined the emotional undercurrents swirling about my fellow leapers. 'I didn't know,' I said at last.

Tryphone offered me a small smile. 'Yes, you think you are so smart, but you don't know everything, do you?'

Turning on his heel, he stalked away.

Slowly, I pulled on my jacket. I was not sure what to think. Elemon had always been nice to me, but now I certainly had a different view of him.

Thaos and Curgis were almost out of the ring. Once they'd corralled the twins, they'd all started back to the dorms. Costi had joined them, although he was trying to stay out of sight behind Thaos. I intended to follow and ask both Thaos and Curgis what they thought of Elemon. I didn't know many men, but I knew them. And they knew Elemon.

Before I did, I stopped by Geos. 'Do you know where Elemon lives?' I asked.

'Why do you want to know?' he asked, looking at me in surprise.

'I wanted to check something with him,' I said vaguely.

Geos shook his head dubiously, he didn't quite believe me, but he answered. 'He lives a little way outside the city, a villa on the southern side. A large bull statue sits just outside his gate.'

'Thank you.' I hurried as fast as I could after Thaos and the others. Although they had a good head start, I could see Thaos's head above the crowd. Fortunately, none of them seemed in any hurry to return home, and I was able to catch up to them as they approached the dorms.

Curgis heard my uneven gait coming up behind them and turned to see who it was. His eyebrows rose in surprise. 'Martis. What are you doing here?' he asked.

'I wanted to talk to you. And to Thaos,' I panted.

'About what?'

'Neither of us ever saw that hair clip,' Thaos said at the same time.

'Not about that,' I said. 'Well, maybe a little bit. I was just speaking with Tryphone.' Both nodded, and Curgis turned and shooed the twins toward the complex.

'We don't know anything,' Thaos said, his voice wary.

'Tryphone doesn't like Elemon much,' I said. From the startled expressions on their faces, I realized I probably should have led up to that statement more gradually. 'He said that many women are fooled by Elemon's looks and charm, and that most men see him differently.' I paused and waited.

Thaos and Curgis exchanged a glance. 'It is true that Elemon does not waste his charm on us,' Thaos said. Curgis nodded in agreement.

'In fact, he is barely polite.' Curgis did not choose his words as carefully as Thaos.

'He doesn't – um – hurt you, does he?' I asked.

Thaos uttered a short bitter laugh as Curgis shook his head. 'Why would he? We have nothing he wants. We can't help him or hurt him. He barely knows we're alive.'

I stared at them. I'd expected them to disagree with Tryphone. Instead, they corroborated his opinion. It was a shock.

'Is that all?' Thaos asked. I nodded, still dumbfounded.

The two young men went around me and continued to the dorms. I did not move. They'd shattered my view of Elemon, and now I wasn't quite sure what to think.

I looked over the fields next to the residence. A crowd of boys were practicing archery. In fact, I thought I saw Telemon. He was not very good. Not only could he not hit the target, but his arrow did not even get close. It dropped to the ground about halfway across the yard.

He must have felt the weight of my gaze. He turned and looked toward me. After a few seconds, he came running up the slope, frowning angrily. 'What are you doing here?' he shouted at me from a few feet away. 'Are you checking up on me? You shouldn't be here.'

'I didn't come to watch you,' I said shortly. 'I was here for something else. I just happened to see you.'

'Well, go away,' he said rudely. 'I don't want you to watch me.'

I gaped at him and then, ducking my head as I fought tears, I limped away. Already, after only a few days, he was turning into someone different. He was not my affectionate baby brother anymore.

THIRTY-ONE

Always impatient, I would have preferred searching for Elemon's villa and questioning him right away, but I knew I couldn't. I was already late going home and I couldn't run. My mother and I planned on attending Ynna's funeral – the nursemaid had arrived home after dark the previous night and would be available to watch Ria – and I still had to eat, bathe and change my clothes to a bright yellow-and-black skirt and yellow jacket.

Although I rushed through my preparations, when we reached Ynna's apartments, we discovered the coffin had already been removed.

'Really, Martis,' my mother said disapprovingly as we hurried to the steps at the front of the complex. 'Why didn't you come straight home?'

The professional mourners had already begun wailing, tearing their clothes and throwing ashes on their heads. We joined the crowd as the pallbearers lifted the coffin to their shoulders and began the walk to the Sacred Grove.

This was a small and inexpensive funeral. The pottery coffin was much simpler than the one we'd chosen for Arge, and there were only three professional mourners. Not too many of us attendees either.

In the first group behind the coffin, I saw a man and a woman. They both bore a strong resemblance to Ynna. Under cover of the mourners' loud wailing, I asked my mother if the man and woman were Ynna's family. She nodded. 'Brother and sister.' As far as I could tell, they were the only family here.

I looked around to see who else had come.

Anesdura was at the back, her eyes red and swollen. I nodded to her, and she forced a smile. Behind her, I saw an older woman, familiar but I did not know at first who she was. It took me a few seconds to identify her as the person who lived across the hall from Ynna. There were several more people I did not recognize at all, but since they walked with Ynna's neighbor, I thought they were probably neighbors as well.

We walked in silence to the Sacred Grove. The High Priestess had chosen not to officiate, but Lavra, the senior priestess after the Lady, waited by the altar to perform the rituals. I paid no attention to the prayers, instead looking around at the small group. Tryphone arrived quietly. I was not surprised to see him; his appearance gave credence to my suspicion he'd been Ynna's lover. Neither Obelix nor Arphaia attended, but then, as far as I was aware, neither of my friends knew Ynna.

It was Elemon's attendance that astonished me. Maybe, despite my doubts, he had once been involved with the victim. Elemon, Tryphone and Duzi? Ynna had had a complicated love life, with a reputation as a lover of bull dancers. Still, Elemon? I could hardly believe it.

He did not acknowledge anyone, not even his fellow bull dancers, as he took up a position at the back.

My mother grabbed my arm, and when I glanced at her, she whispered fiercely, 'Pay attention.'

I looked at Lavra, but instead of listening, I thought about Ynna's murder. Even if Tryphone and Elemon had been involved with Ynna, I could not see any reason why either would murder her. Relationships between fashionable ladies and bull dancers were too common to be scandalous. Not acceptable, perhaps, but not shameful enough to explain murder.

The bearers lifted the coffin to their shoulders and prepared to carry it to the cemetery. My mother fell into step with the other mourners, but I pushed my way to the back to wait for the crowd to disperse. I doubted I could walk that long a distance on my sore ankle.

As Anesdura, weeping, passed me, Elemon joined the throng, and they walked out, side by side. It was another odd pairing. But, of course, they'd both known Ynna well, I thought, and were probably acquainted with one another through that connection.

Then I saw Eile. She acknowledged me with the barest of nods before she swept past. For the first time, I wondered if she could have murdered Duzi and Ynna. I pondered that for a few seconds. Although I could imagine some reason for Eile to murder her former friend, Ynna, I asked myself why now? The two women had fallen out months ago, and I saw no motive at all for Duzi's death. To my knowledge, Eile had not even known him. Nonetheless, I made a mental note to ask Anesdura about the priestess. After all, she'd been part of that group as a young woman.

Once everyone had left, and I was alone, I turned and started home.

The apartment was quiet, and when I looked in on Ria and her nursemaid, both were asleep. The cook brought me fruit and flatbread left over from breakfast and a mug of cold tea. I sat down, and as I refreshed myself, I pondered the deaths. What did I really know about Ynna? I'd paid so little attention to her when she had visited my sisters – and she'd paid even less attention to me. My memories of her consisted of a laughing girl in expensive clothing and glittering with jewelry.

Gradually, my eyes began to close.

'Her father was a merchant,' Arge said. I jerked into a sitting position with a start. 'He traded mostly in precious metals and gems, I believe.'

I nodded; I'd heard that. 'And wine?'

'Yes. The wine from her mother's vineyards is famous.'

I nodded again. 'And what does – did – Ynna do?'

'I don't know. She never learned a craft and, as the youngest, did not inherit the villa or the vineyards and olive groves that go with it. I know she owned a significant amount of jewelry . . .'

'And the apartment,' I said.

'Perhaps. That might also belong to her sister. She may have allowed Ynna to live there after her divorce.' She paused and added, 'You should search it and see what you can discover.'

Since that was exactly what I was thinking myself, I nodded emphatically in agreement.

'You should go now, while everyone is at the cemetery. Go now, Martis.'

I awoke with a start to find the cook bending over me as she took the empty plate and cup from my lap where they'd fallen. 'Did you say something?' I asked, Arge's final words ringing in my head.

'I said, I am going now to market.'

'Oh. All right.'

As she retreated to the kitchen, I stood and stretched. Then I went the opposite way, out into the hall outside.

Here, in the weavers' quarters, the interconnected passageways were crowded with people going about their business. It would be difficult to find a time when people did not throng the building. But the hall where Ynna's apartment was located was quiet. Since the light well was positioned at the other end, shadows darkened this side. I approached Ynna's door quietly. The same guard from before slept against the wall. I tiptoed past him and eased my way into the apartment.

At first glance, it did not look any different from before. But as I moved quietly through the rooms, I saw small changes. Someone had attempted to clean the kitchen. It no longer smelled of garbage and buzzed with flies. But the plate I'd prepared for Ynna still lay discarded against one wall. On a small table was another plate of olives and figs, both shriveled now, and two beakers with the sticky remains of wine dregs dried on the bottoms. I started to move past but then turned around and inspected the food and the cups more closely. The olives and the figs were newer than those I'd offered Ynna. Had her brother and sister taken refreshment here? Or had Ynna been expecting a visitor?

I peered into the sleeping chambers. One, although dusty, appeared recently slept in. Two elaborately carved chests had been placed by the cushioned bench. I opened one and found women's clothing, the skirts and jackets, all in the latest styles, neatly folded. The other chest held men's long robes.

The room connected to it also contained a chest. The occupant of this chamber was not as neat. Women's clothing spilled from the open top, and the cushions on which she'd lain were tossed everywhere.

Three people had come to stay at Ynna's: a couple and a solitary woman. I thought of the two cups set out for wine and wondered again if the cups belonged to them.

I knew the bedroom at the end was Ynna's from the discarded wine cups on the floor and the wine stains decorating several of the cushions. A large sticky red spot on the floor marked spilled wine. I tried to avoid stepping on the discarded clothing lying all around.

Several boxes of jewelry sat on a ledge that ran around the wall. Gold chains, bead necklaces and pearl hair clips lay discarded, both on the ledge and on the floor beneath the boxes. I picked up a gold chain studded with carnelian and jasper beads. I remembered Ynna wearing this long ago, before the competition with Opis escalated.

I opened one of the boxes. Although there was a profusion of rings and chains, few were valuable. I opened another box. This one was barely half full, and most of these again seemed of poorer quality than I would have expected.

A quick search of the other boxes revealed the same. What had happened to the flashy ornaments I recalled Ynna wearing? Had she been robbed? Had she begun selling her belongings? Or had her relatives begun clearing out her things?

'I can't bear to stay here right now,' said a male voice outside.

Heart racing, I flattened myself against a wall and peeked through the door. In the main room at the far end of the hall, I saw three people, pacing back and forth.

'I know. And I haven't even looked in her bed chamber.' That was an older woman. I guessed she was probably the older sister.

'Let's eat.' A younger woman, maybe two or three years older than I was, linked arms with the man. Her skirt and jacket were a dark purple and she wore amethysts in her hair and at her neck. 'We can decide what to do when we return.'

To my immense relief, Ynna's three relatives left and the apartment was quiet once again. I limped quickly to the front door. Although I could hear voices, they sounded a short distance away. I dared to peek out. The guard and the other three people were moving down the hall as they talked. I would not have a better opportunity. I darted through the door and began walking away as quickly as I could.

'Hey, you.' The shout came from behind me.

I turned down the first corridor I saw and descended the set of stairs as rapidly as I could. I had to stop at the bottom. I leaned against the wall and caught my breath. My throbbing ankle told me I'd done too much. I looked around, checking to see where in the complex I was. Recognizing the octopus mosaic across from me, I limped slowly home.

THIRTY-TWO

'Where have you been?' my mother asked when I entered the apartment. I did not reply, instead going to my bedchamber to change my clothing. I wore a black-and-yellow patterned skirt with a yellow jacket – memorable and also recognizable. I did not want to be so noticeable, just in case the guard or Ynna's family saw me and raised some unfortunate questions.

I chose an older skirt, the blues somewhat faded, and a dark-blue jacket. Then I joined my mother in the main room.

'How was Ynna's burial?' I asked, sitting down beside her. The kohl around her eyes was smudged, and her normally perfectly arranged hair was tousled and messy. She pushed her hair back from her face and the strand of onyx beads fell to the floor. She didn't seem to notice.

'Terrible. Such a young woman. Her marriage ended so quickly that she had no children.' My mother sighed. 'I kept thinking that now three of that set of friends – Opis, Arge and Ynna – are dead. Only Anesdura and Eile are still alive.'

Anesdura had said much the same thing. 'Horrible,' I agreed. 'What an unlucky group!'

'Why did so many die?' Nephele wondered aloud. 'Did someone anger the Goddess and she took revenge? Would it help if Anesdura made sacrifices now to atone for whatever they did wrong?'

I shook my head. I was not convinced the explanation was so simple.

My mother and I sat in silence for a moment and then, with a heavy breath, she rose to her feet. 'Are you hungry?'

'Starving,' I replied truthfully. As Nephele turned to go to the kitchen, I said, 'I assume Ynna's family went to the burial?'

'Yes,' my mother said with a nod. 'They all did – her sister and brother, his wife.' She grimaced. 'I didn't care for the wife. She seemed a little greedy. I overheard her talking to her husband about taking Ynna's jewelry.'

The wife would be disappointed. I hadn't seen much jewelry that was worth having. But I did not say so aloud – I did not want my mother to know I'd slipped into the apartment and searched it.

My mother had answered one of my questions, though. I now knew who stayed in each room.

After the meal, I told my mother I had an errand and left. On the way to Elemon's villa – I wanted to question him about the dragonfly – I planned to stop at Dombus's jewelry shop and ask him if Ynna had sold back any of her pieces.

As soon as I entered, the same young man I'd spoken to before left his task. 'More questions about jewelry?' he asked, smiling.

I smiled in return and nodded. 'Different questions this time,' I said. 'Do you know Ynna? She is—'

'Oh, yes. For many years she was a faithful customer. She bought many, many fine items.'

'I am sorry to tell you she has – uh – died.'

'That is a pity. Was she a friend of yours?'

'Um. Yes, I suppose she was.'

'Then I am very sorry for the loss of your friend.' He looked sorry too, and I was touched.

'Thank you. My question is this: has she sold back some of the ornaments this shop made for her?'

The young man hesitated and then finally nodded. 'Since you are her friend, I will tell you. She did. I believe she landed on hard times. I understand she sold some fine sculptures first and then the jewelry. But she only returned to us a few items, not many. Not anywhere close to the number she purchased from us.'

I thought of the jewelry left in her boxes and shook my head in surprise. 'I see. And those she sold were the finer pieces I guess.'

The young man shook his head. 'No. All of our pieces are beautiful, of course, and well made. But some are more unique and more valuable. I would say those items she offered us were mid-range. Here. Like this.' He turned around to the counter behind him and took something from a shelf. When he faced me once again, he held up a gold and pearl-studded neck-lace. I recognized it. Ynna had worn this many times, but the young jeweler was correct: this was not the most elegant or expensive article she'd owned. 'I have a customer for this,' he continued. 'She will pick it up today.'

'I see. Thank you,' I said.

Bemused, I left the workshop. If Ynna hadn't sold her valuable jewelry, where had it gone? Had it been stolen? Maybe Ynna's murder was not connected to Duzi's but had occurred during a robbery? But if that was so, why had she been stabbed, as Duzi had been, by the unidentified knife?

Too many unanswered questions. They whirled through my head as I started walking toward Elemon's villa.

It was not as far away as I feared, although my ankle hurt and I was limping by the time I reached it.

As Geos had said, the villa was marked by the large and gaudy bull statue outside. Although the statue's horns were tipped with gold, the villa itself was not as large as Anesdura's. I heard laughter floating out through the open door.

Suddenly self-conscious, I looked down at my faded skirt. I probably should have changed before I left. I hoped Elemon wouldn't notice. Then I thought about the kohl I'd put around my eyes; was it smeared? Did my hair need to be combed? Besides that, the walk across town had left me hot and sweaty. Well, no help for it now; I was already here. I finger-combed the tendrils hanging over my shoulders, smoothed my skirt and walked around the bull to the stairs.

The laughter and sounds of hilarity increased in volume as I climbed the steps. The servant manning the door looked me up and down in surprise. I guessed I did not resemble Elemon's usual visitors.

'Is Elemon here?' I asked haughtily.

'Elemon?' He eyed me again.

'I am one of the bull dancers,' I said. 'With Elemon. I must speak with him. About something important.' I added those last three words, although it was none of his business.

'Ah.' He did not invite me inside before disappearing into the shadows. I waited outside in the warm sun for so long that I began to wonder if Elemon refused to see me and the servant didn't want to tell me so.

But finally, Elemon appeared. His hair, although combed, was

tied back with a leather thong. Without the unguents holding the
curls in place, it looked lighter. Streaks left by the sun shone red
and gold. I noticed a small birthmark on his temple; a birthmark
that reminded me of something.

Although he was clad in a robe, no jewelry glittered around
his neck or wrists. I wondered if he'd just arisen from bed, even
though it was after noon.

'Martis,' he said in astonishment. He looked me over, his
eyebrows rising in amazement. 'You look nice.'

'Thank you.' That was when I realized I had not planned my
speech. 'You weren't at practice yesterday,' I blurted. I instantly
felt stupid.

'No. We have no more performances for a while. I thought I
could miss it. Why?' Elemon leaned forward a little. 'Oh, I see.
You want to ask me about that dragonfly hair ornament.'

'No,' I began, but Elemon continued, rolling right over me.

'I already spoke to Tinos. It is mine and he returned it to me.'
He smiled at me sweetly. Was it because of Tryphone's opinion
that Elemon's smile appeared artificial?

'Where did you lose it?' I asked.

He glanced at me in surprise. 'I don't know. It could have
been while I was at the ring.'

'You brought it to the ring?' I did not trouble to hide my
disbelief. He shrugged and smiled at me once again.

'What does that matter?'

I thought that mattered a great deal since Costi had told me
he'd stolen it from a pile of clothing at the ring.

'Who gave it to you?'

Elemon, flustered, shook his head. 'I no longer recall.'

I stared at him. He couldn't remember who gave him that
beautiful and valuable piece? I didn't believe it. Why was he
lying to me? 'Huh,' I said dubiously. I would have to go at him
a different way. 'The wanax told me you own two of these.'

'I do,' he admitted.

'I'm puzzled by that. Weren't these love gifts?'

He stared at me. 'No. Now I remember. I ordered them
myself.'

That was proof he was lying to me. Dombus's daughter had
told me she'd made the dragonflies for a woman. Before I could

ask him anything further, a feminine voice called out from behind him. 'Elemon. Are you coming back?'

I peered around him. A young woman, probably my age, had come out from one of the halls. She'd thrown a rug around her shoulders, but I could see she was naked underneath.

She didn't look at me at all. I could have been invisible. But I knew who she was: the daughter of one of the wealthiest merchants in Knossos.

'Coming,' Elemon said over his shoulder. 'Why all these questions, Martis? The wanax gave me my dragonfly. The subject is closed.'

'But I—'

He shut the door firmly in my face. Although I pounded on it for several seconds, no one came to open it.

THIRTY-THREE

At last, I turned and began descending the steps. Since Elemon had lied to me more than once, smiling the entire time, I now believed Tryphone had told me the truth about owning the dragonfly. But where would he have acquired it?

Perhaps Ynna had given one of the ornaments to Tryphone and one to Elemon? That implied both had been her lovers. And where did Duzi and his murder fit into this? I shook my head. Nothing made sense. I still had as many questions as I'd had before. Unexpected tears rose to my eyes. I hated suspecting my friends – my fellow bull leapers – of murder. And I still did not know the truth.

As soon as I arrived home, my mother said, 'What happened?'

'Nothing.' I did not plan to tell her I'd questioned Elemon. My mother did not want me investigating the deaths, and once she found out I'd questioned Elemon, she'd know I was actively disobeying her.

'Martis,' she said sternly. 'Tell me what you've been doing.'

Realizing I must look worse than I realized, I told a partial truth. 'I saw Telemon.' As I remembered his rudeness, fresh tears filled my eyes. 'Sorry.' I rubbed the back of my hand over my wet face. 'He told me to go away.'

'Were you at the dorms?'

'Yes.'

My mother put her arms around me. 'Oh, Martis. Why were you there? He doesn't want anyone to consider him a baby.' But her eyes moistened too. 'It is so hard when one's children grow up.'

'Especially when growing up happens so young,' I said with a sigh. My mother smiled at that but didn't argue. For a moment we sat in silence.

'You weren't checking up on him, were you?' she asked, turning a reproving glance on me.

'No.'

'What were you doing there, then?'

'I walked some of my fellow bull dancers to the dorms.' I wiped my eyes on the edge of my skirt. 'I saw him practicing archery.' I laughed fondly. 'He's terrible at it.' My mother chuckled as well.

Before I had a chance to continue, a sharp knock sounded on the door, Tinos flinging it open before the sound had ended. I saw at a glance that he was furious.

As he advanced on me, I rose to my feet, my heart sinking. 'I specifically told you not to meddle,' he said.

'What do you mean?' I asked, already preparing my excuses.

'Elemon came to see me.'

'He missed practice yesterday and I—'

'Scolding him for it is certainly not your job.' Tinos shook his finger at me. I glanced at my mother. She grimaced, clearly unable to decide which emotion – anger or sympathy – she would adopt.

'But I—'

'Do you believe you are smarter than I am?'

'Of course not.'

'Then why are you following behind me? Why are you inter-rogating Elemon? You were told to leave the investigation of the murders to me. Instead, you visit the victims' homes and question people like Elemon.'

'Martis,' my mother murmured.

'You need to stop,' Tinos said, his voice rising as he grabbed hold of my shoulders. 'Stop.' He punctuated every word by shaking me. 'I . . . mean . . . it.' He released me and I staggered. 'Two dead bodies? Some people are wondering if you had something to do with the deaths and—'

'Some people? What people?' I interrupted. 'Of course I had nothing to do with them.'

'If you don't stop, I'll speak to Geos and see that you are pulled off the team.'

Shocked, I collapsed into the cushions. 'You wouldn't.'

'I would. Isn't leaping the bull enough excitement for you?'

Humiliated, I couldn't look at my mother, couldn't look at Tinos. The man I most admired was scolding me as though I were a child. It felt like a betrayal.

I focused on controlling my breathing so I didn't burst into sobs in front of him.

'I don't want you running around the city searching the victims' rooms or questioning people,' he continued. 'It is too dangerous. Do you hear me?'

I nodded, staring intently at my hands, clasped together so tightly my knuckles were white.

A few seconds later, the door closed with a loud bang.

I burst into tears.

My mother moved over and put an arm around my shoulders. 'We care about you and are only looking out for you,' she said. 'It's dangerous. We don't want you to get hurt. Think about what happened the last time . . .' She couldn't go on. I'd been attacked and might have died.

Although I knew she was trying to console me even as she warned me not to meddle, I shook my head. 'It's different this time,' I protested, sniffing. 'I'm just talking to people. People I know. Bull dancers. None of them will hurt me.'

'That's what you believed last spring.' She heaved a sigh.

'That was different,' I muttered. She shook her head at me.

'Will you listen to Tinos now?'

'I thought he was my friend,' I wailed. Hurt filled my chest until I felt I couldn't breathe.

'He *is* your friend. He's trying to protect you.'

I shook my head. It certainly did not feel as though Tinos were my friend. In fact, it felt as though he didn't like me at all. 'It's not fair,' I said, wounded and resentful both. 'He wouldn't have found Duzi's room or the dragonfly without me.' I angrily dashed away my tears.

'Maybe not. And you made sure he knew too.' She paused while I squirmed. 'I sometimes wonder, Martis, if you even think of your physical safety. You are so impulsive, so reckless. You charge ahead without thinking.'

I did not immediately reply. Reckless? Would I have gone to the part of Knossos inhabited by sailors and immigrants and looked for Duzi's room if I had not been accompanied by Tetis? I remembered the landlord and his leering examination of my body, and I shivered involuntarily. Going alone; that would have been risky.

'I don't think talking to Anesdura is dangerous,' I said at last.

'But you visited Ynna too and she was found murdered,' my mother pointed out.

'We don't know that that had anything to do with Duzi's death,' I argued despite my belief the murders were connected.

She remained silent for several seconds. When she spoke again, she sounded weary. 'I don't understand you at all sometimes. You are never content. You seek out danger. I thought when you became a bull dancer, that would cure you. But it hasn't. I've accepted that you don't want to spend your life weaving, although I don't like it, but what are you planning to do?'

Now it was my turn to go quiet. I didn't know how to explain. I just didn't want to spend my life doing the same thing day after day. It wasn't only the weaving; I was tired of bull dancing as well. Yes, as I faced the bull in a performance, I felt that surge of excitement. But it was the same thing all the time: running up to the bull, grabbing the horns and flipping over. The only part that kept me engaged was the possibility of injury or death, and by now even that risk seemed remote.

I was bored with the constant practice. And now that Geos had me working with the kids, the sessions were even more tiresome.

Besides, my time as a bull dancer was coming to an end. I was sixteen, almost seventeen. Next year I would be living in the women's dorms for my agoge. I'd have less time for bull leaping – and I'd be eighteen at the end. Most of us left the sport between the ages of eighteen and twenty, so even if I hung on, it would be only for a year or so.

Was I more suited to becoming a healer? I recalled the spicy aroma of the herbs and the puzzle laid out by the wounds in Duzi's body. Yes, I was intrigued. But wouldn't choosing another profession hurt my mother's feelings? Be honest, Martis. Tell the truth. What if I wasn't good at it? That was the possibility that truly scared me.

'It's not the weaving,' I whispered.

My mother sighed again. 'You should have been a boy and gone sailing on my brother's merchant ship. Maybe that would have been enough excitement for you.'

I stared at her mutely. I had no answer to that.

'It's almost time for our evening meal,' she said. 'Why don't you bathe first and change your clothes.'

'All right,' I said. I felt limp inside and out and was much too tired to argue.

By the time my warm bath water was ready, I had run through several imaginary arguments with Tinos. In each case, I blunted every one of his statements with a calm and well-reasoned argument of my own, all with such surpassing logic that he was forced to surrender and apologize.

But the bath relaxed me. After sitting in the warm water for a while, I stopped brooding and began to ponder other facets of his scolding. Why, for example, did Tinos so readily believe Elemon and not me? Were they better friends than I knew? Or was Tinos choosing to side with Elemon because I was the one who argued for a different outcome? Was my mother right? Was Tinos offended that I had been two steps ahead of him all along? I did not want to think that. I loved and admired him too much to see any faults, but that possibility would not leave my mind.

I was glad to sit down with my mother and allow her to distract me with inconsequential conversation.

So tired I felt nauseous, I retired to my room immediately after dinner. Since my one window faced west, I was able to stare at the sky, painted pink and purple by the setting sun. I pulled a rug around my shoulders as the cool evening breeze swirled in.

Footsteps paused outside my door. 'Are you awake?'

'Yes.' I sat up and looked at my mother.

She came in and sat on the other bench, the one that had belonged to my sister. 'I know Tinos hurt your feelings,' she said. 'I thought I should explain further.' She paused.

'What is there to explain?' I asked, my voice thickening with emotion.

She hesitated for several seconds. 'This is a trying time for Tinos,' she said at last. 'He is under a lot of pressure. This is not all about you.'

'What do you mean?'

'Of all the ceremonies throughout the year, the Harvest Festival is the one that taxes Tinos the most. He is responsible for performing the rituals – most of them anyway.'

'He's done them for almost ten years,' I replied scornfully. 'He must know the prayers perfectly by now.'

'I am sure he does,' she agreed. 'But he is not usually investigating a murder at the same time.'

I snorted and heard my mother's audible sigh. For a moment she did not speak. The sky outside was now almost dark and I could barely see her even though she sat nearby. 'There is some friction between Tinos and the High Priestess,' she said at last.

I nodded; I had seen it. 'What friction?'

'I don't know. She seems to be angry with him, but I don't know why. She hasn't said, and as far as I can tell, he has done nothing to deserve her animosity. Potnia has been moody of late. Lavra says that is a sign that the Lady is nearing the end of her fertile years.' My mother involuntarily touched the gray streaking her black hair. She and the High Priestess were of an age and could be expected to reach the milestones in a woman's life at the same time.

My mother paused and for a moment neither of us spoke. Once the High Priestess crossed that threshold, she could no longer serve. A younger woman had to be chosen in her stead.

'Does that mean her daughter will become the High Priestess?'

'Hele? Probably, although there are other possibilities. Mind, I don't know if what Lavra says is true. But I have no reason to doubt her. And if she is correct, you can understand that both the High Priestess and Tinos, as her consort, are going through a difficult time. Everything is changing. So don't blame Tinos too much for his ill temper. All right?'

'Yes, all right. Fine.'

My mother rose to her feet. She patted me on the arm before disappearing through the door. I lay back. Although I no longer felt as hurt and humiliated from my quarrel with Tinos, the sour feeling had not entirely dissipated. Instead, I felt rebellious. I decided I would not end my investigation, although I would be more circumspect. I'd helped Tinos, for all that he refused to acknowledge it. He would know next to nothing if not for me. And I would follow this through to the end.

THIRTY-FOUR

I slept poorly that night. I hoped Arge would appear to console me, but, of course, she did not. Instead, I lay in the dark alone for hours, thinking dark thoughts, until I finally dropped into an exhausted doze. I overslept and then, knowing I would be late reaching the bull ring, ran out of the apartment without breakfast. As I feared, everyone else was already there and had begun practice when I arrived. The older and more experienced bull dancers were on the field with the bull. I could tell after a moment's inspection that the beast they faced was young and untried, and therefore dangerous. Unlike the older, more experienced bulls who went through their paces consistently, the younger animals charged in fits and starts and lunged from side to side.

This session served as training for him as well. By next spring, his performance would be more reliable – and safer.

Geos had begun working with Costi, Nub and the twins. When he saw me, his expression changed to one of relief. 'You can take over here,' he said, abandoning Costi on the model without hesitation. Already scowling with anger that he had not been placed with the older leapers, Costi made a rude gesture at Geos's back.

'Where's Arphaia?' I asked as I moved to Costi's side. I did not bother removing my skirt or jacket, although I wore my loincloth underneath.

'Not here.' Geos shot me a look, but he had the grace to refrain from saying he'd told me so. I shook my head. Even if Geos was correct that Arphaia would leave us to marry, I didn't believe she would just disappear without telling him directly.

Shouting at the older members of the team, Geos walked across the dirt to the ring. 'Elemon, you first.'

Elemon nodded. Seeing me, he grinned. I interpreted the cocky grin as triumph; he'd gotten me in trouble with the wanax. Big trouble. I thought of Tinos and his anger and shuddered, my eyes burning. Although I was hesitant to entirely believe Tryphone and his clear dislike of Elemon, I also no longer considered Elemon such a wonderful person.

'Go ahead, Costi,' I said with a nod in his direction. He snorted at me but obeyed. I watched his fluid revolution over the practice bull. If the animal in the ring had not been young and fresh, but an older, experienced animal, Costi would have been able to jump with the older dancers. He already was that good.

I turned to Nub. Although not as skilled as Costi, she flew effortlessly over the model's back and landed easily on her hands before flipping over and springing upright. She landed without trouble on the ground beside the wheeled form. Soon, Geos would be able to start her on a live, albeit old and slow, bull.

As I helped the twins get into position, automatically straightening their arms and legs and gently pushing their backs into the proper position, my mind wandered. I was bothered by Arphaia's absence. Not because I thought Geos was wrong – I didn't. I fully expected her to be wed in a year or so. But it wasn't like her to just disappear either. Arphaia would tell Geos she was withdrawing so that he didn't count on her. Besides, I knew her aunt would put Arphaia to work around the farm if she saw her niece was available. And Arphaia would much rather be a bull dancer than a farmer.

'Have you seen Arphaia?' I asked Obelix when she finished her jump. She glanced at me over her shoulder.

'No. But I know she has other interests.' She cut her eyes to Tryphone and Elemon, and I saw she didn't want to discuss

Arphaia and her handsome young man in front of them. Tryphone, who was standing behind Obelix, frowned and shook his head.

'Was she here yesterday?' I asked. Since I'd been attending Ynna's funeral, I'd arrived late. I hoped Arphaia had come and then gone so I'd missed her.

'No. Last time I saw her, she said something about helping her aunt,' Tryphone said.

I nodded but I didn't believe it. She hated working on the farm; that was why she had come to Knossos in the first place. While I could imagine Arphaia helping intermittently, for one day at a time, this was the third day that she hadn't come to practice.

'Why? Do you think something happened to her?' Tryphone asked, his brow furrowed.

'Probably not,' Obelix replied calmly. 'We all know how indifferent she is to bull dancing. She's likely taking this opportunity to rest and do other things.' She rolled her eyes at me once again.

Three days? Obelix was wrong. Maybe Arphaia was ill and hadn't thought to get word to Geos? I should visit her. I considered the long walk. Could I do it? My ankle was better now. A little better anyway.

What about Tinos's order not to meddle? I quickly dismissed that concern. Surely, I would not be disobeying Tinos if I went somewhere to check on the health of a friend. He couldn't be angry with me for that.

Although I still did not feel entirely comfortable with my decision to hike to the farm, I also felt I couldn't not do it. And what better time than the present? After practice ended, I zigzagged through the city to the road that ran by the Priestess House. I exited across the track from the House and set off, walking southeast. The road surface was muddy and scored by the deep prints of oxen now that the October rains had fallen. I soon fell into a rhythm, striding past the knots of trees without really noticing them. Once I'd left the green fingers of the forest behind, I was glad to reach the beginnings of farmland. My ankle was beginning to ache. It had not healed as much as I'd hoped.

I saw laborers in the fields. Now that the Harvest Festival had concluded, they were planting wheat and barley. The grains, as well as the olives, would ripen throughout the moist mild winter and be ready to pick in the spring.

By the time I arrived at the farm where Arphaia lived, everyone was out in the fields. As the men walked behind oxen pulling wedge-shaped plows, the women in their hiked-up skirts trailed behind, dropping seeds into the furrows. The children were not as busy, although I saw a young boy walking at the head of the oxen, guiding them across the field. Most of them ran around, unsupervised and ignored unless one of the adults needed someone to run an errand.

I crossed the road and paused by one of the stone pillars framing the entrance to catch my breath. It would be noon soon. As I rested and watched, the oxen were unyoked and led to water, and the sacks that held the seeds were closed and put aside. I walked slowly up the muddy track toward the stone building. I hoped I remembered what Arphaia's aunt looked like, I thought as I kept my gaze on the crowd moving toward the house. I saw a sun-browned woman with a strong nose and prominent cheekbones and hurried to intercept her. I wasn't certain she was Arphaia's aunt, but she did look familiar. As I approached her, she looked at me without recognition.

'Who are you?'

'I'm Arphaia's friend. She didn't come to practice today. I was worried . . .'

The woman pushed her hair off her sweaty brow and pointed to another woman. 'You want my cousin.'

I nodded my thanks and hurried to catch Arphaia's aunt before she disappeared into the house. She seemed quite surprised when I asked about her niece. 'She left first thing yesterday. In the morning. She told me she was going to practice.'

I stared at her. I knew Arphaia hadn't been in the ring yesterday, or today either, but I didn't want to say anything. I didn't need to. She looked at my expression and her eyes widened with fright.

'I'm sure nothing happened to Arphaia,' I said quickly. 'I'll talk to her friends . . .'

Before I finished speaking, the aunt called over a young man. He was quite dirty, covered with mud from the fields, but I recognized the fellow Arphaia had been flirting with. 'Do you know where Arphaia is, Zeno?' the aunt asked fiercely.

Zeno shook his head, his eyebrows high with surprise. 'I haven't seen her since supper the day before yesterday. You remember? She left immediately after eating—'

'She was with me,' the aunt said. 'I insisted she help me clean up the kitchen. I saw her into bed.' Now thoroughly scared, she bit her lip so hard that a bead of blood bloomed on it.

'I'm sure it's nothing,' I repeated, although I wasn't sure of anything of the kind. I knew neither Obelix nor Tryphone – nor Geos – had seen her. Had Elemon or Thaos? Elemon had been jumping the bull and Thaos catching when I'd asked my question. 'I'll talk to the other bull dancers,' I promised. 'Maybe one of them knows where she is.' I doubted it, though, and I felt all shivery with worry. 'Um, may I look in Arphaia's room?' I asked her aunt. Her eyes widened.

'Why?'

'Maybe she ran away? If so, some of her clothes would be missing. Or there might be something that will tell us where she is . . .'

Arphaia's aunt nodded. 'Of course. Let me show you.'

She hurried toward the house, walking so fast that I struggled to keep up.

Arphaia had been tucked into a small chamber on the lowest level of the house, down among the storage rooms. With that said, the chamber was flooded with light from one long window high on the northern wall. Arphaia was not a tidy young woman. Cushions were scattered around as though a windstorm had swept through the room. Clothing spilled out of the chest in a profusion of bright colors. Jewelry, a copper necklace and two or three beaded hair chains lay on a table with a pot of kohl.

I turned a questioning look on Arphaia's aunt. 'Is anything missing?'

'Not that I can see.' She went to the chest of clothing and half-heartedly rummaged through the top layer. 'It looks like everything is here.' Her panicky dark eyes jumped around the room. 'She didn't run away.'

I nodded, sweeping my gaze around. I did not see the loincloth or the old skirt and jacket she wore over it when she went to the bullring. That supported the aunt's story that Arphaia had left to attend practice. I crossed to the chest of clothing and glanced inside but it told me nothing.

'Where can she be?' Arphaia's aunt muttered, her voice shaking. I did not want to look at her and see her fear. Instead, I began sorting through the blouses, jackets and skirts in the chest. Although all were of decent quality, none were as dazzlingly fashionable as the clothes my sisters had worn.

Then, way at the bottom, I spotted a golden gleam. I turned to say something to Arphaia's aunt, but once I saw her stricken expression, I thought better of it. I carefully shifted the tumbled apparel. The bottom of the chest was covered with a layer of jewelry: necklaces of gold and silver, lapis lazuli, carnelian and pearl. Rings and beaded hair chains. All were much more valuable than the items that Arphaia had worn every day. And far too dear for a farm girl to own.

I recognized several of the articles. Keeping my back to Arphaia's aunt, I carefully lifted out a necklace with a golden bee at the end. Although I could not examine it as closely as I wished, I was sure I knew this piece. It had once belonged to Ynna. How, in the name of the Goddess, had Arphaia acquired it?

Shaking, that shivery feeling was making me tremble all over, I tucked the necklace under my belt. I was very afraid something terrible had happened to my friend.

THIRTY-FIVE

Pasting a smile on my face, I turned and said, 'There is nothing here. Could she have decided to go home?' I doubted it, but it was a much more acceptable explanation than the others burning through my mind.

'Without her clothes? Without saying anything to me?' The aunt shook her head. 'She would never have done that. Besides, her life is here now. She'd met someone. Someone serious. For the first time, she'd begun talking of marriage.'

'Marriage!' I thought of the young man I'd met here and said quickly, 'Who? Who was the man?'

'I don't know. She wouldn't tell me.'

I ran through the young men I'd seen Arphaia with. Duzi, now dead, the young farmer I'd met upstairs and Tryphone. I recalled him standing with her at the Harvest Festival and said slowly, 'Tryphone. What about him?'

The aunt clutched at my jacket. 'She said he was a fellow bull dancer. A friend. She's also mentioned Elemon. Do you think she might be with one of them?'

I pictured the worry on Tryphone's face. I did not think Arphaia was with him, but I chose not to say that. Elemon? Why would he choose Arphaia when he had the pick of the young women in Knossos? I didn't say that either. 'Perhaps. I'll ask them.' One of them might know where the gold jewelry in Arphaia's chest had come from, but I would be hesitant to ask. I could just imagine Elemon claiming it all as his own.

Arphaia's aunt and I walked upstairs in silence. Forcing a smile and with a cheery wave, I set off down the path. But my smile disappeared as soon as I turned away from her and was out of sight. At the gate, I turned on the road and headed back to Knossos, walking on the north side this time so I was at the edge of the fields. The smell of freshly turned earth filled the air with its sweet scent. Gray clouds boiled up in the sky and I could smell rain coming. As a cool breeze swept across the hills, I huddled into my jacket and linen blouse.

Where could Arphaia be? With one of the bull dancers? Thaos and Curgis both lived in the dorm, so I knew she could not be staying with either of them. But Elemon? Could Arphaia be there? And did I dare visit him after Tinos's scolding?

Or could it be Tryphone? Could he be her new man? Although he would not be my choice, he made more sense to me than Elemon. I pondered that for a moment. I didn't know where Tryphone lived. But I would see him again at practice.

That raised another question: if Arphaia were with a bull dancer, why didn't they both come to practice? Both Tryphone and Elemon had been present this morning.

Then I had another thought. Maybe neither was the new man Arphaia had spoken of. What if it was someone I did not know? If that were the case, I might never find him.

As I pondered, I walked faster and faster until I was breathing hard. I soon left the farms far behind. But my sore ankle began to throb, becoming so painful I had to slow down. I was already nearing Knossos and passing the band of forest that edged the road. As I breathed hard, a faint whiff of corruption caught my nostrils. It was an animal, I assured myself as I glanced through the tree trunks. Of course it was. But I couldn't be sure. I thought I saw something large and dark perched on a deadfall. I stepped into thick forest and was instantly transported to a different world, a shadowy one that pressed around me. I stepped on a dry stick and the loud crack sent the dark form flapping higher into the trees. It was a vulture, and it was far larger than it appeared from a distance. I gulped and stepped back, tripping over a large branch and almost falling. When I looked above me, I could see nests high in the trees.

I was tempted to flee back to the road. I could see the pale dirt through the trees, a much more open and well-lit space. But that awful cold feeling in the pit of my stomach pushed me forward. I had to see what the vulture – vultures, for now I saw there were several – had been feasting on. The birds regarded me balefully from their perches. Even though I knew they only ate carrion, I could feel my heartbeat speed up. What would I do if they attacked me?

I picked my way carefully through the downed trees and around the bushes. With each step, I could smell death more and more clearly, and I clapped my hand over my nose. In a hollow behind a fallen tree lay the dead thing. One of the vultures squawked and reluctantly shifted his heavy body away from me. He looked too large and ungainly to fly, but after a running start, he lifted himself into the air.

As he moved away, I saw a patch of blue. Trying to swallow down my nausea, I stepped closer. First, I saw the legs, sprawled out, and with chunks of flesh missing. Above that, the blue skirt and tight belt, the midriff lightly veiled by a linen blouse. I didn't want to go forward but I had to, even though my stomach was roiling in protest.

Another step forward. I could see the black hair curling down over the shoulders. Another step and then the face came into view. Oh no. I turned away with a gasp. One quick glance; that was all I could manage. The eyes were gone and livid punctures in the cheeks went all the way to the bone. Shuddering and retching, I stepped back. Although I'd been hungry, now I was glad I hadn't eaten anything. The only thing that came up was bile.

Sobbing, I turned and struggled to find my way out of the forest. Behind me, I could hear the flapping sounds of the vultures coming down from the trees, but I couldn't bear to look.

I knew the identity of the body lying in the woods. I'd found Arphaia. She hadn't gone far away at all.

And now I had to find Tinos.

THIRTY-SIX

I broke into a limping run, hurrying as fast as I could all the way back to Knossos. As I passed the Priestess House and turned into the woods across the road, the skies opened up, releasing sheets of water. The rain drenched me in a matter of seconds. My sandals began slipping on the wet path, but I didn't slow down. I was still crying, and now the shoulders of my jacket were wet and my clammy skirt clung to my legs. My sodden braid flapped between my shoulder blades as I hurried. The few people braving the rain turned to stare at me as I pushed past.

I wobbled up the steps of the complex. Once inside, I raced straight to the High Priestess's chambers. I didn't know if Tinos was there, but I had to try. I couldn't think of anywhere else to go. My feet slipped on the smooth floor and left wet prints behind me.

People called out as I rushed past.

'Are you all right?'

'What's wrong?'

'Can I do anything for you?'

I ignored those who were calling to me, desperate to find Tinos and tell him what I'd found. I staggered up the stairs, holding my damp skirt away from me so I wouldn't trip.

I burst through the door and plunged into the High Priestess's chamber. Her daughter, Hele, smiled at me, but the High

Priestess's son stared at me with an obsidian gaze as hard as his mother's.

Dressed in an elegant robe, Tinos was reporting on something as the High Priestess regarded him unsmilingly. I ran straight to him. Grabbing his hand, I shouted, 'You've got to come with me.'

'Who is this young woman?' the High Priestess asked in a cold voice. I bowed to her. 'Martis?'

'Yes. Martis, daughter of Nephele.' Turning to Tinos, I gasped, 'You've got to come.'

'Does your mother know you're here?' the High Priestess asked in an icy voice.

'No, My Lady,' I said. Tinos removed his hand from mine.

'I wish you would not bring your women to court,' the High Priestess told Tinos in a frigid voice.

'She is not—'

'Please, someone remove this young woman,' the High Priestess interrupted him.

'What are you doing here, Martis?' Tinos asked. 'You're wet. Go home.'

'You don't understand—' I began.

'Go home,' he repeated. Several of the Lady's guards approached me.

'I've found another body,' I shouted, my voice hoarse and trembling. A babble of voices from Potnia's ladies rose around me. Tinos stared at me. 'I apologize for breaking in,' I said to the High Priestess with another little bow. Turning back to Tinos, I added, 'It's Arphaia. She's dead. You've got to come.'

'Are you sure? What happened? Where were you?'

'It's on the road to . . . I'll show you. You've got to come with me.'

Tinos turned to look at the High Priestess. Frowning at me, her black eyes flat and unsympathetic, she said to him, 'Go. Take her away.'

He bowed and pushed me ahead of him from the chamber. 'Are you sure?' he repeated. 'Maybe you are mistaken. Maybe she's sleeping.'

'Of course I'm not mistaken,' I said angrily. 'She's not sleeping. The vultures . . .' I shuddered.

'Maybe it's someone else.'

'It is not! I know Arphaia. She's in the woods. Her poor face . . .' I shuddered convulsively and burst into loud ugly sobs.

'All right. I'll take a look. Go home—'

'No. I'm coming with you. And that's final.' I stamped my foot, not caring if I sounded like a child. No one was listening to me.

'Go home and change your clothes. I will as well.'

'No. We can't. Arphaia . . .'

'We can spare a few minutes to change. You're soaking wet. The rain has stopped. Get some dry clothes. I'll meet you on the path to the Sacred Grove.' When I hesitated, he said sharply, 'Go on.' As I reluctantly started away from him, he shouted after me, 'And make sure you tell your mother where you're going.'

I was so afraid he would leave me behind or, worse, that he didn't believe me and would disappear somewhere that I almost ran home to the apartments. When I hurried inside, my mother gaped at me in shock. 'Martis, where have you been? And what are you doing?'

'I have to change my clothes and meet Tinos,' I gasped, hurrying into my bedchamber. I stripped off my sodden jacket and skirt and threw them over the bench.

'What happened?' My mother appeared at the door of my chamber. She held the baby over her shoulder. The sleepy child regarded me with half-closed eyes.

'I found—' My throat closed up and for a moment I couldn't speak.

'Oh, Martis, what happened?' My mother sounded both disappointed and worried.

'I found another body.' I didn't want to say Arphaia's name for fear I would begin weeping again and not be able to stop. I choked back a hiccupping sob. 'I must show Tinos where she is.'

'Is it another of the bull dancers?'

I nodded, tears leaking from my eyes in spite of myself. My mother reached out a hand to console me, but I stepped back. I was afraid I would collapse into tears if she treated me tenderly.

'When you began jumping the bulls, I feared one of them would gore you. Maybe trample you to death. But this – this has nothing to do with the bulls at all.'

I tried to smile. 'At least I'm not in danger this time.'

My mother frowned and shook her head doubtfully.

'I must hurry. Tinos is waiting.' I did not bother combing out my hair. I threw on another skirt and jacket over the linen blouse and hurried out.

'Wait,' my mother said. 'Take this.' She handed me the canvas square.

'Thank you.' I began to run through the door but turned back. 'Don't worry. I'll be fine.'

As Tinos had said, the rain had stopped but the air was still cool and heavy with moisture. Puddles dotted the ground, and the sky remained an ominous shade of gray. We would have more rain soon.

I'd been so afraid Tinos would arrive before me and leave that I hurried. No one was waiting when I reached the meeting place. Then I wasn't sure if Tinos had been and already gone, or whether I was there before him. I paced back and forth several times, trying to decide whether I should go on or continue to wait. Just as I was deciding I should leave, Tinos hailed me from the square below. He was no longer dressed in his ceremonial robe but had changed to a kilt and a rug over his shoulders. Three guards accompanied him, one of them carrying a large canvas sheet.

'I thought you'd left,' I said.

'I don't know where to go,' he pointed out as he gestured me forward.

I started walking as fast as I could. Tinos easily kept up with me and we reached the road very quickly. I stole furtive glances at him, wondering if he was still angry with me. His mouth was set in a thin line.

'Are you sure of the identification?' he asked abruptly. 'You know who the girl is?'

I nodded. 'It's Arphaia. My friend—' My voice broke. I looked away and surreptitiously wiped my eyes.

'Duzi's girlfriend?' he asked.

'No. Yes. She wasn't anymore . . .' I stopped talking, realizing he did not care about the personal relationships among the bull dancers right now.

'Two of you have been murdered,' he muttered. 'As if bull

leaping isn't dangerous enough. But why?' And he looked at me as if I should know the answer.

'I don't know.' I didn't understand it either. 'But there is Ynna. She was murdered too. She's not a bull dancer. Never has been.'

'No.' Tinos spoke so brusquely I knew he was hiding something from me. I stared at him.

'I suspect she and Duzi were sleeping together,' I said.

Tinos glanced at me in surprise. 'Duzi?'

'Of course. At least for a little while. She may have been involved with someone else too.' I threw him a glance. 'I know all about Ynna. She was a friend of my sisters. I know she had a particular fondness for bull dancers.'

'Duzi?' Tinos said slowly. 'Well, Duzi did not murder her. So who do you think she was with now?'

I shrugged. 'I thought it might be Elemon,' I said. I held back Tryphone's name, suddenly reluctant to share it with Tinos.

'Elemon?' He shook his head. 'Not Elemon. Not now, anyway. Maybe once, long ago.'

I looked at him speculatively. He seemed to know Elemon better than I'd thought. I fingered the necklace hidden beneath my belt, glad I'd decided to keep it secret for now. 'You must know all about those fashionable women,' I murmured. Tinos tightened his lips and did not reply.

How strange to think he'd been only two years older than I was now when he'd been an elite bull dancer.

THIRTY-SEVEN

We walked east on the road, avoiding the puddles as much as possible. My feet were soon wet and muddy from the water splashing on them and they began slipping on the leather soles of my sandals. Finally, I took them off and walked barefoot as I used to. The soles of my feet were tender now, though, and it was not comfortable walking over the stones.

My father would be horrified by the condition of my footwear.

I wondered how he and my sister were faring. Last spring, he'd taken her away on a ship. Neither had returned, and although he had promised to come back, I was beginning to doubt he would.

Shaking off those glum thoughts, I steeled myself for what lay ahead.

We left the Priestess House behind. I kept watch for the place where I'd entered the forest. After a couple of false starts – so much of the forest looked alike, especially with the rain dripping from the trees – I found my previous entry into the woods. Once I'd found it, I was amazed it had taken me so long. The broken stems and crushed undergrowth left by my panicked flight out of the forest were obvious.

I went in only as far as I needed to, to the point where I smelled corruption, and then I pointed. I retreated backwards, crashing into tree branches and cutting my feet on twigs as I fled to the road. I could not bear to see Arphaia's body lying in the mud again.

The time passed very slowly as I waited for Tinos to reappear. I began pacing up and down the road. The hem of my skirt soon became sodden with mud and it left smears on my ankles as I trooped back and forth. Finally, Tinos reappeared. His rug had disappeared, and his kilt and chest were smeared with mud and leaves. A streak of dirt went across his forehead as though he'd wiped a hand across his face. He looked at me sadly, and I felt my eyes moisten.

'It was murder, wasn't it?' I asked, my voice shaking.

'Probably.' His mouth curled as though he were tasting something sour.

'How was she killed?' I asked.

'I don't know. The vultures have—' He stopped short and gulped.

I nodded, tears beginning to roll down my cheeks. 'Why didn't I check on her when she missed that first practice?' I muttered. 'Oh, why didn't I?'

'This isn't your fault,' he said sharply. 'In fact,' he added, looking at me with a stern expression, 'how did you happen to find the body?'

'She missed three bull-dancing practices,' I said. 'I know Geos expects her to marry and leave, but she hasn't so far. And it is unlike her to miss practice, especially when she needs it so badly. I walked out to the farm to see if she was sick or something.'

'I told you I didn't want you to investigate,' he said in annoyance. 'Or question anyone.'

'I wasn't planning to,' I said. 'But Arphaia is my friend, and I was worried. It wasn't like her to miss practice . . .'

'Some might say you had something to do with her death,' he said. 'This is the second victim you've found in just over a week. And Arphaia was hidden. Well hidden. How did you happen to discover her?'

I hesitated, remembering. 'I smelled her,' I said at last. 'I didn't know it was her, of course. As I went in, I saw the vultures.' I gulped.

Tinos nodded. 'They can always sense death.' He sighed and rubbed his hand over his face, leaving another muddy streak. 'We will have to bring out the body and return it to her family for funeral rites.' I nodded. I knew. Without the proper rituals, Arphaia would haunt her family for nine generations. Even after performing the proper ceremonies, she might visit them as Arge did with me. It was extremely important to treat the dead with respect.

I heard swearing. I looked past Tinos. Dimly, through the tree trunks, I saw movement. The men were bringing out the body, struggling to avoid the deadfalls. I backed up very quickly as the shrouded body came through the trees. Tinos directed several of the men to take the body to the healer for an examination. As they started west, Tinos looked at me expectantly.

'What?'

'Where does Arphaia live? Her family has to be told.'

'The farm is the first on the left after you leave the woods,' I said. 'There are stone pillars at the entrance.'

'I think you should show me,' Tinos said.

I hesitated a few seconds and then began shaking my head. I did not want to see the grief of Arphaia's family when the body arrived.

'You wanted to be involved; you are now involved,' Tinos said. 'You can manage to show me where Arphaia's family lives.'

'It is only an aunt,' I said hopefully. 'Her mother lives somewhere to the south. I don't know where.'

'The aunt's farm will be fine. It is still family.' He stared at me, his mouth set and uncompromising.

'Oh, all right. Come on.' I began walking east, really limping now from the combination of my sore ankle and the pain as my soft feet stepped on the sharp rocks in the road.

I was too angry to look at Tinos. He did not want me involved – unless it was useful to him.

I did not accompany Tinos and his companion up the muddy path to the farm. Instead, I watched the laborers in the fields, focusing on them as though they completely captivated me even though most of them stopped what they were doing and turned to watch the wanax and his man march up the track to the farmhouse.

Before Tinos reached the door, Arphaia's aunt broke away from her work and hurried across the ground to meet them. I glanced quickly at Tinos and saw him gesticulating. A few seconds later, the woman's shrill cries of grief sliced through the air.

Tears burned in my eyes, and I turned my head away. I couldn't watch.

When Tinos returned to the road, the wailing followed him like thick black smoke. Now, the women – probably the entire farm, in fact – would mourn Arphaia, throwing ashes on their heads and weeping.

When Tinos and his sole guard reached the road, I joined them. Tinos's face was set in a grim mask, as hard as stone, so he looked more like a sculpture than a man. I did not dare speak. He did not look at me but set a rapid pace back to the city. I couldn't keep up and soon the men were far ahead. I did not even try to catch up to them but walked more and more slowly as I thought.

I was sure someone had lain in wait for Arphaia, intercepting her as she went to practice and killing her. Although I had little reason to think so, I suspected she'd been stabbed. Just like Duzi and Ynna. By the same person. Once I arrived in town, I would follow the body to the healer's. She would be able to tell me more.

The rain started again as I limped up the steps into the building. I wove my way through the halls of the complex until I reached

the steps descending to the healer's chamber. The young girl I'd
met previously was not there. Instead, a young man was sitting
at the small table. He glanced at me, and although his eyes
widened, he said nothing.

The healer herself stepped out of the back room. 'Martis,' she
said but not as though she were surprised.

'Where is the girl?' I asked, pointing my thumb at the young
man.

'She decided she was not suited to this life,' the healer said,
somewhat drily. 'I suppose you are here about the body that was
just brought in?'

I nodded. 'Arphaia is – was – my friend.'

'Oh dear, I am so sorry.' She paused and then added, 'I had
a friend who was murdered. I think of her regularly. In fact, that
is why I do this.' She gestured to the back room. 'I try to give
them back their voice – at least, as much as I am able.'

I considered that for a few seconds. Of all the reasons to
become a healer, and work with the dead, that was the best of
all.

For a moment we stood together in silence. Then I shook
myself and asked, 'Have you had a chance to look at her yet?'

'A bit.' The healer glanced at the gray light outside. 'I can't
see very well. But I've noticed a few things.'

I nodded and hurried to her side. The healer examined me
carefully, from my wet hair to the sandals looped around my
neck to my muddy skirt. 'Did you find her too?'

'Yes.' My voice broke.

'I see. Oh dear.' She touched my shoulder. 'Come and
see; I've done a little.' She motioned me to the back room. I
hesitated. I did not want to see Arphaia's remains. The healer
did not notice my reluctance and continued speaking, 'I believe
we know each other well enough now to introduce ourselves
more formally. My name is Despina.'

'Martis,' I said, although I knew she'd heard Tinos call me by
my name.

When I looked through the door, I was very relieved to see
Despina had covered Arphaia's face and lower extremities with
canvas. I'd been worrying about seeing her poor damaged body
again. As I entered the room, I focused on the bare white midriff

between the canvas sheets. The healer – Despina – had already washed away the mud and blood.

'Do you see the knife wounds?' Despina asked. I nodded.

'The edges are mostly smooth,' I said. Quite different from the injuries left by the vultures. They'd torn at the flesh. I shivered and willed my stomach to settle. 'Do you think she was stabbed by the same knife as Ynna and Duzi?'

'I do. You see, it is more of a puncture. And here' – she pointed to a small tear – 'is the same imperfection we saw with Ynna. Same knife.'

'Arphaia was accosted and stabbed to death,' I said to myself. 'Then her body was thrown into the woods.'

'Exactly,' the healer said with a nod. 'One other thing.'

'Yes?' I said warily.

'She was not violated.'

'Violated?' And then, 'How do you know?'

'No tearing, no blood, no bruises. I thought it was interesting since when a young woman is attacked, she is frequently assaulted.'

Appalled and horrified, I stared at Despina.

She smiled at me. 'Oh, you're perfectly safe here. But I wouldn't spend too much time at the docks.' Her smile slipped away. 'I think we can be quite sure she knew her killer, just as Ynna and Duzi did. Your friend clearly did not try to defend herself.' She pulled one of Arphaia's hands out from under the canvas sheet. I looked at the pallid palm and nodded. Although it was muddy and bore a few minor scratches, the hand exhibited no wounds. 'The murderer walked right up to her and stabbed her before she even knew she was in danger.'

THIRTY-EIGHT

I returned home by way of the interlocking halls of the complex, so deep in thought I scarcely noticed the curious stares thrown my way. My concerns about Arphaia warred with my own personal worry: should I apprentice to Despina? The more I thought about it, the more it drew me. But what would my mother, and the family weaving business, do without me? And what if I proved as much of a disappointment as the young female apprentice I'd seen? That I couldn't bear.

'Where have you been?' My mother asked as soon as I entered the apartment. 'I expected you hours ago.' She lowered Ria to the floor.

'Everything took a long time. Why do you have the baby?'

'That lazy nursemaid fed Ria and left again. I suspect she has found a new man.'

'Do you want me to visit Kryse again—'

'No need. I sent a messenger to her. Her sister will arrive tomorrow for an interview. Now tell me, what, in Our Lady's name, happened?'

I threw myself into the cushions. 'They took Arphaia's body to the healer,' I said and burst into tears. 'Ar–Arphaia was murdered.'

'Oh, my dear,' my mother said, sitting down and putting an arm around my shoulders. 'I know she was your friend. I am so sorry.' The baby began to wail. My mother frowned and bent forward to pick the child up. She held Ria on her lap and comforted me with the other arm while I wept.

My tears quickly subsided, and I wiped my face on the sleeve of my jacket.

'I didn't know Ynna, not much anyway,' I said. 'But Duzi and Arphaia were my friends. Someone murdered them and I don't know why. Or who did it.' I looked at my mother. 'What shall I do?'

She stared at me in astonishment. 'Even when you were a little girl, you went your own way. You decided what you wanted to do and you did it, no matter what I or your father said. And you never gave up. I'm flattered you want my help. Even though,' she added with a smile, 'I know you're only asking now because you are grieving and upset.'

I nodded. That was true. I couldn't think over the emotions crashing in my head. 'I just don't understand it,' I said in a low voice. 'Duzi owned nothing and Arphaia—' I thought of the gold in her trunk and stopped. 'Robbery isn't the reason,' I continued after a moment.

'We both know greed is not the only reason for killing someone,' my mother said. 'Love, hate, revenge – any powerful emotion can inspire a murder.'

'Yes, I know,' I agreed, thinking back to the previous death I'd investigated. 'I thought of that. But I haven't seen that kind of emotion this time. While Duzi and Arphaia were together, it was for such a short time. Then they both found someone else. And Ynna – well, I don't know enough about her. I suspect she was involved with someone, maybe Tryphone, but I don't know for sure.'

'Was her apartment broken into?'

'No. Not that I know of, anyway.' I thought back to my second visit. I'd pushed through the crowd before entering. Someone had been talking about a loud argument. I closed my eyes and thought. Who had it been? The woman standing at the door across the hall. An older woman but carefully made up and in an elaborate skirt and jacket of royal purple. She deserved a visit.

Then I thought about the door. The panel was untouched, so no one had broken in to attack Ynna.

'No. It was not broken into,' I said slowly. 'But one of the neighbors heard an argument.'

'With a man or a woman?'

I looked at my mother blankly. 'I don't know. Why?'

'Well, if it was with a man, it is a safe bet Ynna was seeing someone. Him. After all, she wouldn't welcome a man into her home unless she felt safe.'

I had not thought of that.

'And another thing,' Nephele continued. 'I'm curious about the dragonfly hair clip. You never told me who truly owned it.'

'I still don't know. Both Tryphone and Elemon claimed it.'

'They claimed it? I'm confused,' my mother said. 'I thought you said Duzi owned the dragonfly.'

'I found it in his apartment,' I corrected her. 'But I later discovered he did not own it. Cos— um, someone stole it from one of the bull dancers at the practice ring and gave it to Duzi.' I held up a hand to forestall another question. 'But he didn't know in whose clothing the clip was hidden.'

'I see . . . I think. What happened to the piece afterward?'

'Tinos took it,' I said, suddenly realizing I'd forgotten to show him the bee necklace. I'd been too taken up by the chaos surrounding the discovery of Arphaia's body. 'He spoke to both Tryphone and Elemon and decided it belonged to Elemon.' Considering Tinos's disposition of the dragonfly, perhaps it was best I hadn't thought to mention the necklace.

My mother caught the tone of my voice and eyed me sharply. 'You don't agree?'

'I'm not sure,' I admitted. 'Elemon told Tinos he owned the mate. If the dragonfly had been a love gift, why would he have two? The one who gave the dragonfly to him would still own the other one. Unless Elemon chooses to wear feminine jewelry in his hair.'

My mother was silent for a moment. 'Who gave the original dragonfly to Elemon?' she asked at last. And when I shook my head, she continued. 'If the dragonfly was a love gift to Elemon, and that makes sense – he's been a popular bull dancer for some time – someone had to offer it to him.'

'Of course,' I agreed. 'But who?'

'I don't know. But I think you should ask Anesdura. She was, well, she admired the bull dancers almost as much as Ynna did. And since Ynna is now gone—'

'But she told me she didn't recognize the dragonfly,' I interrupted. Of course, I hadn't believed her then. At best, she didn't tell me the entire truth.

'Then she may be able to suggest someone else to talk to,' my mother said.

I nodded slowly, thinking that through.

My mother smiled. 'Are you calmer?'

I realized I was. 'You did that on purpose,' I said accusingly.

She smiled. 'You needed to be distracted.'

'I thought you didn't want me to continue investigating.'

'I don't. But a visit to Anesdura, a friend – well, that's not really investigating, is it?' She widened her eyes innocently 'I doubt Anesdura will harm you.' I smiled. My mother was just as curious as I was, and her desire to know what happened was warring with her desire to keep me safe. 'Besides,' she added virtuously, 'I hope you share these suggestions with Tinos.'

I nodded but didn't promise anything. Tinos had been so irritable with me recently that I was hesitating. I couldn't imagine what I'd done to annoy him so. My curiosity was nothing new. Besides, I no longer trusted him to draw the proper conclusions, as he hadn't when he'd spoken to Elemon and Tryphone. I thought there were still too many unanswered questions about that piece of jewelry – questions Tinos seemed unwilling to ask.

Now that I was calmer, I realized I was very hungry. 'Is there anything to eat?' I asked hopefully.

'You're back to normal,' my mother said with a smile as she put Ria down.

After eating, I changed my clothing again, donning a newer skirt and jacket. I was too impatient to arrange my hair in the fashionable style, but I allowed my mother to line my eyes with kohl. She knew I intended to visit Anesdura and thought I would search for Tinos afterwards. Although she was correct about the first, she was wrong about the second.

My plans were somewhat different. Besides visiting Anesdura, I intended to speak to Ynna's neighbor. If I saw Tinos, I might share what I knew. But I would not hunt him down. He didn't deserve any more of my help.

Since the rain was coming down in sheets, I decided to visit Ynna's neighbor first and traveled through the maze of halls and chambers to the location of her apartment, remembering exactly which door belonged to the woman who'd mentioned hearing an argument. For a moment, I stood irresolute.

Then, as my heart began to thud with excitement, I rapped on the door across the hall.

After several seconds, a young woman answered my knock. She was only a year or two older than I was. This was not the woman I'd seen, and since I did not know her name, I could not ask for the person I wanted. 'Um, um,' I stammered.

'Who is it?' called a voice from within.

As the speaker approached the door and I recognized her face, I sighed with relief. 'I wanted to ask you some questions,' I said. 'About Ynna?'

'Regarding what exactly?' she asked suspiciously.

'I was here the morning after the wanax found her. You said you heard an argument. I wanted to know about it.'

'Why should I answer your questions?' The woman inspected me. 'You're awfully young.'

I couldn't say that I was curious. 'I knew Ynna,' I said at last. 'She was a good friend of my sister's. I visited her the day before her death. I feel terrible . . .' Well, that was true enough.

The woman hesitated a moment. 'I suppose you'd better come in,' she said at last.

As the young woman – I didn't know whether she was a relative or a maid – went to prepare refreshments, I made myself comfortable on the cushions and looked at the older woman expectantly. 'You heard an argument?'

'Oh, yes. It was impossible not to hear it. Ynna's voice was quite loud.'

'Did you hear the person she was arguing with?'

'I could hear enough to know she was quarreling with someone, but I wouldn't recognize the voice, if that is what you mean.'

'Was she arguing with a man? Or another woman?'

She wrinkled her brow. 'I couldn't really tell. The other person spoke much more quietly. But if I had to guess, I would say it was a man.'

'A man?' I clasped my hands together in excitement. I would have to tell my mother her suggestion had been a helpful one. 'Why would you say so?'

'Ynna was seeing someone. A man. Younger than she is – was. He visited her a few times.'

'Do you know what he looked like?'

'Oh, I never saw his face. Only his back. But he was quite lean and tanned dark.' She paused and then added, 'I suspect he was a bull dancer.'

That made sense. I knew Ynna's partiality for bull dancers. 'Did he have any scars?'

'Not that I saw.' As the young woman entered with a plate of fruit, the older woman asked her, 'Did you see any scars on the man who visited Ynna?'

'No. No scars.'

So not Elemon, then. The thick scar that wound around his waist from the time he'd been gored by the bull was unmistakable. I'd wondered if Duzi had been engaged in a relationship

with Ynna; now I wondered if her man had been Tryphone. He
was a bull dancer: slim as we all were, and darkly tanned.

The woman broke into my thoughts. 'But the person I saw
the day Ynna died and the one she argued with were different.
Not the man she'd been seeing.'

'Different?' I repeated in shock. There were two mystery men?
'Different how?'

'I'm not sure.' She screwed up her face. 'The man who visited
her the day she died wore a robe, so I couldn't see him well.
And, of course, I never saw their faces.'

'Could you describe him?' I asked.

'Not really. He was similar to the man she was seeing.' The
older woman smiled slightly. 'All you bull dancers resemble one
another. Thin, muscular, tanned.' Her forehead wrinkled. 'He was
different. Maybe shorter? He moved differently.' She shook her
head in frustration. 'I just knew he was not the same person I'd
seen before.'

'What did the robe look like?' I asked. Her descriptions so
far had been almost no help.

'Purple bands on the sleeves and the hem.'

I stared at her. I knew I'd seen such a robe, and recently
too. I lapsed into silence as I cudgeled my brain. Who had I seen
wearing such clothing? Then I remembered. Tryphone.

THIRTY-NINE

Although I stayed with the two women – a mother and
daughter – for some time longer, I learned nothing further
about Ynna's visitors. The daughter was engaged to marry,
and I heard a lot about the wedding and the stellar qualities of
the husband-to-be. As I left, the daughter impulsively invited me
to attend the marriage ceremony.

During my time inside, the rain stopped. The clouds were
breaking up and shafts of sunlight penetrated the windows and
down the light wells. On an impulse, I decided to visit Anesdura,
after all.

I did not go home first. Instead, I made my way to the front entrance and descended the stairs. The air was cool and damp, and pools of standing water shimmered between the paving stones. As I crossed the city, drops of rain spat from the sky but did not develop into showers.

Anesdura greeted me joyfully and brought me to the courtyard. Outside the awning that had protected the patio from the rain and on the other side of the plants, the stones were still wet from the previous downpour.

Anesdura's daughter was playing nearby. She'd pulled herself to a stand on a bench and was moving some small wooden toys around. When I entered the chamber and sat down beside Anesdura, the child gave me a wide smile, revealing a tooth. I smiled back. 'She's beautiful,' I told Anesdura.

She smiled. 'Someday you will have one of your own,' she said, resting a hand on her swollen belly.

'I plan to dedicate myself to Artemis and remain a virgin,' I said. 'I've always planned to do so.'

'A noble sacrifice,' Anesdura said admiringly.

I did not consider it such a sacrifice. Although my intention may have begun that way, as I'd grown older, I'd seen other advantages to remaining childless. Babies tied a woman to her home. I would not have the freedom to dance with the bulls, go where I wanted or anything else.

'Have they found the man who murdered Ynna?' Anesdura asked, her eyes filling with tears.

'Not yet.' I paused, not sure how much to say. In the end, I decided not to mention Duzi or Arphaia. 'You probably knew Ynna best—'

'Don't ask me about Ynna anymore. I told you – we saw each other infrequently.'

I nodded and decided to step away from Ynna for a few minutes. Anesdura was on edge and ready to take offense. 'What about Eile?' I asked.

'Eile?' Anesdura looked astonished. 'What does Eile have to do with this?'

'Maybe nothing. Did she ever compete with the rest of you?'

'No. By the time she was fourteen, Eile's interests had begun to turn away from clothes and jewelry. Honestly, I was surprised when she married.' She paused. 'I don't see Eile often.' She shrugged. 'We have nothing to talk about anymore.'

'Would she be jealous of Ynna?'

'Why? Eile is – um – important as a priestess. That's what she cares about. She has no time for Ynna, who behaves – behaved – as though she's still sixteen. As far as I know, they haven't spoken in years.' She sighed. 'Eile is dismissive even with me. I'm just an old married lady.'

I thought of the squalor in Ynna's apartment and the stench of old wine. 'I think she worshipped the Wine God more than she should,' I said drily.

'I wish you'd known her better.' Anesdura continued her own train of thought. 'She was so much fun. Opis could be critical—' Realizing all at once that she was talking with Opis's sister, Anesdura stopped, her eyes widening.

'I know better than anyone how critical Opis could be,' I said. 'I was glad when she married and moved to the villa. The apartment was much quieter and more harmonious.'

Anesdura relaxed and nodded. 'Ynna came into her own when Opis left. Arge, of course, was engaged to that barbarian, and Eile was busy at the Priestess House, so usually only Ynna and I watched the bull dancers . . .'

She stopped again, looking at me in embarrassment. 'I keep forgetting you are one of them now.'

'That is what I wished to speak to you about,' I said. 'I have only been a dancer for six months. Although I was training before that, I didn't really know any of the real bull dancers very well.'

'Why? Why do you want to talk to me about that?' Her cheeks flushing, she looked away from me. She shifted in her seat as though I'd made her uncomfortable.

'I think Ynna's death has something to do with the bull dancers,' I said. When Anesdura did not speak, I continued. 'She was seeing one recently. Did you know that?'

'I didn't.' Anesdura's mouth pinched. 'But I am not surprised. Even then' – she looked away, toward the courtyard outside – 'it was a competition for her.'

'A competition? What do you mean?' I thought I might know but found the idea so repellent I didn't want to believe it.

'A competition to see who slept with more bull dancers.'

I stared at her, aghast. 'Really?'

'Yes.' Anesdura, embarrassed, looked away from me. 'She always won. I met someone early on. Then I thought the whole contest was stupid.'

'Someone you preferred to spend time with?' I tried to keep the shock out of my voice. Had Opis engaged in such activities before her marriage? Of course she had. I didn't want to know any more than that.

Anesdura nodded, her cheeks coloring. She was rescued from responding by the maid who brought in a platter of fruits, nuts and pastries. Anesdura took a pastry and stuffed the entire square into her mouth. In the sudden silence, I could clearly hear her daughter.

'Babababa,' the little girl said. I turned to look at her and she smiled at me. I smiled back.

'Babababa,' I repeated to her. Anesdura stretched out her arms and lifted the child to her lap. As she brushed back the light hair, I saw the birthmark on the child's temple. Where had I seen such a mark before?

Since it was not important right now, I put the question out of my mind and went on to another topic. 'The dragonfly hair clip. You told me you didn't recognize it?'

'I've seen jewelry like it. Maybe not as beautifully made. But similar.' She burst into speech, her eyes sliding away from mine. 'But not that piece, no.'

'Ynna recognized it,' I said. 'She claimed it as hers. Do you know anything about that?'

'I don't.'

'Anesdura,' I said reproachfully, 'I know you're lying to me. If Ynna owned it, you've seen it before. You did recognize it. Why won't you tell me the truth?'

'That trinket has nothing to do with Ynna's murder,' she said. Her voice was trembling.

'Maybe not. But we don't know that for certain right now.'

Anesdura, the woman who could talk without pausing for breath, said nothing.

The silence stretched out. This time I did not break it with a question. Instead, I chose a fig from the platter and took a small bite. Anesdura's daughter stretched out her hands.

'Are you hungry?' I asked her. What did babies eat after they were weaned? Opis's baby had not been weaned yet, and I did not remember what my mother fed Telemon at this age. 'Maybe some fig?'

I glanced at Anesdura for permission as I broke off a small piece of the soft, sweet fruit. She shook her head and chose a honey-soaked pastry, offering a small piece to her daughter.

As the little girl looked up at her mother and opened her mouth for the treat, I remembered where I'd seen that birthmark. 'Elemon,' I blurted. 'Elemon.' The realization struck me like an arrow from the Goddess. 'Elemon is her father.'

Anesdura looked up at me, her eyes wide. She opened and closed her mouth several times, but no words emerged.

'It's true, isn't it?' I leaned forward.

She hesitated for several seconds and then she nodded. 'Yes.'

'You gave a dragonfly ornament to Elemon as a love gift?'

She hesitated but finally answered. 'Yes. I fancied myself in love with him, foolish girl that I was then,' she said bitterly as she made her way to the cushioned bench beside me.

'What happened?' I asked, thinking of the girl standing behind Elemon when I'd visited him.

Her eyes filled with tears. 'He didn't want me. I asked him to marry me, and he refused.'

'He refused?' I was astounded. Marrying Anesdura would have given Elemon status and property, just as becoming consort to the High Priestess had done for Tinos.

She nodded, tears running down her face. 'He didn't want to surrender his freedom. That was before the bull gored him, of course.' She forced a smile. 'It was for the best. I might have become an early widow. I was already pregnant then, although I didn't know it.'

I did not think it was for the best. She was still yearning for Elemon.

I sat back. I no longer wondered why Anesdura had not admitted she recognized the dragonfly. She must have been humiliated by his refusal as well as heartbroken. 'Then you married your husband?'

She sighed. 'Yes. Well, I had to do something. But I'm afraid now that the marriage may have been a mistake. We really are not very well suited.'

'I'm sorry to hear that,' I said truthfully. For a moment, we were both silent. I reflected that none of the relationships my sisters and their friends had been in had ended well. Opis married Uncle Pylas and was miserable, Arge died on her wedding day, and Ynna's marriage ended almost immediately in divorce. And now here was Anesdura, married to a man she did not love. None yielded compelling arguments for marriage, and I was even less interested in tying my fate to another than I had been.

'But Ynna said the dragonfly belonged to her. Was she lying to me?'

'No, she wasn't lying.'

'So, if she owned one of the hair clips, how did she come into possession of it?'

'I gave it to her,' Anesdura said.

'What?'

'I had the pair made at Dombus's,' she said. I nodded; that I knew. 'After Opis moved to the villa with her husband, I gave one of the dragonflies to Ynna. I thought it would make us better friends.'

'Did it?'

'Yes. For a time. But after I met Elemon, I wasn't interested in hanging around with the other bull dancers. I stopped going with her. We lost touch.' She smiled weakly. 'I gave the second dragonfly to Elemon when I still thought we would marry. You know what happened after that.'

I reached across and touched her hand. Elemon had behaved badly, and I liked him even less than before.

But I still had questions. Who had brought the second hair clip, the one that had been owned by Ynna, to the bull ring? Once I'd thought it belonged to Duzi and that he was Ynna's lover. Now I realized I'd been wrong. It had to be Tryphone. He had claimed the dragonfly as his own, and I now believed him. If he had been the man Ynna was seeing, everything made sense. But then, who was Arphaia involved with?

I had to talk to Tryphone and get answers to these questions.

FORTY

arrived early at practice again the next morning. Geos had only just reached the ring himself and glanced at me in amusement. 'This is becoming a habit with you,' he said. 'From coming to practice late, you've switched to early.'

I nodded, trying to find the words to tell him about Arphaia. 'How is the ankle?' Geos asked.

'Fine.' I held it out. My feet still looked battered from yesterday's walk in the rain, but the ankle looked much better. Although still a little swollen, the bruises had faded and it no longer hurt so much.

'What did you do?' Geos asked, staring at the scratches on my feet.

I sighed. 'I have bad news,' I said. My voice broke and tears flooded my eyes.

The smile dropped from his face. 'More bad news? What now?'

'Arphaia—' My throat closed up and I couldn't continue.

'Oh no,' he said. 'What happened?'

'She's dead. Murdered. I found her body—' I stopped again.

'I don't understand what's happening,' Geos said, his own voice hoarse. 'Why is someone targeting my bull dancers?' I had no answer to that and shook my head. 'Does anyone else know?'

'Tinos. I alerted him as soon as I found her.' I inhaled a deep breath. 'None of the others know . . .'

He nodded and passed his hand over his grizzled chin. 'We'll have to tell them.' He looked over my head. I turned. Thaos, Curgis and Tryphone, laughing at some joke, were approaching us. When they saw Geos and then me, and our sorrowful expressions, their laughter faded.

'What's happening?' Thaos asked.

Geos pointed to Costi and Nub, who were trotting toward us. 'Let's wait for everyone.'

Finally, all the remaining bull dancers had reached the ring.

'Gather round,' Geos said, gesturing at each of us. He waited until everyone stood in a circle facing him. Then, to my surprise, he looked at me. 'Martis has something to tell you.' All eyes turned to me.

I frowned at him reproachfully before looking around the circle. Expressions ranged from mildly curious to worried.

'Yesterday . . .' I said, struggling to speak through my emotion. I stopped and took a deep breath. 'Yesterday I visited Arphaia's home to find out why she had not been attending practice.' I looked around at my team. The twins gazed at me, perplexed, too young to understand what could happen.

Obelix bit her lip and stared at me. 'Did something happen to Arphaia?' she blurted anxiously.

'What happened?' Tryphone's voice was hoarse with worry.

'Is she hurt?' Obelix asked at the same time.

'Arphaia's aunt told me she'd left the farm the day before, in the morning.' I stopped, fighting the tears that threatened to choke me.

'Go on,' Thaos said, his own voice shaking.

'I found her body on the way home. In the forest.'

After a few seconds of shocked silence, everyone began talking at once. 'What happened? Was it an accident?'

'Dead?' cried Tryphone, his eyes reddening. 'She can't be.'

I nodded sorrowfully. 'Her body will be returned to her family so that all the proper rites . . .' I couldn't go on. Obelix began to cry, and after a few seconds, Nub joined her.

'But how?' Elemon asked. I had never seen him look so shocked. 'How did she die?'

I thought of the stab wounds. I did not want to mention them. Then I thought of the vultures and shuddered. 'I don't know,' I said. 'I found her in the woods. I don't want to talk about it.'

'But Arphaia is – was – so young. How could she die?' Tryphone's voice was so thick with sorrow I could barely understand him.

'I don't know,' I repeated. I suspected Arphaia must have known something about the murders, but I could not imagine what that would be. Not yet anyway, although I would find out. I was determined to.

'Considering this news,' Geos said, 'practice is canceled for today.' He gestured at us, his hand shaking.

I watched my fellow bull dancers turn away, paying particular attention to Tryphone. Everyone was shocked and upset, but he was distraught with grief. As he would be if he was the man in Arphaia's life.

'Tryphone,' I called after him. 'A word.'

Tryphone did not slow down or even look at me. I sped up and grabbed his elbow. 'Tryphone.'

'Leave me alone.' His shoulders shook with his sobs. Burning tears ran down my cheeks.

'Please, Tryphone.' I darted in front of him. 'We both cared about her. Let me help.' He looked at me.

'Was she murdered?'

I nodded. For a moment, we just stood there, tears streaming down our faces. I swiped at my face with my arm. 'Please help me find out who did this to her.'

Asking him for help was a calculated risk. I knew better than to assume he was innocent – in fact, I thought he was likely guilty – but I hoped I would learn something.

After a moment, Tryphone nodded. 'What do you want to know?'

'Do you know of anyone who wished to harm her?'

'Harm her?' he repeated. 'Why would anyone—' He stopped and took a deep breath. 'No, I don't know anyone who would do that. Even that old man her mother wanted her to marry took her refusal graciously. And he lives far away.'

'I saw you at the Harvest Festival,' I said. 'Standing with Arphaia's family. I didn't realize you two were so close.'

'We planned to marry,' he said, his eyes filling with fresh tears.

I stared at him. 'Marry?' I repeated. Arphaia and Tryphone. I still had trouble believing it.

'We were saving everything – all the gifts we received from our performances . . .' His eyes slid away from mine.

An involuntary giggle bubbled up in my chest and escaped as a muffled grunt through my closed mouth. Arphaia had been such a poor bull leaper that I did not believe she'd earned anything more than the most basic copper bangle. Tryphone, believing my crazy laughter to be a sob, looked at me sympathetically.

'I know she was your friend.'

I nodded. Arphaia was probably one of the few women I could

call a friend. And I'd been highly critical of her. I regretted that now.

'But you knew Ynna too,' I said. It was not a question, although I was not entirely sure. He nodded.

'Yes. She approached me . . .' His voice trailed away. He pushed the long tresses of his black hair to the back.

Since, from all accounts, Ynna had a history of seeking out bull dancers, I said, 'I believe you.' I thought of the bee necklace and the rest of the hoard tucked into Arphaia's chest of clothes. 'She gave you love gifts, didn't she?'

Tryphone did not answer for a moment, and when I looked at him, he was staring at the ground. Finally, with a sigh, he nodded.

'Including the dragonfly hair clip?'

He nodded again. 'I gave most of the pieces to Arphaia to keep.'

That explained the hoarded gold. 'Did you tell Ynna you were marrying someone else?'

He looked at me in surprise. 'I did. Just a few days ago.' He scowled. 'Why is that important?'

'Did you and Ynna argue about it?'

'Yes. How did you know that?'

'Her neighbors heard the quarrel,' I said.

He glared at me. 'You talked to her neighbors? By the Lady, you are nosy. I've never met anyone so eager to pry into other people's lives. I could almost believe you murdered Duzi and Arphaia just to give yourself a reason to poke your nose into other people's business.'

I stiffened and stepped back but did not reply as he shouted at me. Now that his initial shock had eased, grief was turning into anger. I understood. Anger was easier to deal with than despair, and I made a handy target.

'You could have saved her. Why didn't you stop it?' he demanded. 'You knew someone was out there murdering people. Why didn't you keep Arphaia safe?'

Realizing his grief had made him irrational, I did not try to argue.

He moved forward, crowding me. I refused to show any fear, although my stomach threatened to dump my breakfast on the ground.

'Hey, hey,' said Geos, inserting his beefy arm between us. 'Calm down and shut up, both of you. This is an emotional time for all of us. I don't want anyone to say anything they will regret.' Neither Tryphone nor I moved. 'Go home. Now.'

Tryphone finally stepped back. Once he moved away, I also retreated a step. I was trembling so hard that my legs felt weak. Tryphone's grief had boiled over into rage so quickly I'd been caught by surprise.

Although several of my questions had been answered, the most important one remained. I still did not know who had murdered Duzi, Ynna and now Arphaia.

Geos dropped his arm and moved away. Shaking, I turned around, only to realize most of the other bull dancers had witnessed the clash. Only Nub and the twins were out of earshot.

And Elemon also was red-faced with fury. When I caught his eye, he folded his arms and glowered at me. He looked as enraged as Tryphone, almost as though he could strangle me on the spot.

FORTY-ONE

Neither Elemon nor Tryphone approached me while I was in the arena. They knew Geos was watching and would intervene. But I wasn't sure what they might do outside, so I hurried up the steps to the hill outside. I heard someone pursuing me, and when I glanced over my shoulder, I saw Elemon right behind me.

'Wait. I want to talk to you,' he shouted.

I broke into a run, holding the skirt away from my legs. But he took several long strides and caught up to me. Grabbing my arm, he jerked me to a stop.

'What are you doing?' he asked angrily. 'Are you trying to get someone in trouble? Tinos is wanax, not you. And he is satisfied that dragonfly belongs to me.'

'Three people have been murdered,' I retorted. 'And two of them have been bull dancers. Part of our team, Elemon. People we know. Don't you care?'

'Of course I care—'

'You don't act like it. You seem more interested in grabbing all the prizes. You know that dragonfly did not belong to you.' I wrenched my arm away from him.

'Oh, and who does it belong to, then?'

'Tryphone – just as he said. It was a gift. Two dragonflies were made in Dombus's shop, and you genuinely own one of them. Isn't that enough?'

'What do you know about it?' he demanded, his face reddening.

'I know where your hair clip came from,' I shouted at him, staring into his furious face but too angry myself to think about what I was saying. 'From Anesdura. Oh yes, she told me all about it. You know her daughter is yours, don't you?'

'You little bitch.' Shame added fuel to his fury. 'You're meddling in things that don't concern you.' I noticed he did not deny my accusation.

'Anesdura is a friend and she told me all about you.'

'You know nothing,' he snapped. 'You have a family. You can take over your mother's weaving business after your time with the bull leapers is finished. Why did you become one of us anyway? For fame? I don't believe you did it to honor the Goddess. Most of the rest of us do this for the prizes. Our time as a bull dancer is short, and most of us do not have the option of retreating to the loom. Or get chosen to serve as a wanax, as Tinos did. So, yes, I take everything that is offered to me. Most of us do.'

'That is not what this is,' I shouted. 'You could have married her. But no. You chose not to.'

'Yes, I could have married her, and I would have brought nothing to the marriage but my fame as a bull dancer. If that even lasts. Anesdura would have regretted it eventually.' Remorse clouded his eyes.

'You don't know that. If what you told me is even true.' I recalled Anesdura's expression as she confided in me. 'She loves you still. Besides, I don't think stealing from one of your teammates is a wiser choice. It makes you nothing but a common thief.'

His face went from red to white. 'I ought to—'

Suddenly, I could easily imagine him losing his temper and lashing out – and stabbing someone to death.

'What? Hit me? Stab me as Duzi and Arphaia were stabbed?'

'What is going on here?' Obelix appeared beside me and grasped my arm. Gently, she pulled me backward. 'What is the matter with you? With both of you? Arguing out here where everyone can watch.'

I took a deep breath and looked around me. Women carrying baskets, craftspeople on their way to their workshops and even the slaves had turned to stare at Elemon and me. Now the heat I felt was one of embarrassment, not anger.

Elemon did not appear any happier to be the center of attention than I was. He took several deep breaths and gradually his color returned to normal. Making a disgusted noise in his throat, he stamped away. But before he'd taken more than a few steps, he turned back. 'This isn't over, brat,' he warned.

Breathing hard, I watched him disappear into the crowd. I realized I was sweating and shaky. 'Thank you,' I said to Obelix. She nodded.

'You should be more careful. Elemon has a temper.'

I nodded. 'I know that now.'

'I'll walk you home.'

'Thank you.'

My trembling legs could scarcely hold me up, and after a few seconds Obelix took my arm. 'Elemon is arrogant,' she said. 'If he's guilty of the murders . . .' She shook her head. 'He's dangerous, that's all.'

I was unable to speak. Although my heart rate had begun to slow down, I still felt as though I couldn't catch my breath.

After we'd walked a short distance, she spoke again. 'Elemon is right, you know,' she said.

'About what?'

'About why we became bull dancers.' She glanced at me and looked away. 'Most of us want to better ourselves. Duzi was a former pirate and owned nothing. Costi is an orphan and lives on the streets most of the time. Tryphone is from somewhere outside of Gortnya, a village wiped out by the brigands. He came here with nothing but the clothes on his back. And me?' Now she stared at me. 'Do you think I don't know people call me Fish Guts behind my back? That they flinch when I go near them, recoiling from the fishy smell in my clothing and hair? I bathe and wash my clothing often, but nothing seems to help—' Her voice broke and she looked away from me. 'Even Arphaia. My friend.'

'I'm sorry,' I muttered, flushing with shame. I hadn't been a good friend, to either Arphaia or Obelix. I'd called her Fish Guts more than once. And I could smell her now, a strong fishy odor like one would smell on the docks. 'You're a good bull leaper,' I said in a small voice.

'I hope so. That's why I became one, despite the danger. I do not want to be a fisherman's wife or work with fish my whole life.' She smiled bitterly. 'I don't enjoy the smell of fish any more than anyone else.'

I thought of Kryse, a former bull dancer who'd been seriously injured during a performance. She'd married a fisherman and still worked on the docks. But her time as a dancer had earned her enough to buy a fishing boat for her husband. Unconsciously, I nodded.

'I see. If you don't marry a fisherman,' I said now, 'what will you do?'

'I don't know. But once I have some resources, some jewelry and such, I can choose something else. Who knows, maybe I'll become a rich man's wife.'

Although uncommon, that was not unheard of. I looked at Obelix, inspecting her as my mother would me. 'Yes,' I said. 'That's possible. With kohl around your eyes, fashionable clothes and jewelry, you would be pretty. I think a merchant might marry you.'

'Thank you,' she said drily. 'So happy to have your approval.'

Seeing I'd offended her, I said quickly, 'I'm sorry.' That only made it worse; she grimaced.

'I'll leave you here,' she said. The complex where I lived was still some distance away. I looked around but saw neither Elemon nor Tryphone. Besides, the square was busy. No one would attack me with these crowds around. 'Thank you for walking with me,' I said as raindrops spotted my clothing and darkened the stones around my feet.

Obelix looked up at the sky. 'I suppose practice will take place in the caves again,' she said. 'Be careful.' With a nod and a wave, she veered away and soon disappeared into the crowd.

With one final glance around to make sure no one was watching me, I hurried home.

First, I went to the High Priestess's chambers to look for Tinos. I wanted to tell him about Elemon. I wanted to say, 'See, your friend might be guilty.' But when I peeked inside the throne room, only the High Priestess and her ladies were inside. I did not feel I could question the High Priestess. She scared me. Then, thinking that he might be visiting the healer, I descended to the lowest level where Despina worked.

'No, I haven't seen him,' she said in answer to my question. 'Why? Has something happened? Not another body, I hope?'

I shook my head. Biting my lip, I turned to leave.

'Martis.' The healer called me back. 'I wanted to tell you. I sent Arphaia's body to her family. Her funeral is this afternoon.'

'This afternoon?' I was shocked by its suddenness. 'So soon?'

She nodded. 'Her family were eager . . . A messenger should be arriving at your house.'

'Thank you.' I flew up the steps and hurried home.

My mother was not alone. A young girl who looked vaguely familiar, although I was sure I didn't know her, sat on the cushions having tea with my mother. Ria sat on the carpet between them. 'Do you know Kryse's sister, Eris?' my mother asked me.

'We've never met.' I smiled at Eris. 'You resemble your sister,' I said.

'I hear that often,' she replied with a smile.

'Eris is interested in the position of nursemaid,' my mother said, just as though I hadn't suggested it.

I sat down beside Eris. 'You don't wish to dance with the bulls, as your sister did?' I asked her.

She shuddered delicately. 'Too dangerous. I'm sure I would be frozen with fear.'

'Or become a fisherman's wife?' my mother asked.

'It is a messy job, cleaning fish. One might be as easily injured with a knife as a bull's horn, and there is all that blood and scales. No, it is not for me.'

My mother hesitated. I knew Ria was still not weaned, and Eris, a young girl, had not borne children yet. 'Why don't we have a trial,' she suggested. 'You can work every afternoon for a bit. If we are both satisfied, you can move in permanently.'

Eris's face lit up. 'That is very satisfactory,' she said eagerly. 'When shall I begin?'

'Tomorrow? Say, the hour after midday?'

As they began discussing compensation, I rose and went to my bedchamber to change my clothes. I moved more and more slowly as my thoughts turned once again to the murders.

Duzi had been the first. I still didn't understand why. Was it because Costi had stolen the dragonfly and brought it to Duzi? Or was that piece of jewelry simply a distraction? I thought I now understood the chain that connected the dragonfly to several people. Anesdura had purchased the pair and given one to Ynna. Sometime later, Anesdura had given her hair ornament to Elemon, and Ynna had given hers to Tryphone.

But Arphaia had no connection to that trinket and yet someone had murdered her. I sniffed and pushed aside the image of her body in the woods. Arphaia did not deserve to be murdered and discarded like trash for the vultures to find.

Bringing my unruly thoughts back to the dragonfly, I thought of Elemon and Tryphone. Elemon owned one of the dragonflies, and he still lived. As did Tryphone, who I now believed had owned the other one – before Costi had stolen it. I began to pace the length of my small chamber.

Tryphone knew all the victims. We all did. All of us were connected to one another, so that was not a strong argument for the guilt of either Tryphone or Elemon. But who was connected to Ynna? Her neighbor had claimed someone other than Tryphone had visited her. Had she been seeing one of the other bull leapers as well as seeing Tryphone? I'd thought Ynna had been involved with Duzi, and she might have been, but he could not be the man who'd murdered her. By then, he was already dead.

Who else was there? Not Costi and the kids, but I'd never suspected them anyway. Thaos and Curgis were young, still in the dorms, and not at all famous. Would Ynna be interested in either of them? Doubtful. So who could it be? Elemon?

But why would he – or Tryphone, for that matter – murder any of the three victims?

Elemon had always been friendly with Duzi. He'd ignored

Arphaia and, as far as I knew, had no relationship at all with Ynna. Although Elemon had a temper, I saw no reason for him to murder any of the three victims.

I turned my thoughts to Tryphone. What did I know about him? A bull dancer in his small town, he'd moved to Knossos recently. He made no secret of that. He'd come from the west. And Obelix had just told me his village had been destroyed by pirates.

Duzi had once been a pirate. Would that give Tryphone enough motive to kill him?

Tryphone admitted he'd quarreled with Ynna, an argument so loud and acrimonious the neighbors heard it. Could that have led to her murder?

I struggled to understand the reason for Arphaia's murder the most. Had she decided she was no longer interested in him? Were they fighting over the gold?

But when I'd announced Arphaia's death, Tryphone had been devastated. He'd begun sobbing uncontrollably. I shook my head. I couldn't believe someone so grief-stricken was the murderer. What was I missing?

FORTY-TWO

My mother and Eris walked to the front and said their goodbyes. A few seconds later, my mother appeared at my door. 'I think she may do very well,' she said. 'She is comfortable with Ria, and the baby likes her.'

'But Ria isn't weaned,' I pointed out.

'Not completely, no. But our current nursemaid missed feedings so often lately that I doubt it will be difficult to finish the process.' She smiled. 'We'll accomplish that during this trial. Are you hungry?'

Her sudden change in topic caught me by surprise and it took me a few seconds to respond. 'Yes.'

'Come and eat.'

My mother and I settled into the cushions in the main room.

A few moments later the cook brought out a plate of flatbread, olives and fruit and two cups of cold tea.

'A messenger came while you were away,' my mother said. 'Arphaia's funeral—'

'Will be held this afternoon. I heard.' I looked at the bread in my hand. 'It seems like I've attended one funeral after another recently.'

My mother nodded. 'It has been a difficult time. Are you planning to attend?'

'Of course. Arphaia was my friend—' My throat suddenly closed up, and I put the bread back on the plate.

'Martis,' my mother said gently, 'you will not help anyone if you faint from hunger. Eat your olives and drink your tea.'

I ate the olive and spat the pit on to the plate. I took a sip of tea. Feeling a little better, I slowly nibbled my bread. 'I just don't understand why Arphaia was murdered,' I said, my voice catching.

'Have you discovered the reasons behind Duzi's and Ynna's deaths?' my mother asked. I shook my head. 'I suspect you will understand everything once you know the connections between the three victims.'

I pondered that a moment. 'Well, Arphaia did not know Ynna,' I said at last. But she had known Duzi, and I was pretty sure he and Ynna had been involved. At least for a little while. 'Maybe I'm wrong about Arphaia's connection to Ynna,' I muttered. 'Maybe Arphaia did know her or had met her at least.'

'There has to be something,' my mother said. 'You just have to find it.'

I nodded, recalling Arge telling me that the bull dancers were at the center of this. At the time, I'd been annoyed to hear her state something so obvious; now I considered her suggestion again. She'd been correct. Tryphone and possibly Elemon were connected to all three victims.

But I couldn't remain here, brooding. I had a funeral to attend. I changed my clothes and applied kohl to my eyes. My mother handed me the canvas sheet, since it had begun raining again, and I once more set off for the farm where Arphaia had lived. I carried a small pottery bull so she would have companionship in the afterlife.

* * *

I expected to see farmers in the fields. I knew from my uncle Pylas that the work on a farm had to be completed at the proper times, no matter what else was happening. But these fields were empty.

I paused at the gate to catch my breath. From here, I could see a crowd massing at the back of the house. I climbed the muddy slope and approached them.

I had barely reached the house when Arphaia's aunt broke away from the others and hurried to meet me. 'What do you want now?' Although beautifully dressed in a matching red skirt and jacket, she wore no makeup. Her red and swollen eyes bore mute witness to her grief.

'I am so sorry about Arphaia,' I said, my own eyes filling. 'She was my friend.'

The woman looked away from me. 'The wanax said you found her?'

'As you know, I was looking for her,' I said. 'I was worried.'

'I suppose I should thank you.' She looked back at me, her mouth trembling. 'We were able to perform the necessary rites . . .' She broke off on a sob. I reached out and touched her arm, tears running down my cheeks.

For a moment we wept together. She pulled herself together first. 'The wanax has no idea who might have murdered her,' she said, her voice thick.

'No, he doesn't,' I said, my voice shaking. 'How is her suitor taking this?'

'Her suitor?' The other woman looked confused. 'What suitor? Do you mean the man her mother wished her to marry? He is at her mother's villa, some distance from here.'

'I meant Zeno,' I said. The young man Arphaia had been flirting with. I wondered if Tryphone knew about Zeno. 'They seemed very friendly.'

The woman's expression cleared.

'Zeno. He is her cousin. He is not – they are not together. Nor will they ever be. They are friends only. It is a game for them. Was a game.' She put her hands over her face. The stifled groan was more moving than a sob would have been.

I impatiently dashed away the tears filling my eyes. I couldn't succumb to grief now; I had to think. 'I know Arphaia – I heard she and Tryphone were together . . .'

Arphaia's aunt shook her head as she scrubbed at the kohl streaking her cheeks. 'Arphaia told me they were friends. Nothing more. Only friends, as you and Obelix were her friends.'

I realized Arphaia had not told her aunt about her relationship with Tryphone. I opened my mouth to say something but realized I had no right. It should be Tryphone who confided this secret. Instead, I said, 'Are Tryphone and Obelix here?'

Arphaia's aunt nodded and pointed. 'Geos also.' I followed her finger and saw my fellow bull dancers. Obelix clung to Tryphone's arm, weeping convulsively. Geos stood just behind them. I would not have recognized him if Arphaia's aunt hadn't pointed him out. He wore a robe instead of the loincloth I was accustomed to seeing, and his gray hair was neatly combed and tied back.

Maybe Arphaia had confided in her cousin, had told him something that would help me. 'Could I speak to Zeno?' I asked tentatively.

'If he will,' she said, wiping away her tears with her fingers. 'Come in.' She gestured to the farmhouse. 'Refresh yourself after your journey.'

I knew that this woman, this family, did not want to entertain company at such a sad time, but I understood the habits of hospitality were almost unbreakable. The Goddess frowned on those who did not treat visitors well. 'Thank you,' I said. 'Maybe some water.' Grief tied my stomach into knots and I was too nauseous to think of eating.

'Are you sure you won't take wine or beer?' she asked as we entered the covered pergola. Grape vines snaked over the stakes overhead. During the summer, when the grapes were ripening, this would be a pleasant, shaded spot.

'Just water,' I said. I would have taken tea but did not want to put her to any trouble. She poured a cup of water from a jug.

'Wait here,' she said and disappeared into the house.

I waited for some time, standing awkwardly under the pergola. At last, the young man appeared. 'What do you want?' he asked, staring at me with eyes bruised by weeping.

'I'm Arphaia's friend—' I began.

'I remember you,' he interrupted. 'We've met. And she talked about you sometimes. And about the girl she called Fish Guts.' His expression lightened as he remembered happier times.

I hesitated, wondering what she'd said. But I had more important issues to worry about.

'Did she ever talk about the men she was interested in?' I asked.

'Sometimes. Why?'

'Well . . .' I paused again, wondering what I should use as my excuse for questioning him.

'She told me you were the nosiest person she'd ever met,' he said with a sudden grin.

I relaxed and nodded. 'I am. And the wanax doesn't seem to be getting anywhere . . .'

'No,' he agreed, sounding bitter. 'I suppose he thinks a farm girl is not important.'

Although I was peeved with Tinos myself, I doubted that was the reason. 'He is stuck. Arphaia is the third person to die this week,' I said. 'The wanax seems no closer on Duzi or Ynna either. Do you know if Arphaia was seeing someone new?' I thought about adding 'besides Tryphone' but elected not to. Arphaia might have met someone entirely new.

'Maybe.' He stared into space. I realized he was trying to decide whether he should tell me or not.

'Knowing who he is may help me find her murderer,' I said.

Still he did not answer. I held my breath. I was on the verge of saying something else to encourage him when he finally answered.

'First, she was interested in Duzi.'

I nodded. I'd suspected so. 'But I don't think it lasted,' I said.

'No,' he agreed. 'He owned nothing – no jewelry or property of any kind. And Arphaia found Duzi's insistence on marrying and settling down distressing, especially since he seemed too interested in her farm. Too much, too soon. You know? Besides, at that time, she did not want to marry.'

'Yes, she told me. We agreed about that,' I said.

'After Duzi, she began seeing Tryphone.'

'And?' I said impatiently, maddened by his slow progress.

'He wasn't interested at first. I think she said he was involved with some rich woman. A woman who gave him expensive gifts,' Zeno added drily.

'Ynna,' I said to myself.

'Maybe,' Zeno nodded as though I'd spoken to him. 'But he and Arphaia did begin seeing one another. Eventually. She began talking about getting married. She finally seemed happy.' His face crumpled and for a moment he could not speak. I waited in silence until he pulled himself together. 'Is that what you wanted to know?'

I nodded. 'Yes. That's helpful.'

'Do you think he killed her? That Tryphone?' Zeno's face flushed with anger, and he clenched his fists.

'Maybe,' I said. 'I'm not sure, though.' While it was true that almost everything I knew led back to Tryphone, I still wasn't satisfied he was Arphaia's murderer. I couldn't stop thinking about his grief. Would he have killed someone he cared about so much? I couldn't be sure. I knew people could do any manner of awful harm to one another in the name of love, but Tryphone? I didn't want to believe it of him. Besides, I couldn't see why he would murder Ynna, especially if she was giving him expensive gifts. Had Ynna threatened him? I recalled her heartbroken wail; she seemed too desperate for affection to threaten anyone, and I could not imagine why he would resort to murder. I doubted she'd asked him for a dedicated relationship. The thought was almost funny. She'd spent years pursuing attractive bull dancers; how could she ask for faithfulness now?

I was certain if I tried hard enough, I could come up with a solid argument for accusing Elemon. Perhaps he wanted to make it seem Tryphone was guilty. The competitiveness between him and Tryphone was sufficient to make me wonder.

'Hello?'

I suddenly realized Zeno was speaking to me. 'Sorry. What?'

'Are you all right? You looked Goddess-touched.'

'I was thinking,' I said stiffly.

'Hmm. Are you finished asking me questions?'

'I have just one more. Did Arphaia ever mention Elemon?'

'Once or twice. She said he was always nice to her. But she noticed he was nasty to Duzi and Tryphone.'

'Not just them,' I murmured.

'She saw him trip Duzi once, in the ring. That made her

nervous around him and so she tried to avoid Elemon whenever she could.'

'Thank you,' I said. Someone had tripped me too, just as I started my run at the bull. I could have been badly hurt. Had that been Elemon? I considered that for a few seconds. Although likely, I finally concluded I couldn't prove it. It could have been anyone. I did not trust any of my fellow bull leapers now – and that was one of the saddest consequences of all.

FORTY-THREE

The sudden beat of a drum drew Zeno's attention away from me. 'I must go,' he said, staring at the crowd. 'The funeral is beginning.' He didn't wait for my response but brushed past me and hurried to join the other mourners. I followed more slowly. As Zeno squirmed his way to the front, I took up a position at the back, clutching the little clay bull I carried to put in her coffin.

To the measured beat of the drum, we began walking forward. Instead of heading to the road and the cemetery that lay between Knossos and this farm, we trudged to the back of the property. Arphaia had many more of the professional wailing women than Ynna had had – at least ten, parading behind us and crying so loudly I could not hear the sobs of the truly bereaved.

The track led past the fields, through an olive grove and into a copse of trees. I expected a field dotted with tholos tombs once we exited the woods; instead, we approached a rocky escarpment. Green vegetation fringed the top like hair on a head, but the rough side facing us was bare and pocked with holes. At the bottom of the bluff gaped a large cavity. It was clearly our destination; the men carrying Arphaia's coffin headed directly toward it. I was surprised; although caves had been used in the past, most people I knew had switched to underground tombs with a brick or stone dome on top.

The rock blocking the entrance was pushed aside, and I followed the procession into the darkness. An unpleasant damp, musty smell billowed out of the interior. The coffin was lowered to the ground. A clay lid had been placed on the top of the sarcophagus. Under that, a linen shroud covered her face, chest and lower extremities. I knew why. To hide the damage done by the vultures.

The family brought articles for Arphaia to carry on her journey. A mirror and a pot of kohl were put in first. I found that a trifle surprising since, as far as I knew, Arphaia rarely primped. Bowls of fruit and grain were snugged in with her so that she might have nourishment on her journey. Tryphone added a chain of pearls to go through her hair and a gold necklace.

The clay bull I slipped in beside the valuables looked like a poor gift, and I was tempted to retrieve it. But when I looked up, it was not only Geos and the other bull dancers smiling at me in approval but Arphaia's aunt as well. Comforted, I moved away to make room for another.

When all had passed by, the lid was pushed into place and the coffin was lifted to the pallbearers' shoulders. I followed the family a few yards as the terracotta slipper disappeared into the darkness at the rear of the cave. They were gone a long time and I began to wonder how large this cave was. How long had it been used for burials? If I followed Arphaia's coffin all the way to her resting place, how many generations of this family would I pass on my way? I knew the pottery caskets had not always been used. Would I see human remains just lying on the ledges? The thought of all those eyeless skulls staring at me made me shudder, and I turned and fled back into the sunshine and the fresh, salt-tinged air.

I found myself walking with Geos and the other bull dancers. Although most of the family and the other mourners returned to the house, we continued on to the road. Obelix had stopped crying, although her eyes were still swollen and puffy. Tryphone was no longer weeping, but he stumbled as he walked. Grief eddied off him in waves.

I took Obelix's hand. 'Arphaia could be so much fun,' I said. 'When she laughed, you couldn't help but laugh with her.' When Arphaia laughed, her cheeks rounded into fat globes like pomegranates and her eyes disappeared into slits of hilarity. 'We should remember her that way.'

Obelix looked at me, her eyes bruised with weeping.

'Do you remember when we went to the beach, instead of going home?' I'd been in trouble for that and I was sure both Arphaia and Obelix had as well. We'd just wanted to walk along the sand and talk. 'Arphaia started throwing water at us . . .' We'd ended up running in and out of the creamy water, laughing hysterically as we splashed one another. I'd gone home soaked and stiff with salt.

A slight smile touched Obelix's lips. 'She was funny. But she could be cruel. Remember that time in the market—'

'When she imitated Thyia?' I nodded, smiling involuntarily. When the High Priestess's niece had been born, seers had predicted she would become High Priestess one day. I doubted it. What about the High Priestess's daughter? But Thyia behaved as though she was already the High Priestess. We'd seen her flouncing through the market, sneering and behaving as though everyone was dirt under her shoes. Arphaia had flounced after her, imitating every flick of Thyia's fingers, every tilt of her head, until Obelix and I were helpless with laughter. Even the stall keepers had grinned.

In retrospect, maybe that had been unkind, but I still thought Thyia had deserved it.

'But Arphaia could be kind too,' I said. 'She gave that little girl her lunch.' Knossos was a wealthy city, but we still had our poor. Arphaia had seen the little girl begging and, without hesitation, had handed over her flatbread.

'I knew you were going to say that,' Obelix said, sniffing as fresh tears rolled down her cheeks. My eyes stung as salty water filled them.

'She was very special,' Tryphone said, his voice shaking so I could barely understand him.

No one spoke again until we were almost to Knossos. Then Obelix looked at the clouds massing in the north and said, 'We'll have rain tomorrow.'

'If so,' Geos said, his voice hoarse, 'we'll practice in the cave.'

'It will be good to get back to normal,' Obelix said, her voice quavering.

'Will we ever be normal again?' I asked.

No one spoke. Then Geos said in a hearty voice, 'Of course we will.'

I shook my head slightly, not sure that was true.

'How did she die?' Obelix asked suddenly.

I glanced at Tryphone and found him looking at me. For a moment, neither of us responded. Finally, I said, 'She was murdered.'

'Murdered?' Obelix stared at me. 'Are you sure?'

I nodded. 'I spoke to the healer.' I recalled the stab wounds but, glancing at Tryphone's haunted expression, chose not to mention them.

'How does the healer know?' Obelix asked. 'Maybe she's wrong.'

I hesitated for several seconds. 'She showed me the stab wounds,' I admitted reluctantly. 'She thinks the same knife was used on all three of the victims.'

Obelix began weeping once again. A low cry broke from Tryphone's lips and he turned his face away. 'This is your fault, Martis,' he said.

'It isn't,' I retorted, hurt.

'Why did you meddle?'

After that, none of us spoke again.

Despite Obelix's prediction, the following morning was dry. Clouds covered the sky in a gray film like dirty milk, but no rain was falling when I left. Not yet anyway. I took a chance that Geos would prefer to hold the practice at the ring and went there instead of to the caves. I was right: he was standing in the ring, his face turned up to the sky in concern.

I could hear a bull in the pen behind him. Obelix, who'd arrived before me, was chatting with the bull handler.

Tryphone and Elemon arrived separately but at the same time. Elemon looked at Geos and said crossly, 'I went to the caves first.'

'Rain will only become more frequent as we go into winter,' Geos said, gesturing to the distant mountains. The tops already glistened white with snow. 'I want to take advantage of the dry days as much as possible.'

'I don't need this much practice,' Elemon grumbled. Geos did not speak. Instead, he stared pointedly at the scar circling Elemon's waist.

Avoiding both him and Tryphone, I deposited my skirt and jacket to one side. As Costi and Nub arrived, closely followed by Thaos, Curgis and the twins, Geos gestured to me. 'Pull out the practice bull.'

I wheeled the horned cart to the side of the ring. I couldn't decide how I felt about working with the kids. On the one hand, I thought it a boring task. On the other, I did not want to stand anywhere near either Tryphone or Elemon. But after I had the bull model set up and had arranged the children in a queue, Geos assigned Elemon to them and told me to practice with the real bull.

'I don't want to—' Elemon began. Geos grinned, showing all his teeth.

'You told me you thought you didn't need so much practice,' he said. 'So I thought you could share your expertise with the younger members of our team.'

I hid a smile.

'The rest of you, line up,' Geos said. 'Tryphone first. Obelix, you catch.'

I made sure I moved into position behind Thaos and Curgis.

I recognized the bull that trotted toward us. This was the young bull, still partially untrained and very energetic, that we'd worked with before. Snorting and tossing his head, he ran into the ring. An only partially trained auroch was more dangerous than one of the older, steadier bulls. At least only a small audience watched our every move, judging us as we jumped, so we would not be too ashamed if we fell.

I glanced at Tryphone. He was rubbing his hands nervously together. 'Go,' shouted Geos. Tryphone took a breath – I could see his shoulders rise – and then he broke into a sprint across the dirt. His hands stretched out, and he flipped easily over the bull's horns. But this young bull was still moving and Tryphone kept rotating past the black back to the tail. Obelix grabbed him as he staggered.

Thaos and Curgis exchanged a glance and switched places so the younger Curgis was next in line. As the bull wheeled around and raced after Tryphone, the handler came out shouting and waving his pole. The bull returned to the center and pawed at the ground.

Thaos ran at the bull, but as the animal galloped toward him, he turned aside at the last minute. Now, with a new target, the bull went after him and sent him fleeing up the rows of stone steps.

Curgis, perspiring with fear, gulped audibly.

When the bull returned to the center, Curgis burst into a run before he or the bull were ready. But Curgis made the jump, falling awkwardly on the bull's back before sliding to the ground.

Now it was my turn. My heart began to pound in my chest. The bull took up his position in the center of the ring and stared at me with his small black eyes. For several moments, we stared at one another. Huffing, he began to run at me.

Time slowed down. I felt as though I were running very slowly toward the bull that was racing toward me. I reached out for the horns and felt their smooth ivory slide into my hands. I jumped at the same time as he tossed his head and I went sailing over him. My feet hit the warm hair of his back. Time reset to normal and suddenly I was falling toward the side. Obelix lifted her arms to me. I grabbed them and jumped to the ground. My shaky legs could not hold my weight and I fell to my knees on the ground.

The handler ran into the field to restrain the bull.

FORTY-FOUR

After I staggered to my feet, Geos called us together. He looked at me. 'What happened to you, Martis?'

I shrugged. I didn't know. My heart was still thudding in my chest like a hammer.

Geos nodded. 'Martis, you take over for Obelix and catch. Curgis, you work with the children. Elemon and Obelix, join the queue. I want you two to jump next.'

We moved into our new positions and the practice began again. Elemon executed a perfect leap but wobbled as he jumped to the ground. He refused my assistance, however. Obelix came next.

I watched, my heart in my mouth. It looked as though one of the horns would snag her, but she shifted her position at the last moment and flew over the bull. It was not a graceful jump, but her technique was solid.

Geos kept us practicing all morning, rotating us around from position to position. By the time he called a halt, the bull was too tired to gallop. All he could manage was a slow trot. The handler came into the ring and took the weary animal back to his pen.

All of us dancers were sweaty, out of breath and worn out. Every muscle in my body ached, and my hands were so tired I couldn't completely close them. But I still planned to ask Geos my questions.

He grinned at me, self-satisfied.

'You did that on purpose,' I accused him.

'I thought I'd settle all of you down. There has been far too much emotion among you.'

'Hmm.' I glanced around me. Tryphone and Elemon were several feet away, but still within earshot. The only other bull dancer anywhere near was Obelix. She paid me no attention as she pulled on her faded skirt. I lowered my voice. 'Elemon has been tripping some of us while we are in line, waiting to run at the bull,' I said. Geos looked at me and did not reply. 'Did you know about that?' I persisted.

'This is a dangerous ceremony,' he said, his eyes shifting away from me.

'Yes, it is,' I agreed. 'But do you want to see him put one of the others of us in harm's way?'

'Did it happen to you?'

'I was tripped,' I said.

'Did you see who did this?'

'No,' I admitted.

'Did you tell me then?'

'No. Well, I wasn't sure . . .'

'No one was hurt. If I thought there was a danger of that happening, I would have stepped in.'

I stared at him. In the past, he'd kept me from jumping, and now I wondered if he'd done so not because he thought the bull might hurt me but from worry about some of my teammates. 'You know Elemon may be the murderer,' I said.

'Elemon is the best among you—' he began, but I interrupted him.

'I see. So, it doesn't matter what happens to the rest of us?' Growing angrier by the second, my voice began to rise. 'I know who murdered Duzi and Arphaia and when I tell Tinos—'

'Enough.' Geos gripped my arm so tightly I grunted involuntarily in pain. 'Everyone can hear your shouting. We'll discuss this later.'

I looked around. Everyone was staring at me. From the expressions on Elemon's and Tryphone's faces, I realized they had overheard my angry lie.

I directed furtive glances at Tryphone and Elemon as I crossed the ring to my clothes. I tried to behave as though I were unaware of their scowls as I bent down and picked up my skirt and jacket. I thought they would not approach me here, where Geos could intervene, but they might follow me out of the ring.

Suddenly, instead of drawing on my skirt, I bundled the clothing under my arm and began running. I took everyone by surprise as I crossed the ring, went over the slope and raced into town.

'Martis, wait,' shouted Tryphone. 'I want to talk to you. Come back. I won't hurt you.'

I tried to run even faster.

Instead of heading straight for the apartments, I darted into a lane and navigated the maze of interlocking alleys to the back wall of the courtyard behind my kitchen. I hurled my clothing up over the wall and then scrambled up the bricks. I was startled to realize it was not as easy as it had been. A year ago, I'd spent more time in the boy's kilt than a skirt, blouse and jacket. This rear wall had posed no barrier then and I'd climbed it frequently. Now it was more difficult, and once I reached the top and clambered over, I lay on the cool damp bricks to catch my breath.

Finally, I stood up and pulled on my clothing over my sweaty loincloth. I wished I hadn't lied to Geos. I didn't know the identity of the murderer; I only suspected Elemon and Tryphone. Now it was critical to figure out who the murderer was – before he came after me.

As I crossed the yard, a fine drizzle began to fall from the sky.

* * *

When I entered the main room from the kitchen, my mother looked at me in surprise. 'Martis. Where have you been?' Then, as she took in my appearance, her nose wrinkled. 'You are filthy. Bathe before you eat.'

Since there was no time to heat the water, I bathed in cold. At first, the cool water felt pleasant on my hot skin. But it soon became uncomfortable, and my teeth began to chatter. I washed quickly and jumped out of the tub, suddenly so ravenous I couldn't wait to eat.

I threw on clean clothing and hurried to join my mother.

She already had cold tea, flatbread, roasted meat and figs waiting for me. I filled my plate and popped a fig into my mouth before I sat down.

'My goodness,' my mother said, watching me in disapproval. 'There is no need to eat quite so fast.'

'I was hungry,' I replied. 'Geos worked us very hard.'

It felt odd to discuss bull dancing with my mother. A year ago, I'd kept it secret from her. She hadn't wanted me to engage in such a dangerous activity, and I'd sneaked out to practice. Now I was talking to her about it; that felt strange.

'Do you think you will continue as a bull dancer next spring, when you enter the dorms for your agoge?' Nephele asked, just as though I'd spoken my thoughts aloud.

I shrugged; I didn't know. I would be seventeen then, with only a year of freedom left before taking on adult responsibilities. I'd worked very hard to become a bull dancer. But . . . but. I thought of the constant practice. About Elemon, tripping the dancers he saw as competition. About the complicated romantic relationships between the various members of the team – something I'd been blind to when I'd first started. 'Perhaps not,' I admitted at last. 'There are no old bull dancers.'

My mother smiled. Before she could reply, someone knocked on our door. Raising her eyebrows, my mother glanced at me. I shook my head; I wasn't expecting anyone. My mother rose and, after a few seconds, I followed her.

A boy – a small, ragged boy – stood outside. 'What do you want?' my mother asked.

'Geos sent me. He says there's another practice this afternoon. In the caves.'

'What?' I mentally reviewed the aching muscles in my arms and legs. 'He didn't work us hard enough this morning?'

The boy lifted his shoulders and glanced hopefully at my mother. 'Wait here,' she told him and disappeared toward the kitchen.

'Have you told other bull dancers too?' I asked the boy suspiciously. I wondered if the murderer planned to lure me to the cave and kill me there.

He nodded. 'Yes. I brought the message to Obelix, Tryphone and Costi.' He ticked them off on his fingers.

I relaxed, reassured.

My mother brought out a dish of food for the boy – almost the same meal I'd just enjoyed. He sat down cross-legged and quickly began eating. He was unexpectedly neat, although he wiped his greasy fingers on his ragged loincloth.

My mother took back the empty dish. 'His dirty hands,' she muttered in horror as she shut the door. 'Oh, those hands.'

'Maybe you should have offered him water to wash with first,' I said.

FORTY-FIVE

G rumbling, I went to my bedchamber and climbed into my grimy loincloth once again. I could barely stand to touch it; it was still damp with sweat from the morning's work. I slipped into my old jacket and skirt. Since I did not feel fully confident that this invitation was not a trap, I looked around for a weapon to carry with me. I tiptoed into my mother's room. My father hadn't taken all his possessions when he'd left. I rummaged through his bag until I found his old knife. I slipped it under my belt – just in case this was an ambush.

Since it was now raining heavily, I also took the square of canvas. I still got wet but at least it protected my head as I ran through the city.

I used the tunnel closest to the ring, cautiously walking toward the dim reddish light cast by the dish lamps. The smell of bull remained, intense under the odors of burning oil and damp. Something was off; I knew it when I heard no voices. I put my hand on the hilt of the knife and tiptoed forward.

As I rounded the final curve, I saw Obelix outlined in the dim light. Breathing a sigh of relief, I walked forward. 'Obelix. Where are the others?'

'We're early, that's all. Geos and Tryphone are in the back.' She gestured to the rear of the caves. 'Geos is scolding Tryphone.' She smiled at me. 'Geos said he wants to talk to you too.'

'Oh, all right.' I walked past her, on my way to the rearmost niche. I was not looking forward to Geos's scolding; I was sure that was what I was going to receive. 'What kind of mood is Geos in?' I began, turning back to Obelix.

To my shock, I saw she had pulled out a knife – a thin sharp knife. As she raised her arm, orange light ran up and down the shiny blade. Shaking off my stunned paralysis, I began back-pedaling away from her. I was not fast enough. She slashed at me, catching the sleeve of my jacket and ripping it.

'What?' I scrambled backward. Blood was crawling down my arm from the stinging wound. Although it hurt terribly, I did not think it was very deep or long. 'What are you doing?'

'I tried to warn you off,' she said as she advanced upon me. 'But you won't stop. Honestly, Martis, I like you. I don't want to hurt you.' She sniffed. 'But you won't stop.'

'But why?' I struggled to wrap my head around this sudden surprising twist.

'I would have married Duzi,' she said, breathing hard as she lunged for me. I twisted away, hurling the canvas sheet at her. It hit her and knocked her back, giving me time to run toward the pens at the rear of the cave. 'But he didn't want me.' Her voice caught on a sob. She advanced, her knife held out. I recognized it now; it was a knife used by the fishermen to scale and gut their catch.

'What happened?' I gasped out. Anything to stall her until I found a way to escape.

'When Duzi first arrived, I helped him. He lived with my family then. With me. I thought he cared about me. But he didn't want me.' Her voice broke. When she spoke again, she sounded angry. 'He called me Fish Guts. He was a pirate, with nothing except what I gave him. And he still didn't want me. He preferred that old drunken woman.'

'Ynna?' I gasped as I struggled to free the knife from my belt. 'Did you kill her too?' Another slash of Obelix's knife communicated her answer. 'Ynna wasn't even a bull dancer,' I protested.

'Ynna saw me arguing with Duzi,' Obelix said. 'She'd come to the ring to fetch him.'

As I recalled the description of Ynna's visitor, I blurted, 'You were the one at Ynna's.' The neighbor had described a tall, lean bull dancer. Now I realized that portrayal fit the slender Obelix as well as the two men. 'You stole Tryphone's robe and wore it when you went to Ynna's.'

'I had to. I knew that if I wore it, any witness would assume I was a man.'

'But why did you kill her?' I jumped backward a few more steps.

'She mocked me,' Obelix said. 'Even though she was sleeping with Tryphone by then and didn't care about Duzi anymore. She mocked me.' Obelix lunged forward again, but this time, distracted by her grievances, she did not come close. 'Duzi preferred an old drunk to me,' she wailed. I pictured Ynna rubbing Obelix's nose in her humiliation.

'I understand. That must have been hard,' I said sympathetically. 'But Arphaia? I can't forgive you Arphaia. She was your friend. You loved her.'

'I did. I truly loved her. But Arphaia didn't love me back. First, she took Duzi from me. She claimed to be my friend but she didn't hesitate. Then she saw the blood on my loincloth and realized it wasn't my time of the month. Once she figured that out, she knew the blood had to be Duzi's. She blackmailed me. She took the trinkets I won in the performances for herself.' Obelix sniffed. 'I didn't want to kill her, but she left me no choice.'

I thought of the exchanges of gold jewelry I'd seen and nodded.

Obelix suddenly lunged forward again and slashed. Distracted, I'd dropped my guard. I jumped back with a gasp, realizing only then that I was being driven even further to the back. If she trapped me against the cave wall, I would have nowhere to run, and she would kill me.

I fought to wrest the knife from my belt and finally pulled it free. I parried Obelix's next blow. But my father's dagger was ornamental, and when she struck it with her blade, my weapon broke with the force of her blow. As the top of the bronze edge skittered across the rock floor, I jumped backward again.

'But we were friends,' I shouted.

'We were never friends. I like you but I always knew you derided me behind my back. You, the daughter of a well-known weaver, one of Geos's favorites. I was your pity friend.'

'That's not true,' I said. But as shame swept over me, I knew it was. She lunged again, and I stumbled back, almost tripping as I tried to move away from that dangerous glittering knife.

She laughed. 'That's it. Keep going. It will look as though you and Tryphone died together.'

'Tryphone? What does he have to do with this?'

'You are such an idiot. Tryphone and Arphaia were together. Didn't you see it? I'm sure she told him everything. And then he told Ynna too. He was sleeping with both of them. I know it. I couldn't trust any of them to keep silent,' she added bitterly.

'But Tryphone is still alive . . .' I began. As Obelix moved forward, I stumbled over something on the floor and almost fell. Obelix's wicked dagger whizzed over my head.

'Not for long,' Obelix said as I stared down at the form I'd blundered into.

It was Tryphone, sprawled unconscious on the ground. Blood seeped from a wound on his head and puddled on the cave floor.

As Obelix approached again, I gathered my legs underneath me and propelled myself forward, butting her hard in the stomach. She staggered back and went down on one knee. I ran at her, but she jumped up and retreated, her knife flashing in the orange firelight. She laughed.

'It's all right,' she said. 'I won't stab you. I won't need to.'

She backed up, but not far enough for me to run past her. I couldn't abandon Tryphone anyway. 'How were you planning to explain this?' I asked, gesturing to the injured man sprawled on the cave floor. 'Tinos will see the stab wounds.'

'No, he won't,' she said with a tilt of her head. Now, in the sudden silence, I could hear something echoing in the tunnel nearby: a low groaning interrupted by a huffing. Although rendered hollow and strange by the cave's rock walls, I recognized that sound. It was a bull.

FORTY-SIX

'There's a bull in here?' I gasped.

Obelix laughed. 'I told the handler I wanted to practice . . . The fool believed me.'

She stepped back again, craning her neck toward the tunnel that led to the sea. I looked behind me. The pen here had not been used recently. There was no gate, but it would have to do. I took Tryphone's arm and struggled to drag him through the opening. He groaned but did not wake. He was so heavy I could barely shift him and succeeded only in pulling his upper body over the threshold. I intended to roll his legs into the pen but I couldn't do that now; I'd run out of time. I could hear the clicking of the bull's hooves on the stone floor. His huffing had transitioned into short bark-like sounds. He was angry.

But I might still escape an aggressive bull's attack if he didn't see me. I peered around the corner of the pen. Obelix was shouting and waving her arms so that the auroch was sure to see her. Roaring a challenge, the bull ran for her. And she turned and pelted right for me, turning aside at the last minute and vaulting over the wall of the adjacent cage.

The bull ran straight for Tryphone.

Several thoughts ran through my head at the same moment. This was the young bull, still only partially trained and more aggressive than an older, more seasoned animal. Although I could hide in the pen, Tryphone could not. I had to draw the animal away from the injured man. That meant leaving the relative safety of the enclosure.

I ran out of the opening and raced as fast as I could to the other side of the cave. My skirt clung to my ankles so I held it as high as I could. I knew the bull saw me; he roared as his hooves beat a rhythm on the floor. The pen in which my sister had been imprisoned – only a few months ago – was straight ahead, almost invisible in the shadows. I couldn't tell if the gate hung open or was closed, so I made a sudden turn, into the darkness. I pressed myself against the wall. The bull ran into view and stopped. His white horns glimmered in the faint light. He turned his head to one side after the other, and I could hear his deep snuffling breaths as he tried to smell me.

Slowly, I began to edge around the side of the cave. This was dangerous, I knew. The cavern wall bent inward here and I would be perilously close to the animal. But I was hoping I could shuffle around the wall to approach the center of the cave. Only there would I find room to run. If he found me here, I would be pinned down with no avenue of escape.

He grunted and took a few steps toward me. I sidled right and held my breath. He sniffed the air once again, his tail lashing. I removed my heavy belt and threw it at him with all my strength. It sailed over his head, missing him entirely. My disappointment turned to jubilation when the metal made a solid clinking noise on the cave floor, and he turned to look. He trotted toward the sound to investigate, and I took the opportunity to run along the wall toward the tunnel I'd entered the cave by.

'No, you don't,' Obelix said, emerging from the pen and racing forward to cut me off.

I stopped short and considered my choices. Obelix still held the sharp pointed knife. I did not want to approach her too closely. But the bull was on my other side, turning to face us now that he'd heard her speaking. I'd rather take my chances with the bull. He'd turned and trotted toward us.

'Oh, oh, oh,' Obelix caroled at the beast. He began to gallop toward us, faster than I would have thought possible. I quickly dropped my skirt and kicked it away from my feet. Could I jump over him? Was he trained sufficiently to react automatically? There were no other bull dancers to intervene and distract the bull from me or Geos to call the handlers in. I had no catcher either, and a fall on the hard rock floor might hurt me.

But I would give myself more room to run.

As the bull ran for me, I sprinted toward him, stretching out my hands for those dangerous horns. Although the sharp tips had been trimmed and the ends blunted, those spikes could still kill me. I gulped but I didn't stop running.

The bull lowered his head. I grabbed the horns. He lifted his massive cranium – and I went flying over his back just as though this were any performance. I landed near his tail and slid to the ground.

Roaring, he rotated, searching for me.

I darted into the shadows to hide and catch my breath.

'You can't run forever,' Obelix said, her voice bouncing off the cave walls. I knew she was correct. I was already tiring. My heart thudded so loudly I did not know why the bull didn't hear it.

He began trotting toward the sound of her voice, and I quickly tiptoed across the cave. I picked up my belt and my skirt, the only weapons I possessed right now, and retreated to the cave wall.

Obelix disappeared. I guessed she'd taken refuge once again in one of the cages. The bull lunged this way and that, searching for his quarry. I froze, hoping he would choose to leave the caves rather than continue pursuing me. I tried to calm my panting but couldn't. I was breathless with fear and exertion.

And then my belt, my fashionable heavy belt that cinched in my waist, fell to the floor with a clang. In an instant, the bull turned and started for me. He was too close for me to run toward him and grasp his horns. He moved much faster than I could believe and was almost on me. In a frenzy of fear, I hurled my skirt at him and turned to flee.

The fabric tangled around his horns and fell in a drape over his eyes. Blinded, he staggered around shaking his head, trying to dislodge the heavy cloth shrouding his eyes. And I took the opportunity to bolt across the cave to hide in the black shadows at the very back.

Trembling like a leaf in a high wind, I leaned against the rough stone of the back wall. I did not know how much longer I could run away from the bull. Obelix must have thought the same; her voice came out of the darkness like a prophecy of doom. 'You must be tired,' she said. 'And you are now a distance from Tryphone. Thank you for covering the bull's eyes. I can easily slip across the animal pens until I reach him. I'd hoped the bull would gore him and trample him to death, but if that isn't going to happen, I still have my knife.'

I knew she meant to lure me out of hiding. I knew as clearly as I knew my own name that this was a trap. But I didn't see what else I could do, so I cautiously felt my way through the darkness toward the front of the cave. Tryphone was helpless. I couldn't allow Obelix to stab him to death.

The bull had managed to shift my skirt, so it hung rakishly from one long horn. His eyes shifted from side to side as he searched the cave. In the dim and smoky light of the dish lamps, his eyes glittered orange. I inched along the side of the rearmost pen and peered around the corner. Obelix must also have been immobile, because I saw no movement save for the bull. He snorted and moved a few steps toward the place from where Obelix's voice had come. I knew she wasn't still there. But I didn't see her anywhere else either. Was she hiding in one of the cages? Or was she easing her way toward me with her sharp and lethal knife?

As I backed up, Obelix vaulted over the wall of the pen beside me, landing right next to the place where I'd stood. The tin knife in her hand shimmered as she brought it down. If I'd still been in that spot, she would have cut me, maybe killed me.

I turned and fled into the darkness, tripping and falling to my knees. Pain shot through my legs. I stifled a groan and staggered to my feet. Blood began running down my right leg. I limped the last few steps to the back of the cavern and pressed myself against the back wall as though the stone would protect me.

Obelix was close to me, too close. I sidled right, following the cave wall. I couldn't run anymore.

But although the bull was coming toward me, he was much nearer to Obelix. The sound of her feet slapping on the rock floor had attracted his attention. He began trotting toward her, following the footsteps that echoed from the walls. She glanced over her shoulder and broke into a sprint, her feet thudding on the stone. I could see the terror on her face.

As she raced toward me, the bull's trot became a gallop. He grunted angrily, and I saw the exact moment when she realized she might not make it to safety. Gasping, she tried to run faster. But he was already on her. His horns caught her from the back. He tossed his head, and she went pinwheeling through the air to land with a horrible smack on the stone floor behind him. My skirt drifted to the ground beside her. He turned around and trotted back to sniff the broken form lying on the rock. He pawed at her, but she didn't move.

FORTY-SEVEN

I sagged against the wall, incapable of movement. My stomach twisted itself into knots; if I'd had anything in it, I'd have thrown it up.

'For the love of—' From the cave entrance came Geos's voice. 'What is going on here?'

'Watch out, watch out.' That was Tinos, shouting a warning as the bull galloped in their direction. He disappeared from my view. As quietly as I could, I tottered forward, to the end of the pen.

'Where's the handler? Why is this bull here?'

'Martis? Martis?' My mother cried, despite the efforts of the others to hush her.

'I'm here,' I shouted. 'So is Tryphone. He's seriously injured.' I shut up when I heard the snap of the bull's hooves on the stone floor, rapidly approaching me. A few seconds later the animal came into view.

'Hey, hey,' shouted Geos. 'Where is that damn handler?'

As the bull vanished around the pens once again, I flattened myself against the walls, moving forward until I reached the opening into the cage that held Tryphone. I slipped inside and knelt by him. He groaned and opened his eyes. 'What's happening?' he muttered. 'Obelix . . .'

'Hush. I know.'

He struggled to sit up but I pressed him back.

'An angry bull is roaming around the caves,' I whispered. 'Wait until Tinos and Geos capture the animal. Then you can sit up and talk.'

'Obelix hit me,' he said.

'I know.' I put my hand over his mouth and shook my head.

I did not believe the bull could hear us over the shouting at the cave entrance but I certainly did not want to take chances.

'Here, I brought water and the juice of the poppy.' Another, deeper voice spoke from the entrance. 'He is sure to be thirsty. Once he drinks, he'll become more docile . . .'

The bull wheeled in front of the cage's opening and disappeared in the direction of the tunnel.

'What is he doing here anyway?'

'We don't know. Yet.' Tinos sounded grim.

'Where is Obelix now?' Tryphone whispered.

'The bull got her.' And even though I knew she had tried to kill me, kill us, the tears rose to my eyes. Tryphone looked up at me and took my hand.

'I know she was your friend,' he murmured.

The bull did not reappear for some time. As the perspiration dried on my body, I began shivering with cold and wished I'd kept my jacket. Tryphone was trembling as well. His eyes kept closing, and I was afflicted with a new worry – that if Tryphone fell asleep, he would not wake. 'Stay with me,' I whispered as I lay beside him and attempted to warm him with my body. 'Don't go to sleep.'

It seemed like forever before I heard my mother calling me. 'Martis. Martis. Where are you?'

'Here.' I released Tryphone and stood up. 'Here.' I stepped through the cage door just as my mother ran into sight.

'By the Lady, I was so worried about you.' She caught me in her arms and hugged me tightly. 'I am so angry with you right now.'

'Mother, I want to apprentice with the healer,' I blurted. I don't know why I thought this was a good time to tell her. She blinked at me, too shocked to speak. 'I'm sorry . . .' I began.

'If it means you will give up bull dancing, I approve.' She glanced at Obelix's body. 'You could have been killed.'

'Why did you come after me?' I looked over her shoulder as Tinos and Geos came around the corner. 'I thought . . . we thought there was a practice.'

'Geos came to the apartments,' my mother said, tears of worry and stress filling her eyes. 'He wanted to talk to you. When I told him you were at practice, he said there was no practice.'

'Are you all right?' Geos asked gruffly, hurrying forward.

'Fine. Cold. But Tryphone . . .' I gestured behind me. 'He's badly hurt. Obelix hit him.'

'Obelix?' Geos turned to look at the body several yards from us.

'Yes. She was the murderer.'

'*She* was?' Geos sounded shocked.

'Why?' Tinos asked, striding around the pens toward us. He'd belted the long robe up so that his legs from the knees down were free. 'I don't understand why she murdered Duzi or anyone else.'

'Duzi turned down her advances,' I said.

'Enough,' my mother said, very loudly and firmly. 'She's cold and she's had a terrible experience. I'm taking her home. You can ask your questions later.'

'Tryphone is in the pen,' I said over my shoulder as she pulled me inexorably away. 'Obelix hit him. You need to bring him to the healer right away.'

'We will,' Tinos promised. But I heard him call after me as my mother pushed me toward the tunnel entrance, 'I told you not to involve yourself.'

I was bathed, dressed in fresh clothing and fed when Tinos and Geos arrived at the apartment several hours later. 'How is Tryphone?' I asked, starting up from my seat.

'Despina says he will recover,' Tinos said, dropping down on the cushions across from me as though he were exhausted.

'How did you know it was Obelix?' Geos asked me.

'I didn't. But I knew the murderer had to be one of us. A bull dancer.' I'd believed the guilty party was Tryphone or Elemon, but I saw no point in mentioning that. 'Duzi humiliated her,' I continued. 'Arphaia connected both Duzi and Tryphone—'

'Boyfriend one and two?' Geos asked dryly.

'Yes. And Tryphone was also involved with Ynna.' I paused. I suspected Tryphone's relationship with Ynna was purely mercenary and that he'd shared nothing important with her. Despite Obelix's fears. 'Ynna gave him valuable gifts. Like the dragonfly.' I looked at Tinos meaningfully. 'Elemon lied about owning the clip. He does own the mate, but it was given to him by . . . by another. I think Tryphone and Arphaia were collecting everything they could so they could wed.' I sighed and rubbed my bandaged knee. 'All the gold they amassed, the items they won in the ring, as well as the trinkets given to Tryphone by Ynna are stored in a chest in Arphaia's chamber at the farm.'

'I knew she wouldn't last,' Geos said. 'I knew she would leave to marry. I can always tell.'

'Was Obelix jealous?' Tinos asked, looking at me. 'Was she interested in Arphaia?' He glanced at Geos. We were all aware of the limits on the female dancers; a pregnant woman could not jump the bull.

I shook my head. 'Arphaia guessed something wasn't right and blackmailed Obelix to keep silent.' I mentally berated myself for my stupidity. 'I blame myself for not seeing what Arphaia saw,' I admitted now.

'And what was that?' Tinos asked.

'When we found Duzi's body, Obelix had blood on her loin-cloth. Arphaia realized it wasn't her time of the month. So where did the blood come from? It had to be from the murdered man.'

Both men looked startled, and I saw the sudden realization that only another woman would see and understand that clue.

'Arphaia's mistake was in blackmailing Obelix,' I continued. 'I saw the exchange of a piece of jewelry after a performance, but I didn't understand the significance at the time. Obelix knew it would never end, so she . . .' I stopped short.

'And you were too focused on the men,' Tinos pointed out in a supercilious tone. I glared at him, wishing I could smack his smug face. But he was correct.

'I was. I mean, both Obelix and Arphaia were my friends . . .' My voice thickened and I fell silent, shaking my head. Both Tinos and Geos looked at me sympathetically and did not speak while I struggled to compose myself. 'The blood wasn't the only clue,' I continued at last. My voice shook only a little. 'The stab wounds were made by a particular knife . . . well, I should have guessed they were caused by a fish knife. I saw Kryse using one when I visited her.' I looked at Geos and he nodded.

'I remember her,' he said.

'What about Obelix?' I asked cautiously. 'Is she still alive?'

Tinos sighed. 'The Goddess herself punished Obelix,' he said.

'She's dead?' I asked the question even though I was already sure of it. I did not think anyone could have lived through that landing on the cave floor, even if she'd survived the bull's goring.

Both Tinos and Geos nodded.

'I will give an offering to Her,' I murmured. 'In thanks for my deliverance.'

AUTHOR'S NOTE

Bull dancing and bull leaping
Most people who have heard of this practice learned of it first through the Greek myth of Theseus and the Minotaur. In that telling, King Minos of Crete required the defeated Greek King Aegeus to produce seven young men and seven young women every nine years to be eaten by the Minotaur (half man, half bull) in the labyrinth. Since the Greeks conquered Crete, their version of bull dancing (the demand for captives to appease a half man, half bull) is suspect in my opinion.

The archaeological exploration of Knossos among other sites in Crete revealed mosaics of young people of both sexes leaping over the horns of a bull, and it is theorized that the practice is part of (probably) religious ceremonies, but no one knows for sure.

The transition from local children aspiring to become bull dancers to the use of immigrants and prisoners is purely my own invention. I just thought, considering the Greek myth, that the change made sense.

The number nine is also thought to be sacred, and a floor mosaic depicting a maze, or a labyrinth, has also been found.

The root word for labyrinth, *labyrs*, however, refers to the double axe that was sacred to the Goddess. One of the hypotheses regarding the labyrinth is the interconnected rooms and halls of the complex discovered in Knossos. I've visited Knossos, and the structure of the large complex, which probably contained religious functions, workshops and apartments, is a maze of rooms that flow into one another. Another possibility is that it means 'place of the double axe'.

The Minotaur is a myth, but it is true the bull was revered by these ancient people. One of the sacred symbols was a stylized representation of the bull's horns called the Horns of Consecration.

Money

Like so many other things, money had to be invented. The Babylonians were using metal for money – the shekel – by about 2000 BC. The Egyptians were using something as well, but coins did not come into common use until several centuries later. Since money was not common, as far as we know, I suggest a form of barter. The use of money, or the financial system in Cretan society, is still a mystery.

Dionysus

Dionysus is a very old god. Tablets with his name have been found at Pylos and date from the twelfth or thirteenth century BC. Since all attempts to find an Indo-European root for his name have failed, some scholars believe his name is pre-Greek in origin. Traces of a Dionysian cult have been found in Bronze Age Crete. Some of the myths surrounding him, such as his birth in a cave on Crete, pre-date the myths surrounding Zeus. In later myths, Zeus was elevated to Dionysus's father (with Semele.)

As early as the fifth century BC, Dionysus became connected with Eleusis, and for centuries after part of the worship involved induction into the Eleusinian mysteries. Although plenty has been suggested for those mysteries, we still don't know what they involved.

The elements of Dionysian ceremonies were set early. Dionysus was not immortal. Born in the spring, he matured through the summer and died in winter. A harvest god, he was in charge of fertility, he was the Master of Animals and, of course, the Lord of the vine and of wine. Throngs of inebriated women, the Maenads, followed him. Rituals included tearing apart animals and eating them raw. Ceremonies for Dionysus involved the sacrifice of bulls, goats and sheep.

He was also the God of the Theater and was widely believed to have invented it.

Because he was a harvest god, some scholars have conflated him with Demeter and Persephone.

Worship of Dionysus was brought to Rome; his name changed to Bacchus. (And the wild ceremonies were called Bacchanalia.) Throughout the Middle Ages and Renaissance, sculptures, paintings and more were created of him.

Pirates

By about 1400 BC, the so-called Sea Peoples began to sweep out of Anatolia. In the thirteenth century, Egyptian hieroglyphics from Ramses II refer to the Battle of Kadesh against the Hittites. In the text, Ramses mentions people who campaigned alongside the Hittites. Hieroglyphics picture men with different headdresses and clothing. At least three of the tribes were circumcised.

Since Crete had a powerful navy, the pirates did not attack the island often. They kept their eyes on the wealth in Egypt to the west. It made sense to me that Egypt would apply to Crete for help. They were trading partners. Some scholars suggest the Keftiu were Cretans. With their powerful navy, they could defeat the Sea Peoples on their ships. Some scholars suggest that the Sea Peoples set up colonies on Crete before finally returning to what is now Turkey and Israel.